Socks In The Dryer
the secret power of non-attachment

Paol Seagram 1999   ISBN 0-9654451-1-9 © copyright

Seabreeze Publications & Events
p.o. box 5620
Santa Monica, California, 90409

310 288 6588

Cover design and art by Paol Seagram.
Digital scans by Smart Art, Venice, Ca.

Acknowledgments

I thank God for providing me the ways, means and ever expanding support to do this work.

I wish to acknowledge those who assisted in the creation of Socks in the Dryer. Firstly, Bill Cunninghame whose brilliant and patient computer expertise is responsible for my preparation and printing of both *No Boundaries* and *Socks In The Dryer*. Bill Benjamin of Honolulu for providing the space and atmosphere for creative writing while housing me in Hawaii. Peggy Clifford for wonderfully, efficient and non-partial line editing. Last and anything but least, Carol Folley for her brilliant guidance and content editing.

Special thanks to Domenick Polifrone for his insightful support and gratitude to Joe Eckre for always knowing what to say when the chips were down. All have provided a beautiful structure that allowed me to do my work and supported me with the best of friendship along the way.

SOCKS IN THE DRYER

Table of Contents

Chapter   **Page**

INTRODUCTION

Socks In The Dryer

The arrival of the third millennium marks the first real significant awakening in the human race since the discovery of fire. In the rising light of a new spiritual age, traditional patriarch-founded structures that humanity historically felt obligated to live by are beginning to dissolve. For centuries, religious politics backed by military muscle, enforced dogmatic strict controls, maintained the borders of nations and shaped the texture of their cultures.

Now, a new paradigm based on Spiritual Oneness, trust and a desire for freedom outpour from each individual who is in resonance with Divine Unity. With a snowball-like speed the *power of love* clearly becomes the impelling force of *Creation* in the twenty-first century. As the Divine Momentum of this love paints itself onto the landscape of our history, it will reveal clear and obvious ways for a one-world-people to live in harmony, balance and peace.

As babies, you and I were full of magic. Each of us came to this world as innocent beings filled with light and love. It was not long before we were taught to feel fear, suspect the unknown and to doubt love. Believing we were separate from our Divine Parent and our own inherent Divinity set us up to be players in an earth-bound game of struggle. As children we were surrounded by adults who believed that Real Power lies somewhere outside of the self. So, we grew up to live in individualistic division from one another and came to rely upon competition for survival.

As a result of the division that comes from feeling separate, humanity engaged in battles to settle differences and stake claims on resources. It casually polluted our planet in exchange for profit and willingly forfeited personal responsibility for those actions (or lack of). A people who accept disease to be natural and normal fail to see that stewardship of a delicate environment is connected to its own health and future. **Until fundamental change is made, any culture which chooses to ignore *the primal connection* to its source operates at the most basic and primitive of levels.**

I know from my own experience that once we become consciously alive with a Self-Realization of Divinity within, we automatically become attuned to a knowing that all of the peoples of earth are members of the same world community. As the old boundaries of separation, segregation and judgment fall away, the inhabitants will participate and integrate into an awakening, harmonious, one diversified community. We will manage and share our resources with a spirit of cooperation to see that all are fed, housed and educated. As this age of enlightenment unfolds, the global tribe of earth will prosper well beyond its current levels of imagination, and will live in a new era of peace. Although barely out of the infantile stages, this metamorphosis is now obvious to many on spiritual pathways.

Boy to hot dog vendor; **"Make me one with everything."**

The transformation in our world we see now is unprecedented. For you and me to thrive during this millennial paradigm shift it is necessary for us to stop insisting on being the driver of our lives, and to be willing to allow Spirit to lead the way forward. As we awaken to merge our thinking into a spiritual base that is the root foundation of our origins, we will exceed all expectations for expansion into every arena of life.

Focus On Thrival Rather Than Survival

To survive and even thrive during these times we may be called upon to dive into the unknown on a daily basis. In order to experience the good that change creates we must be a part of its free-flow. Be willing to let go of dependence upon past conditioned responses and learned thought reactions. How you and I faced challenges in the past was founded upon a neatly controlled and historic, structured order. With this shift and transformation, we will see the clearest path open before us as we make higher, more conscious choices. Decisions that are rooted in heart create success and free the spirit! By learning to rely upon our own spiritual guidance and think past old limits, we reveal and discover new ways to create solutions to the challenges of change. We gather knowing from the field of unlimited possibilities. What is revealed to us may not be like anything we have known in the past. We become free to live in the energy and magnificence of Creation. I know this because it is already happening to me and to everyone I know. **The people of earth are beginning to awaken to who we really are: God/Goddess Beings in a symphony of Oneness.**

The Infinite Mind of the Prime Creator knows trillions of new ways to experience Itself through you and me. As we surrender to It, appropriate, new awareness reveals to us ways of living true to who we are. We awaken to the light that is already within, and we are able to let go of who we were taught to believe we must be. We release the doing of all of those things that we thought we should do but did not enjoy. We become free to celebrate our talents and true purpose. In this great awakening, we become people of a loving planet knowing Oneness with our Source and we enjoy life freely.

Non-attachment is the greatest gift we can give to any situation - to ourselves and to others. The key secret to revealing success at all times (even when confronted with challenge) comes when we surrender our need to control conditions or their eventual outcome. The Infinite Intelligence within each of us knows perfect balance and rightful Divine Solutions to every situation. The free flow of Spirit love-power brings the highest good to all involved!

In order to accept the gifts of the new world he sought, Columbus had to be willing to leave the shores of his old beliefs. We must be willing to do the same.

Internal Activation Of The Highest Order

I write with intention and the knowingness that the expansive, Intelligence of Spirit is flowing through me. As an impelling idea comes, I get excited because I know that as you read an energetic activation will take place for you. Even if I am not aware of it at the time, subtle keys to spiritual awakening and subconscious prompts for your individual interpretation are buried throughout the context. Spirit knows every person who will read the stories contained in *Socks In The Dryer*. Each illuminates how true power is revealed to us by practicing oneness and non-attachment to outcome.

Other than going within, there is nothing required of you and me to find our own personal connection with God. Each of us is already One with The One Primal, Divine Awareness that created the magnificent perfection of the Universe. All the understanding and power necessary to create what we require or desire, lives at the center of our beings. It is often said that what we are looking for, is what we are looking with. In humanity's never ending search for answers, we could not expect to see the Divine Father that we seek to find outside of ourselves until we first begin to look into a mirror and into the eyes of one another. The God/Goddess, Christ-Being is an integral part of who each of us already is.

"Ye are all Gods." Jesus

Humanity will find the peace it seeks, as we accept that a pure and simple truth exists in every moment. The Creator lives within the core of our being, right where we are now. As each individual awakens to a Realization and acceptance of his own Divinity, we expand collectively as a people into peaceful enlightenment. Our Divine Parent designed us to be able to live in ease, free from struggle, and gave us free will so that we could discover it for ourselves. Without free will, the image and likeness factor would be a farce. **A Child of God has the power to make choices, affect them and experiences the fruits and results of those choices.**

Once we know that we are One with the Creator and one another, we come to live in a liberated state free from anxiety. We co-exist in a balanced state of harmony and unity and we handle our dominion comfortably as children of a Divine, Knowing God would. There is a great natural power that one assumes by practicing non-attachment. When combined with complete acceptance of our Oneness with Spirit, it is the simplest formula to know that there is more than enough of everything here and now that we could require to thrive.

Non-attachment activates an invisible power within each individual who applies it. The changes it spawns will ultimately fulfill the Divine Goal of Humanity: to be One with Its Creator. It will propel us towards our personal purpose and to the formation of heaven on earth. The first wave of this new paradigm may seem unfamiliar or challenging. It may be necessary to adjust your attitude to understand the greater meaning of its dynamics. It will unfold as Self-Realization in the self as a Oneness with All that is. To experience this greatest awakening of your life it will be essential to let go of running the show and surrender it to God.

INTRODUCTION

For an idea whose time has come, no manner or force can stand in its way. It must be fulfilled.

Heaven on earth is now at hand.

CHAPTER ONE

Exiting the Fast Lane

The last light and warmth of a lingering Indian Summer was quickly fading. I arrived at the outskirts of Sedona in time to catch a final majestic view of the flaming-red mountain tips as they slipped into the darkness of nightfall. I rounded a bend in the road and my headlights illumined the thick forest before me. The rich welcome of cooling pine filled my nostrils with the essence and scent of Sedona. "This is heaven, and this is home," I thought. Without warning, the cars ahead of me slowed abruptly. "Now what?" Five minutes from my own driveway and there is a delay on the road." I was stiff from sitting behind the wheel for eight hours and more than ready to be out of the car....and at home.

Suddenly the car in front of me sharply braked and veered across the yellow line of the narrow highway. As it did, the reason became all too apparent. Before me in the roadway was a doe. She had been hit and was on her back - all four legs churning in the air. My heart leaped into my mouth. I too, swerved to avoid hitting her and began to pray, calling for the help of angels, and for peace. Tears of compassion filled my eyes and I knew I had no choice but to turn back. I braked and doubled round, bouncing over the rough, gravel shoulder. My heart and breath picked up. I felt a sense of urgency, lest another car hit her again, or that she wander off, injured into the black night of the Junipine forest.

I parked with my headlights flooding onto the wrong side of the road and ran to her, praying all along. "Dear God, help her, help me. What can I do?" I stooped beside her and laid my hands on her side. The churning of her had legs stopped by now and I could feel the rise and fall of her chest as she struggled for breath. I continued to pray and speak softly to her. She was so sweet and helpless, and infinitely magnificent. It felt like a sacred blessing to be with her and a privilege. I could not recall feeling such strong compassion before.

A car raced up beside us. I looked up to see four or five curious, tourist countenances gawking at the two of us from open van windows. In the glare of headlights they asked; "What's wrong?" "She's been hit." I pleaded, "can you help me move her?" Before I could say another word they sped away, not wanting to have anything to do with the delicate and fragile circumstances. I knew in that moment that this was my gift. To be with her at this time and to share her moment of transition from this world to the next was sacred for both of us. She died under my hands. I cried.

I kept my hands on her and continued to pray for her journey to be into light. As I did, I felt an immensity of peace coming from her. I had never experienced such an incredible feeling before. It was as if everything in all of the Universe was well. And it was as if by her passing from this world, a powerful yet subtle vibration that goes beyond any description of words was transmitted into me. I felt a tremendous sensation of peace flow through me, and I was overwhelmed beyond any sentiment.

I carefully picked her up, bracing my knee under her so as to be able to lift the great weight. Surprised at how easily I was able to carry her, I gently laid her on an embankment by the side of the road. I was completely enthralled by the essence and beauty of her grace, even in her limp condition. As I stood up, I looked down at my arms and hands. I felt her energy in them, and in the dark light of night, I could almost see and feel my own limbs as fur-covered legs with hooves of marrow. The vibration and strength of the animal kingdom surged through my arms. It was an extremely stimulating and unique feeling. She had given me her energy and life force. I will never forget that moment. As I said goodbye, I stood misty eyed over her, feeling so privileged to be of service to her and to God in this sacred moment. I drove home and knew that I had just been present for something extraordinary, rare and special. I gave thanks for the privilege over and over.

When I arrived at my house, I noticed that my hands and arms were covered with her blood. As I washed her blood away, I continued to feel transformed by her passage.

In the deep peace and sanctity of my own bed, I thought about the prior week's journey. The time in Los Angeles had been intense yet satisfying. I would start the day with an early morning meeting with a client and be busy all day painting on an on-site art commission, and round it off later with another meeting. I rarely took more than five minutes for lunch. The nights were equally busy, beginning with a workout at my fitness gym and followed by a catch-up, late dinner with long-time friends. This trip driving across the desert from my former home to my new one in Sedona had provided a soothing and peaceful transition. It gave me time to reflect, listen to some empowering and inspiring tapes, and prepare to be at my new residence. It was comforting to know that I would have complete serenity and rejuvenation in my own private mountain-top retreat, distant and far removed from the vibration of the city. I returned to thoughts of the doe. This had not been an ordinary day.

The next morning, I hiked with a friend in an area called North Fork, a magnificent part of Oak Creek Canyon. It's meadows were once home to a sequestered settlers ranch and gardens. There, it is not hard to find an abandoned apple orchard. I always climb one of the old unpruned trees to pick some ripe, succulent fruit to take on my hike. The floor of the steep canyon is forested with pine, maple and ancient sycamores and is lush with desert wild flowers of sage, Indian paintbrush, and lupine. Both great and small Arizona wildlife abound. Mountain lions, goats, bears, and a variety of squirrel and birds inhabit the area. I have seen the most delicate of hummingbirds fanning from flower to tree. More than once, I felt privileged to capture sight of a Bald Eagle soaring overhead. I have lazily watched caterpillars inching across a rock and over my fingertips while I lay sunning. I have peered into the clear waters of the creek as they reflected majestic, red rock towers and a stunning blue sky. I have swam side by side with fish in the cool, green water, and peacefully observed a snake glide within inches of my face. All brought gifts of understanding about myself and my Oneness with everything, and the ease in which God's creatures live in perfect harmony. In those canyons, I could see how rushing about is counterproductive to the natural flow of life. All who visit Oak Creek Canyon and Sedona are captured by it's unparalleled beauty. For a nature-lover like me, it is heaven.

On the way back to the parking lot, I spied another doe. Several clusters of hikers were enjoying watching her from afar. After they left, I approached and knelt on one knee before her. As I held out my hand as an offering, she came directly to me and nuzzled her nose deep into the cup of it. We looked into one another's eyes. It took me right back to the night before. Perhaps she smelled the other doe. As for me, I felt a symbiotic connection with her. As our souls met, I remember thinking to myself: "We are one, but now I feel sad because I know that the specialness of these moments are quickly fading into a memory." Indeed, I knew that I had come full-round with the two deer and experienced a sacred rite and bonding within the animal kingdom.

A few days later, I was driving with a friend near the place where the first doe had been hit. I had not shared the story with him. However, as we reached the spot, he began to talk about St. Francis of Assisi. I recalled how a psychic a few years before had told me that St. Francis was going to be working with me sometime in the future. Now, my friend was reawakening the memory of a past prediction. There was no mistake here. This was a sign. Some great, deep, spiritual initiation to Sedona had taken place for me with the doe.

Deer have always reminded me of the essence of love. From that night on the highway forward, I began to have a new personalized feeling and thoughts about what love really means. I know that the unconditional, Divine love of Spirit encompasses ultimate peace. Indeed, in that experience I discovered that it is a peace that passes all understanding.

All of our animals live by unconditional love. If only we could follow their knowing and take their examples of non-resistant being and be spontaneous living in the moment. Animals may remember the past, but they do not begrudge it. Our own pets demonstrate unconditional love to us over and over, every time we walk in the door they greet us. Our pets live for love. I wondered; why don't we? Or perhaps we do, we just do not know how because we search so hard to find it. The truth is that the love we seek to find, is *what we are* at the core of our being.

Exiting The Fast Lane.

After six month's time, driving to Sedona from Los Angeles had become nearly routine. Once a month, I made the trip for business. The first year away, the space between my monthly fixes of city life and my time away from it, turned out to be a gift that provided the space I needed to break my addiction to believing that I had no choice but to reside in L.A.. Twenty-three years is a long time to live in one town. I had tried to leave it many times. Every few years, I would attempt to escape its traffic and multi-level, ivy-covered freeway bridges and retreat to the wooded canyons of Topanga or the grassy hills of Malibu. Just close enough, but not too far away. Eventually, I would throw in the towel and move back into town. By now, the intensity and density of what L.A. had grown to be were more than I cared to deal with on a daily basis. Every day for the last three years that I spent there, I would be driving down some crowed boulevard and ask; "God, how much longer do I have to put up with this?" I finally made the choice to migrate....and broke the spell.

Everyone who lives in Southern California experiences some sort of love/hate relationship with it. At one time or another most residents flirt with the idea of finding a simpler way of living.

Being the kind of place that Los Angeles is, it deludes one into believing that in order to survive and thrive, one must be there. It is a common thread. When you ask an Angeleno what would be the options for relocating somewhere else they will tell you that there is no place like L.A.. (It's true!) I can't tell you how many times I've heard, "I'd like to leave but where else can I go and have everything that I have here!"

In a way, Los Angeles is a city of illusion. Based on facade, it makes one believe there is no place better. L.A. needs that kind of illusive relationship with its residents to make it the great place it is. I, too, love it.

The City of Angels is extremely seductive. People gather there from all over the world in search of their dreams. Many find them fulfilled. But she requires the passion, love and energy of her residents in order to thrive and to give her rewards. She seduced me by providing a lifestyle I could only have dreamed about in the Midwest. I owned my own home surrounded by palm trees, open to the outdoors, with every latest amenity. I lived near and shopped with movies stars, and made a great living by creating my own art for them. I could go to the beach in the morning, hike in the mountains in the afternoon, have any kind of food for dinner, and party at night with fantastic people....all in L. A.. And Like a lover who hands out just enough goodies to make you believe you would go crazy without her, she sends you away and refuses to marry you. It is a culture that distributes overages of perks and rewards of money, cars and cutting edge glitzy experiences just for staying. It dangles much more before you in endless possibilities, and makes one believe that one truly could not exist away from it, especially without the seduction, and illusion of its surface effects and rewards. This time I had managed to slowly cut my cord of dependency upon the illusion. Still, I would miss my elusive lover, were it not for frequent visits.

In traveling between Sedona and L.A., I quickly discovered that it would be essential to time my departure just right so that the drive would conform to the space between the morning rush hour in Los Angeles and the afternoon commute through Phoenix. Multiple corridors of concrete, blue carbon monoxide haze, and frequent off-ramps line one hundred miles and as many minutes on the way out of Angel City. Endless nondescript tracts of communities devour more than two hours of one's behind-the-wheel time, before one escapes the urbanization and sprawl of the city. Finally, the traffic lightens and the road opens, and the hazy film of Southern California is finally in the rear view mirror. At the same time, I would see a beautiful expanse of desert spread across the glass screen before me like a majestic scene from *Lawrence of Arabia*. And only then, in that first year of commuting by car, could I feel relaxed enough to settle into a meditative drive.

I see that journey as an analogy for our world's history unfolding at this time. Humanity is now at the juncture where we may depart from the chaos and confusion of the past. **The landscape our Creator intended for us now lies before us**. We are emerging from the smog and veil of dark and limited illusions upon which we formed our judgments and knowing.

We are just now coming out of a two-thousand-year history of struggle that humanity has experienced ever since Jesus walked the earth. He delivered his powerful messages in parable form, which contained **how-to** instruction for the creation heaven on earth. However, the message was not always accepted as simple and direct guidance for living as it was intended to be. Much was misconstrued by dogmatic churches and deluded by politics. It was used as a tool of feudal-like control to manipulate the collective thoughts of the populace. It was redesigned, utilized and enforced to keep the people *in and of the dust*, in their social strata, under a blurry filter of control that only sometimes alluded to the *truth*.

As we come into the age of enlightenment, we can be freed to shed the skins of limitation that have clothed humanity in fear for thousands of years. At last, you and I may be in the light living as One with our Divine Parent.

Peace That Passes All Understanding

Today our world is a dichotomy between the shadows cast by war, pollution and over-population, and the light of inspiration shining from the rapid transformation in those who are awakening to spirituality. Peace is spreading over the surface of our planet. We watch via satellite while the old, habitual war game is still dying on the vine as a viable means of settling differences. As violence makes its last stubborn stand to exist, it reveals its futility to those who would fight to perpetuate it. Finally exhausted, the oppressors and the oppressed lay down their weapons and agree to a cooperative peace.

Never before in our history, has there been an evolution so dynamic and unprecedented as the one that is overtaking us now.

The Industrial Revolution that created the modern world spanned the course of three hundred years. It forever altered the way humanity lived. Freed from an agrarian domicile of horses, lanterns and fireplace heat, we live and travel in comfort and ease and communicate instantaneously around the globe. Now, we are a world leaping in technological and spiritual transformation. It is an evolution that is more dynamic on a global scale and uniquely personal than any development or force we have previously known.

The age of spiritual awakening is moving upon the face of the earth. It will take only a few decades or the course of one human lifetime for it to unfold and weave itself over the globe.

You and I are here to participate in this great awakening. We are part of a world that is yearning and learning to live as One. As God's countenance illuminates our awareness and recognition of Divinity within one another, we come into balance with the natural state of life. We live in harmony with a Divine Plan unfolding for an age of global peace and enlightenment. The illusion of darkness and the bounds of material, doctrinal and superstitious beliefs dissolve in the clear illumination cast by Oneness with the Divine as It shines in the face of each human being. To connect, we must take time to tune in and listen to what is already inside of us.

Tuning In

Deep into a river-filled canyon in Northern Arizona, my hiking partner and I meandered. From time to time, we left the marked trail and worked our way up the babbling creek by stepping from stone to stone. Occasionally we would drift back to one of the two trails on either side of the stream. About an hour into the pass, we ran into a couple who were confused and disoriented. Apparently, they had wandered from the trail and lost their way sometime before. They had been searching for a trail out of the canyon for a long time. Slipping from wet stones into the water only agitated and perplexed them further. By the time we found them they were shaken and arguing. "Its just ahead," I nodded towards the trails on both sides of the river, "you can choose either way." Indeed, either trail was no more than twenty feet away and in plain sight. Yet neither of the hikers could find the beginnings of either path, and both appeared to be fearful and uncertain about moving forward.

After they had safely found the trail and were out of ear-shot, my friend who had been quiet up till now commented; "Those two probably get all of their information from the Internet." I had to laugh, I knew what he meant. Sometimes we rely on a road map or a written formula to pull us through, when all we need in the first place is to be at peace and go within. Listening to our own inner guidance will always pull us through. It is the strongest and clearest hearing device we have. Even though we have been taught to deny its power, in times of challenge, it may be necessary to forget what the so-called statistics or experts tell us. For healing to take place, it may be necessary to take focus off the prognosis or the threat of a legal suit and surrender to trusting Spirit. Learn to use your own knowing. As you become adept at trusting it by sharpening your greatest tool within, you will come into tune with higher awareness. Although doctors and lawyers may be helpful, many only know or practice what they have been taught or what is in the text book. However, the Infinite within each of us knows all ways, means and solutions.

We each have an inner knowing and guidance system. When we take the time to get centered and go within, getting in touch with that which knows all, will reveal what we require in order to function smoothly and find entrée to creating our own Divine Solutions.

Use The Field of Infinite Possibilities to Create Change!

Spirit within Knows infinite ways and means to reveal to us what we need to know under all circumstances. When we speak our Word in affirmative prayer. we activate the essence of our desires and begin to bring them into form. Divine Co-Creation with the Infinite is necessary for perfect results. The great secret to receiving the fruits of our Co-Creation is to have a passion for our desire, and at the same time be willing to be completely non-attached as to how it may come. When we remain non-attached to outcome, what we seek can only be revealed as we put the principles of manifestation into action by moving forward as though we expect to receive. It may be a fine line to walk or it may sound like a contradiction. However, non-attachment to outcome always brings the most successful results possible.

Letting Go

Donovan, an Irish-born, folk-rock singer from the British Isles' music invasion of the sixties, went on a spiritual pilgrimage to India. He had heard of the Dali Lama and wanted to meet him and give him a gift that would be unique to the Holy City. He searched and searched, racking his brain, thinking and thinking, "What could I possibly take his Holiness that would be something he does not have?" To be one of a kind and memorable it would have to be an object that would offer some kind of special use or function. He finally came up with what he thought would be a totally unique and perfect idea. When he arrived at the Holy City, it was arranged for him to have an audience with the Dali Lama. On first seeing the unusual gift, the Dali Lama politely declined to accept it. Donovan, certain that there had never been one in all of the holy city, felt that it could be of great use to the other monks in residence. Arguing that it would make their lives easier, he continued to insist that if his Holiness did not want to receive it for himself, he should accept it for the other monks.

Finally the Dali Lama agreed to receive the gift, saying "We have much gratitude for your gift. I will accept the vacuum cleaner, but only on one condition....**no attachments please.**"

The Dali Lama and all mystics know that true power is engendered by letting go of one's attachment to outcome. For centuries, great mystics and teachers have spoken of the gifts that one experiences as a result of surrender. When we release our need to control outcome, we send this powerful signal to that which creates all. "I am willing for my dreams to come true and for them to come right to me. I release struggle and accept that the Infinite will bring my desires in ease. I have an absolute trust and faith in Spirit, that It knows the best ways and means to bring my desires to me, and me to a point of receptivity to them."

In times of shift within any culture, the only constant that endures is change. Adjustments appear within the mesh and fabric of the way things work. (Whether radical or subtle in nature, eminent results of the shift follow any societal alteration). These changes ultimately force us to examine ourselves and the roles we play in our world from a fresh perspective. While the transition is taking place, we may feel a sense of loss for the old and comfortable structures. Unfamiliar and unexplored, uplifting feelings with a new vitality often come with of the arrival of a new paradigm. To those who resist letting go of the old, the shift might feel painful or jolting. But in the end, a revolutionary, new, unifying bond remains as an outgrowth of the metamorphosis that those who have experienced the shift felt collectively.

"We can do this rough - or we can do it easy." Tina Turner.

For a three-year period, my life was impacted dramatically by the ravages of natural disasters that hit Southern California. I rode out the Northridge earthquake with six million others as it rolled through and hit Los Angeles with a hard jolt in early 1994. Just as in the floods, fires, and not-so-natural riots, those of us who shared it have a simultaneous remembrance of the details and the effects of its aftermath. It was more than a physical jolt. Angelenos know first-hand how the people of a city in shock feel. In each case, afterwards it was as though everyone was treading lightly on eggshells. For the few first hours, days, and weeks after the quake, an entire city lay in waiting, stunned in disbelief that the much talked-about quake could have happened at all. Everyone hoped and prayed that the next series of aftershocks would continue to decrease in volume and subside altogether. Rumors of the *BIG ONE* abounded.

When President John F. Kennedy was shot, everyone who was around at the time recalls exactly where he was and what he was doing. A nation watched as actual assassinations played themselves out on television. An entire generation of children grew up becoming familiar with the sound of an oddly pitched obnoxious, horn that interrupted TV and radio broadcasts regularly warning; *This has been a test of the national early warning system. Had this been an actual emergency or nuclear attack you would have been instructed to....* Most children of the sixties were well rehearsed for nuclear Armageddon. By squatting under the desks at school they were assured safety, as if doomsday could be survived. Later, in the days when I was busy dating in the singles scene, I applied that same phrase in qualifying or negating the validity of short-lived romantic relationships. "This has only been a test. *Had this been an actual relationship you would have been instructed to tune in to your partner."*

In 1989, the people of Berlin shared the dramatic experience of The Wall coming down with the rest of the world. As we watched on television in surprise and gratitude, we knew that our prayers and meditations for world peace had collectively been effective. Its disassemble marked the real dawning of a new age of freedom for humanity. With its fall, came the official end to the cold war. It was the first significant sign that the fear of annihilation we had come to accept as a natural part of life could be released. The day it came down forever marks the first real and visible, significant surrender and agreement by mankind of any generation to live in trust and peace as one, earth people.

It's fruitless to resist. Change is going to happen anyway.

Anyone who resists change inevitably leaves claw marks on the old walls as they crumble and fall. Nobody wants to go down with the walls of the past. Out of apparent chaos, ultimately comes order. The most graceful and the highest thing we can do when a climatic, political, governmental or spiritual shift comes upon us is to surrender to its course. Let go, use wisdom by stepping out of the path of the storm, and enjoy the ride. The way to experience change in grace and ease is to detach and allow Spirit to guide us into the new. When we do, we automatically arrive in the right and appropriate place to accept the new that is to come.

Good is present all of the time, in every experience. Often we are so busy trying to make things happen in our lives that we fail to see that many blessings and much good already exists all around us. As we begin to open to the acceptance of new potential in our experience we learn to depend upon the trust that there is a higher knowing of Spirit that flows *through us.*

Our Creator has designed her own intuition into our psyche. Our gut feelings are almost always leading us towards our rightful path of fulfillment. On following our instinct, we are always guided to the very highest and best in every situation - the same Intelligence and Knowing that makes the whole of the Universe tick, so magnificently synchronized with every part of itself. When we listen and follow it, we are in tune with the natural flow and order in all things.

Life is something that happens *through us,* not to us.

As we surrender to the discrimination of Spirit within we automatically have immediate access to the unlimited field of infinite possibilities that exists in all situations and we receive the gifts found in non-resistance and become one with the flow.

The great secret, overlooked by all the known information in all the libraries of the world....

The more we let go, the more we find that the journey and the destination are one. Each is essential to the other. This is the key to enjoyment of the whole course of life, not just your arrival at a goal or destination. **Surrender to living in the moment with *unconditional trust, allowing Spirit within as the guide to being in harmony with your higher self.* At first it may feel like you are winging it, and you may be, but as you come to realize a greater awareness and the power in it, you will uncover the hidden keys to being a master manifestor. You begin to harness the Divine, Inherent Power to fulfill the desires of your life.**

Despite what we may have learned, life was meant to be easy. You and I can choose to experience the bliss of being in a greater receivership with ourselves and those around us by letting go of carrying the burden and responsibilities of the world. In contrast to the tough paradigms for success we grew up with, when we let go and allow for spiritual guidance, we become emancipated. Accept a higher course of action by surrendering the need to control and determine outcome. In doing so, you may greet life's challenges with a deeper trust that the Infinite Intelligence of Spirit is in everything. The Creator within knows everything about each one of us. As we learn to accept this truth in ease, we become One with, and open to the natural order, flow and rhythm of the whole of the Universe. We unify with the workings of life and everything automatically falls into place with perfect synchronization.

Guess what? the Creator in all of Her Infinite Intelligence, knows what She is doing today. All things we require will be revealed to us and coordinated through Divine Order when we align ourselves with the Spirit in, around and through us. We are now free to let go and let God do her thing without interfering!

Socks spells out the Universal Cosmic Laws. Once understood and applied successfully, you can use them to lay out your personal pathways to successful living. In getting the message of the power that can be employed for you in being non attached to outcome, you will own the freedom that comes with it! As you put non attachment into action, your life will change and you will know for yourself that it works. In beginning to live the new paradigm, you will see that indeed the truth is; *"My Father maketh me to walk in green pastures, and lie by still waters."*

"I've learned you can get by on charm for about five minutes.   After that, you had better know something." Tallulah Bankhead

CHAPTER TWO

Let Ease Light The Way

At twenty-three, I was charged with excitement to be exploring New York City alone for the first time. Enticed by the prospects of unknown adventures that the Big Apple surely would expose me to, I had ventured courageously from the sanctity of my humble Arizona adobe. Still, a Midwestern bred vulnerability, (translation: fear of the great unknown), enforced my uncertainty that I might get lost or suffer wild misfortune at any moment from being so brave. Perhaps the element of risk added thrill to my going it on my own. My initial excursion in getting from point A to point B and making my way from Upper Westside Manhattan to Soho downtown, involved taking a city bus line. Sweltering August heat and a standing-room-only-ride gave me claustrophobia to the degree that I disembarked after one or two stops still a great distance from my destination. The brief journey had been so grim that I swore that I would never board a bus again. The only excursion I recall that compares to this day was a hellish excursion I took on the Athens subway in 1994. Try no air-conditioning, in August, with a crammed train, filled with twelve and thirteen-year-olds who had just completed their afternoon of soccer games! A memorable journey.

Next, I tried taxicabs. Although extremely convenient, taking them quickly began to eat a hole in my budget. Whether I rode in one or not, by the end of each afternoon, I always wondered what had happened to the money I had started out with that morning. It was as if there were strings attached to the dollar bills in my pockets. I wondered if they were being mysteriously whisked from me by invisible, sticky fingers Pete or slick pickpocket Pearl.

Finally, I established that my favorite modus operandi - walking was still the best of all choices. To this day I would swear that it is by far *the way* to get the real essence of the sights, sounds and smells of New York City for the first time. Sworn off public transportation for the time being, I began my trek downtown in SoHo, and continued to walk up Broadway all the way back to the Upper West Side where I was staying. That day I walked eighty-eight blocks! I saw much, however it was exhausting.

One day, aided by a friend who was a seasoned resident, I agreed to venture underground and try the subway for the first time. As we rode the train from one destination to the next, I relaxed and became more comfortable, and I fell in love with its speedy efficiency. The cost was certainly a boost to my traveler's budget, so I decided to get a map and brave it alone. In striking out on my own, I found that one could rapidly get from point A to B in literally, a few minutes. It was a wonderful discovery to be able to integrate the street map with the subway map. It was like a bright, light of awareness had been turned on. Suddenly the Big Apple did not look as ominous as before. With my new perception about logistics came a sense of freedom that allowed for easy, confident mobility. Before, I had walked everywhere, feeling like a stranger in a strange land, never quite sure of where I was, and never knowing when I was being taken advantage of. I had heard the stories.

In integrating the map of the subway with its relationship to the city streets and landmarks, I was able to pursue my bliss of taking in as much art as I could fit into each day. Knowing how to get to where I wanted to go made everything fall into place with comfort, safety and ease. With a new awareness of how to manage getting around New York, I was able to travel about without being escorted. I enjoyed the freedom of independence and moved with confidence, exhilaration and purpose to get the most out of each day. At night I was able to meet my friends for Broadway shows, cutting edge, underground plays in the Village, and the best of live art performance, music and dance.

I discovered a similar emancipation and understanding when I began to apply basic principles of metaphysics to my everyday life. For the first time, I could see clearly how to get from where I was to where I wanted to be, and how to get there. Before, like so many in this work-a-day, fast paced world, I had felt trapped in daily chores doing things I did not want to do, and was suffering the pain of it. The idea of enjoying life all of the time eluded me and seemed to be pre-destined just for those who were born into affluence. Now, for the first time, I found that I was able to enjoy using tools that work in concert with all things to create and instigate my own changes from within.

To be emancipated from constraints or conditions of limitation is a primary focus or goal of anyone on a spiritual path of growth.

As I developed a resonance with the secret rules and workings of the Universe, I began to realize my *ability to creatively select experiences.* I had long suspected a connection to creation in mind picturing and the speaking of my word. When I began to consciously practice spiritual creation it was similar to having a map before me of the subway system. By studying and applying metaphysics to my daily life, I could observe the direct results of cause and effect as they unfolded in my experience. As I became clearer, pathways opened before me that lead to new vision and purpose. You, too, can consciously use the principles to create expansion. One great benefit of the learn-by-doing technique is that Light is shed into and through your heart and mind. As it does, it forever expands the love of Spirit within the self.

The Cosmic Law Of Cause And Effect

There is One, Great Divine Intelligence in the Universe that is in all life and that governs all things. We are designed in the image and likeness of that Intelligence, our Creator and have the ability to create in the same way. Our thoughts, words, and belief move upon the Universal Awareness present within us and through It to create our experiences.

As what we have created comes to us, we become aware that we draw to us what is equal to the level of our acceptance and clarity. What comes to us will reflect exactly what we are willing to receive and be equal to our belief of what is appropriate and possible. Spirit operates at the level of cause in consciousness.

You will come to an understanding of the basic Laws of Mind by applying them consciously in the practice of a co-creation with Spirit. As you do, you will automatically gain an awareness of the underground workings of the universe. And by delving deeper into the cosmic map, you assume a natural and working-knowing of how to apply spiritual awareness to what is simply a mechanical, unseen creative force of Spirit. It works with or without our being aware of it. Practicing principles consciously reveals knowing.

Going to the Source of Creation within is *the way* to reach your rightful success in the world. Experiment in creating what you desire by speaking your word, establishing expectations of success, and observe the magnificence of your Creations as they unfold.

A first-hand knowing of the simple *laws of Mental Science* gives us the freedom to rise above the pre-conditioned limits of the human race that we previously accepted along with the rest of the tribe.

Once we become adept at commanding a conscious use of the mental laws, we receive insight through gifts of awareness, and claim power over problems once and for all. It is a *conscious choice* to deal with fears and doubts. One that requires courage. But in doing so, we will stake a claim on greater understanding and graduate into owning the kind of real spiritual power that comes with emancipation. Anyone who remains living at the level of the problem and the limits they impose, would attract them time and again. The circumstances and people might change, but the challenge would always remain the same until one clears the cause of the pattern within the self. Anyone who grew up with a tyrannical parent, will attract and become involved with the same type of individual as an adult, until they heal the need (cause, habit or pattern) within themselves to repeat the scenario.

The Bridge

Trips over the great silver and orange, steel bridge were terrifying. However, traversing it gave entrance from Iowa to Wisconsin for a wonderful day of shopping and fun. There were many spaces and cracks in the narrow wooden roadway. Some so wide that one could easily see the dark and mighty Mississippi River rushing a couple of hundred feet below. The bridge swayed in the wind and vibrated with the passing each car we met. Built in the nineteen-twenties for narrow Model T's and the like, its single narrow lane of traffic going each way, posed a challenge for the heavier, wide and chrome-adorned car bodies in America during the fifties and sixties. Should a semi-trailer truck approach on the narrow roadway, the bouncing became frighteningly wild and rhythm like. There was always a construction crew hanging on ropes somewhere above, making repairs or spraying orange colored rust proofing paint or holding up traffic while replacing floor boards. There was a constant effort to keep up with decay and deterioration.

I never looked forward to the ride over the bridge. From the back seat I could only look out of the side windows, where by peering through the glass, over the broad curve of the fifties fenders I could see straight down through the openings between the tar and gravel covered floor boards to the deep, green river below. The worst and most dreaded part of the crossing would be on our approach to the summit of the tall, swaying structure. My view over the back of the front seats, towards the front windshield, afforded only a clear look upward at rusting steel that soared a hundred feet up or more. The hood of the car pointed towards the sky until the car passed over the steep arch of the summit that marked the halfway point before we took a sudden downward journey to the safety of the other side and when I could let go of the tension in my body and anxiety in my mind.

For many years as an adult, I dreamed about that fearful crossing over the rickety bridge. The dream would always come at a time when I was about to confront a challenge or embark upon a venture that I felt anxious or uncertain about. At that time, I created my own challenges in order to force myself to expand and overcome my childhood fears of not being good enough, or man enough to create or deserve what I desired. In taking them on, I did succeed in growing past the limits. However, until I changed my fear-based thinking and released a belief that life did not support me the bridge would continue to challenge and threaten me. In the dream the bridge would be far taller, steeper and more dangerous than the original one. I would grasp my steering wheel, tense with fear until I reached the other side. Perhaps that was a metaphor for how I handled the challenges of life at the time. When I began to relax my grip and came to trust life accepting that God was on my side, I stopped having the dream altogether.

The old bridge has been torn down and replaced with a smooth flat, firm modern concrete span. I am certain that children and adults alike, and all who passage it can rest easier as a result. I am happy to not be having that vision of terror repeated. When we come to the awareness that we are supported, we are able to trade our fears and doubts for freedom from limits. Learning how the Law of Mind works, and using it consciously, brings the emancipation from our past.

Dark Ages

For thousands of years, humanity slept under the spell of a heavy blanket of limitation. The belief that we are subject to an all-inclusive law of materialism, kept us bound to a *what I can see and touch must be real* sort of mentality. Illumined and enlightened moments recorded in the sketch book of our history were introduced by visionaries, and mystics. However, until now, most of humanity has remained unconscious to the truth, awakening only in increments that are hardly discernible. Humanity has yet to discover many of its innate God-like abilities and gifts. In our awakening to an acceptance of the mysteries from within, we will naturally discover the gifts and secrets of the universe.

By nature people are beings of habit. Historically, religion and politics working hand-in-hand with one another taught us to believe that we were separate from one another, and from God our Source. The traditional belief that this being is an old man in the sky naturally alienates a progressive thinker from wanting to deepen any relationship or involvement with Spirit.

As a result of living with primitive, fearful beliefs, our semi-conscious race was trained to accept violence as a solution to conflict. Anyone who is based in fear can be easily controlled. The dominant leaders who determined dogmatic belief controlled politics and religion. Politics, as defined by Webster, is *manipulation or influence peddling*. This atmosphere of control and limitation bred a usurious and competitive attitude into the race and made man suspect the unknown as being dangerous or morally wrong. Many of the learned reactions are based in fear, egocentric in nature and rooted in ancient, time honored myth.

Thus the unknowing, asleep children of God have lived in denial of their roots. Living shrouded to their true nature of Oneness with Spirit has kept us feeling lost and powerless to change. Historically whenever man has connected with Something Greater he has felt hope, inspiration and power that was naturally his Divine Birthright.

Until now, humanity has lived in darkness, denying its innate and primary connection to our Source within.

Spirit Alive

In awakening to its Divine heritage, humanity begins to clarify the need for change and makes corrections in it's culture. A shift is reflected from the consciousness of the world peoples as an out-picturing of rapid alteration in the landscape of nations. As each member of the tribe awakens to his or her true nature of a personalized, inherent Divinity, each is able to *embody a union of perfection with Spirit. According to Jesus, "Ye will do these things and greater."* Jesus had no doubts concerning His relationship to the Father and Creative Principle. As a result Jesus easily manifested light over darkness. He lived in the Light, as the Light. To bring heaven on earth to life We must emulate and embody what Our Brother Jesus taught. It is up to us to put the principles into action for ourselves. Living by example becomes the best way to teach those around us and the cosmic law of cause and effect will create balance for the rest.

Love Points The Way.
Universal Law Makes The Way Possible.

You and I have an innate, God-given power to materialize our desires into form by speaking our word into the law of mind. When we understand and consciously apply the law we become free to live our own salvation and reveal the atmosphere of heaven on earth. Knowing that we are One with the natural law makes things flow in ease. We may detach from having to struggle to make things happen.

Love is the primary force and glue of the Universe.
Its unifying power brings everything together.

As we apply the focus of love to what we want, it cements our desires to us. I believe that the ultimate wave of love on earth will be the essence of the *Second Coming* of Christ and Self-Divine-Realization within each human being. It will be the first real, awakening of self-love in humanity, and it will unfold as it embodies all of its glory within Its many individualized versions of its unique self. That light-wave within each soul is beaming now. Slowly at first, it begins to awaken those who are ready, willing, and searching. Soon, more members of the same tribe find themselves snapping to attention as Spirit shouts a wake-up call in outside personal or world events. The snowball of spirit coming to life in humanity is irreversible and irrevocable. It must and will saturate every person and event upon earth in the twenty-first century. Others will leave the planet, and heaven on earth will prevail in all of its forms, cultures, religions and peoples.

That is my prediction. It will not come about overnight, or without the threat of darkness or injustice. We may be witness to shocking or disturbing events. But for one who is centered in spirit, all will be well, because one who knows God....knows peace, truth and love and is prospered and protected in all ways at all times. He or she is free to live from that place where all is well. The attitude and posture of peace and plenty always creates more of the same. The more who know, assume and live it, collectively will magnify the force upon the earth. Join me in knowing the truth.

Speak your Word to set yourself free.

I am at my essence, One with the Creative Principle. I choose right here and right now to embody a greater understanding of how to apply the Universal Law of Creation to my experience. Spirit in me is peace and perfection. Therefore, perfection and the perfect Knowing of Spirit resides within me. I accept and give thanks that It reveals to me greater understanding so that I may enjoy use of the cosmic law to create what I choose. In doing so, I am guided in the right and highest choices that serve the greater good right now and at all times. I am in agreement to living in peace and light.

I accept this as my truth. Spirit in me supports me in revealing knowing and right activity in all areas of my life. I accept Oneness with the Creative Principle of the Universe. I am thankful that I know that I am One with my Source and that I am supported, prospered and protected in all of my ways, now and always. I am an emissary of peace, light and abundance. I maintain this attitude of gratitude and Oneness with my Source, now and always. I accept permanent revelation of my love of self, fellow humans and Spirit as one being. We are one in all the world because it is Gods universe and atmosphere we reside in. And so it is!

CHAPTER THREE

Faith and Creation

As infinite spirit beings, you and I might enjoy cloud floating. From our vantage we could easily observe our temporal selves below traversing the river of life. Our view would reveal a passage of broad smooth flows and sudden unexpected turns. We could see our physical journey as it exists within a linear, earthly time-frame, and ascertain that most all of our wisdom, judgment, and actions are derived from experiences gathered along the course. Since our world is balanced by light and darkness, rich and poor, joy and pain, it is easy to see why we rely upon comparatives for our logic and decision. If we were unable to discern differences and felt only exhilaration, and fun we would miss the knowing that comes with melancholy or sadness. It might be difficult for us to appreciate our accomplishments. So to be able to feel the joy that satisfaction brings and bask in the sunlight of fulfillment, the shadows of sorrow and disappointment are necessary for balance.

In this earthly life we experience and feel the contrasts between passion, dread, excitement, fear and thrill. Occasionally our course drifts into boredom. Even with that, comes a subtle balance that soothes drama by feathering our ecstasies and healing pain. It too, is a part of the wholeness of yin and yang and necessary for completeness. **All of our experiences contribute to the wealth of awareness that we collect on our river of life.**

The Mississippi River

When I was a boy, I spent parts of many summers at my cousin's cabin on the Mississippi. The great river was wide and deep between Northeastern Iowa and the Southwestern tip of Wisconsin. At night the water was black, formidable, and silent. More than a mile wide at that point, it was a great challenge to be brave enough to steal a quick swim from the dock at midday. The mighty, fast-moving, Mississippi carried many mysteries in its flow. With swirling, deep currents, and treacherous water moccasin snakes occasionally passing by the dock, most of the time we children played on the safety of its shores. From there, we could watch huge barges headed towards the Southern Gulf Stream. We were on hand to run behind the cabin and wave at the engineers of the passing trains that traveled the tracks between the cabin and the highway a hundred yards behind. Towering along the road stood a backdrop of giant, rocky, wooded bluffs. My summers there were filled with the kind of fun that felt like those of Tom Sawyer and Huck Finn.

My cousins were generous, loving and fun to be with. Their father had made enough in the stock market to live comfortably on just the interest income. The family was fun to be with. Free from normal stresses of making a living, they enjoyed a relaxed life at the summer and weekend cabin. Even driving to town to get fresh, drinking water was an adventure. Riding in the third seat of a station wagon, rear window open, balancing tall, aluminum, milk cans, as we cruised beside the tall, green bluffs and inhaled the smells of the river, are memories I will never forget. Trips to the bathroom revealed a double-seater, outhouse. Bath time took us on a boat journey to a sandbar, located upriver in a cove. A few weeks at the cabin was always great fun.

Faith

One evening, the grown-ups included us children in an excursion to an adult nightclub, dinner lounge, located on an island in the middle of the river. This was a major adventure for a child, since it consisted of a small, motorboat passage into the blackness of the night, over the deepest, and widest part of the water. On this moonless, night the river looked particularly spooky. From it's center, all I could think about was anticipation of the trip home to the safety of the shore. The little boat sped across the river to the piers and planks of the landing dock at the exotic, Pink Elephant nightclub. We enjoyed a good meal and the nightlife. It was fun being with the adults, but the discomfort of knowing we had yet to cross back in the dark permeated my evening. My swimming skills ended with easy dog paddles and a couple of circles near the safety of the dock in full daylight.

When it came time to leave the island I was relieved that this fear-filled adventure would be over soon. Yet I dreaded it. We set off. Near the center of the river, the darkest and spookiest part, we spied one of the enormous barges coming our way. We would be forced to wait in the dark rather than risk crossing his path. As the looming hulk approached in the black silence, the pull of his draw on the water began to rock the boat. Silently and relentlessly churning and eating water in his roadway, like some behemoth monster, he rumbled past. I held tightly to the side, clenching my jaw as tightly and praying for the whole thing to end. I was a chicken no doubt. As he passed beyond, the hungry wake churned us further. The little motor finally started up and we picked up speed planing over his wake and safely onward to the comfort of the shores and my bunk. The nights adventure would be complete.

For a seven-year-old boy, not prone to risk danger, it was a terrifying adventure. As adults, we all face personal challenge. We all know what it feels like to make rough, river crossings in the black of night. A fear of the darkness and of the possible unknown contains all kinds of challenge and illusions. Until we learn to trust and accept unconditional spiritual guidance and protection the shadows will continue to threaten, coming upon us like the wake of a giant barge to rock our faith. I am sure that my cousin driving the boat was confident and comfortable. He had complete faith that he could handle the river crossing at night, regardless of what came along. We all have a small child within, who requires the firm hand of an adult to steady his courage when his boat is rocked. Practicing the three P's; prayer, patience and persistence will get you across the rivers and support you. They add strength to your faith in Spirit and yourself. They are one in the same.

Faith is a mental attitude that is so convinced of its own idea and completely accepts it so that any contradiction is unthinkable and impossible. **Ernest Holmes.**

Creation and the Creative Process

Reverend Carol Carnes of the Calgary Church of Religious Science, writes about two musicians who were trying to describe the creative process. Both agreed that they didn't know "where the music comes from." One heard it in his dreams already completed and the other concurred that "we don't write music, we hear it." Rev. Carol states: "Music exists in the universe as vibrations which the composer arranges in a form that allows it to be experienced by others. To be completed, the creative process requires a human partner." As a working artist, I can tell you that I draw or paint what I feel from within, yet I see that my work is interpreted differently by everyone who views and experiences it.

Futurist Barbara Marx Hubbard said that we have evolved from the "creature human" to the "co-creative human." We no longer think of ourselves as children of God, we are in partnership with God. Rev. Carol continues; "Humanity is directing the path of evolution. We are not standing outside of reality; we are participating in its creation in the immediacy of the moment. Our moments strung together, build our future. For those of us who are interested in shaping a future that will celebrate and support all humankind in love and abundance, our part is to heal this moment and set it in the right direction."

"Each moment is consciousness on the move." Rev. Carol Carnes

Life is an experiment acting upon itself to see just what it chooses to create for Itself. You and I are the Individualized Self constantly making choices and moving upon the waters of Spiritual Creation as we call forth our desires. We are the Creative Spirit within of God Itself, every minute of every day. Be in the Now!

Life.... the never-ending cycle

We walk the earth filled with the same water and air of the life substance as the mother, planet herself. The Divine blueprint within each one of us contains an internal, automatic knowingness of how to create new life along with the cellular memory and DNA codes for self-healing. Just as the earth perpetuates its life with the flow of the rivers and the rains, so does the Spirit of the Source of life within each man and woman. We are One with the sea of Infinite Mind of the Creator, and we arrive on this planet with the keys to Creation within our soul. It is a wonderful system God designed. For these things are ordinary, everyday occurrences. At the same time they hold magic and mystery for us. The beauty of birth and the body's ability to self heal are miracles to behold in their own right, yet to be fully understood or duplicated by science.

Causation And Its Effects

You and I are forever creating everything in our experience by use of our image and likeness power. The simple mechanics of the creative principle automatically give back to us in equal measure what we put into our subconscious in expectancy, acceptance and belief. If we think and speak negative thoughts, we will experience equal negative results. When we think and speak in the positive we enjoy the affirmative benefits. By dancing our own dance of joy, by doing what we love, and by being true to who we are, we expand in self-realization and expand into real purpose. As we imbue this satisfaction and joy into the cells of our being, it flows outwardly to our creation. Everyone around us benefits because it connects deep within our own subconscious mind to the subjective of the rest of the human race, (the whole of humankind's subconscious mind is connected through the God Mind).

What we sow, we shall also reap.

The Prime Creator of All Creation created the Heavens and the Earth by use of the Word. It is our Divine Right as offspring of the One to speak our Word and have an effect on the *Waters* (Pure Spirit out of which all is Created) to create good in our lives. Speaking our Word to create is in essence, the Image and Likeness of our Creator made manifest within us. The creative principle is Individualized by free will and activated by our power of decision.

We contribute to humanity by "dancing" our own version of the dance, whatever individualized form it may take. We do not have to be a Baryshnikov or a Picasso to express our creative nature.

Each one of us is a part of the Creator's divine plan. Its intelligence moves us to express our own unique version of the dance of life. By doing whatever we do, our own talents and natural abilities flow through our work and our play. Whether we consider these endeavors to be creative or not, the creative juice of Spirit is involved. **Creative thought is as creative thought does.**
It is the quest for and enjoyment of increased dharma or life-force that is the impelling energy each of us resonate with when we are involved in any passion-filled act. The soul of creation within us seeks to experience that life-blood and flow of creation while here. When we are participating in creating the things we love, we find and feel the fulfillment and joy we seek. Creation has proven itself to be part of the key to living a rich life. It keeps one engaged in happy life-producing activities and expands our dharma.
It is a sad but obvious fact that those members of our social family who surrender involvement in conscious creation experience a deterioration of life force. The fact that we force retirement upon the most wise and experienced in our culture by isolating and compartmentalizing them into nursing homes is an enormous detriment to the dharma, productivity and creativity of our community.

Life Is Art - The Art Of Doing What We Love

Creation by its own nature, must flow in order for it to fulfill its purpose. As it streams outward from an inner well, it requires a place to go where it can be received. True artists do what they do and create what they do because they have little choice. Their innate need to express their creativity is always present inside. As artists share their passion, they project and transmute a personalized, essence of what is felt on the inside, outwardly to their respective audiences.

Anyone who has ever created anything has become attuned to a resonance with the love of creation that emanates and springs from this inner well. A spontaneity of living comes from being one with the creative process. Artists who tend to be some of the most free and child-like of the adults on the planet, breathe their joy and energy of living into their gifts as they pass it on to those who are able to receive. This spontaneous creation is similar to the play we all experienced as children. Although disciplined, a dancer who is flowing with the music in interpretive movement or a painter who emotionally lays his paint on canvas draws from the same place as the child on the ballfield or in the sandbox. Whether it be a mechanic who loves to tinker with cars, or the cook who is in ecstasy when busy in the kitchen, it is the love of doing what we love that propels a real passion for a project and increases our dharma - life - force.

We cannot all be artists, but in our own right, each of us is a creator. Whenever we put our thought and energy into a project, and become inspired or impassioned with a spawning that comes from urges of the soul, we come into co-creation with the Greater Spirit within. That energy takes us beyond the normal limits of everyday life. In becoming involved in doing something we love, it is not unusual to lose track of the time. I recall instances when I was so deeply absorbed in my act of creation that I lost all sense of time and place. It would not be unusual for me to look up from a drawing only to discover that many hours had passed. That is living art.

Dance As If It Were So!

Dancing is another great way to express the joy of creation. When our human spirit feels free enough to be compelled to get up and boogie, we can do it with plenty of spontaneous energy. For me, I am free enough just about any time I hear the right music. The beat and harmony work within to amplify a feeling of Oneness. I feel the life force rise and flow within, like a river of music with all its currents until I become so consumed by its flow that my spirit and body feel absolutely air-borne. It is as if waves of passion, emotion and sensuality unite to choreograph an exuberant awareness of Spirit within. The wave merges with an intentional quest to join with its Source. Just as the river flows until it spills into the sea, the sea is irresistibly drawn to the heavens seeking to return home and circulate to a greater part of itself.

Mindless Bliss

When totally consumed in the flow of creativity, whether it be art, dance, sports or whatever, one may enter a blissful state of mindlessness. The highest knowing where pure freedom, ecstasy and creation merge as one with the life force of pure spirit. Once entered into that state of nirvana, One may experience the utmost in release by letting go of the world's thoughts and becoming one with absolute non-attached joy. In that place of total joy and release, I have received some of my greatest guidance and awareness directly from my Source and realized what it was that I would next create. When I begin a new project I act and dance as if it were so. Soon I am looking at my creation because I have already imaged it mentally, and become spiritually engaged in its activity.

Having Passion And Enthusiasm With Non-Attachment To Out-Come Always Creates Success!

The Cycle of Life

Water flows through channels on the surface of this earth as the lifeblood of the blue planet. It recycles to the sky from where it falls to the land again and again, back to the streams and rivers completing its never ending course. Where did it pass, what did it pick up, and what did it drop along the way? The river and its path of flow are an analogy of the journey of your life.

If we were to know with certainty that we too would flow from one life to the next, ever anew with a collection of feelings and experiential wisdom, we might accept the passage of time in our lives with more grace and ease and pace ourselves accordingly. Reincarnation gives fluidity to the idea of returning to life in a cyclic path from one incarnation to the next. Belief in it brings us the opportunity to have the freedom to release a fear of death. The journey on the river is a metaphor for the passage of life we all experience from youth to age. Reincarnation gives credence to the cycle of moving from one life to another, with a non-physical, spirit life in between.

Yet there are no guarantees that death is not the end. No one left us a handbook telling us the cosmic rules. So we are to find our own truths and discover our own path of understanding. Each of us learns how to dance our own dance and devises ways to swim the currents and waves on the river of life as they come along. We apply what we have learned from past experience or we end up going through a process of trial and error. This may work but it takes time and effort that may or may not achieve desired results.

You and I can streamline the manifestation of our desires and create free flow by going within before we create. Seek guidance from Spirit in all things, in advance. Be willing to step into action by moving on the intuition you receive. I prefer the learn-as-I-go method. It reveals the path of least resistance, involves open doors rather than blocked passageways, and requires me to do a bit of spiritual surfing, dancing or improvising. By trusting my own intuition, and moving into the activity of what I desire to experience, and taking one step at a time, I own the experience at its completion. It requires absolute, unconditional trusting of Spirit and listening to the strongest urge. The benefits of free flow are revealed when unencumbered by my control to having to have things be a certain way. *Non-attachment* to the ways and means of outcome is essential, and *flexibility* in being willing to go with what works with the least amount of effort is the key to ease in demonstration. ***The way of Spirit always is smarter, not harder.***

Going With The flow

To be on the path of least resistance and enjoy its gifts, one must stay present in the moment. It is the only way to discover the opportunities that exist in being non-attached to outcome.

On past visits to New York I frequently enjoyed attending the ballet. One performance presented by the American Ballet Theatre stands out as being most memorable. I have forgotten what the ballet was but I recall my disappointment when an announcement was made that the lead dancer for the evening would be replaced by a little known, stand-in. Sighs and moans of polite, but obvious disappointment rolled across the audience.

Several people got up and left in disgust, assuming that the whole evening would be a let-down. I thought "How bad could it be?" I settled in to my seat feeling disappointment but open to enjoying the performance anyway. As it turns out those of us who remained were in for a treat. The stand-in for the evening was Mikael Baryshnikov. At the time he was an unknown. As he leapt across the stage and began to dance, everyone was captivated by the magic of his skill, strength and grace. He continued to share throughout the years what he came to this world to give, becoming one of the most well-known and admired dancers of all time. It just goes to show us that we never know what spirit has lined up for us. Those who left at hearing the announcement never knew what they were missing.

It never pays to judge in advance. Be sure, however to follow your gut instinct. If it tells you that it is time to leave, it is best to follow its message. Should you be uncertain about whether to stay or go, ask for more clarity, or a sign. It most always comes, and you participate in the right experience where you will enjoy the gifts of the moment that are there for you. It is about learning to trust yourself as one with Spirit.

The secret to staying in the flow and to feeling afloat in times of doubt is this; **Practice the three P's. Prayer, Patience, and Persistence. Putting them into service allows you to relax into, trust and accept results without attachment to outcome. Whatever you choose to do will be enhanced by practicing the three P's; Each enhances the flow of the other. I find this to be the formula that gets me through the rough rapids on the river of life. It is especially helpful during those times when the going is flat and nothing appears to be happening. The three P's gives me the extra strength and courage to flow with the river of life and enjoy the peaceful feeling it brings.**

Sometimes embarking on a course may take you to a place that feels like virgin territory. What the three P's add up to is a greater trust of Spirit and Yourself as One. When you activate this higher trust you will create a new energy to enjoy. What might formerly have been a fearful trip into the unknown, instead becomes a wonderful new adventure.

The cycles of your life will take you in greater confidence and ease to your rightful place. Bumps in your journey are only like snags on the river that may contain gifts.

What comes to you as a result of dealing with them will prompt you to reach a greater awareness that enhances your navigational skills and ability to relax and enjoy the ride. You are not alone. Trust that Spirit is with you and will provide whatever you need. That belief of its own accord magnifies your power and courage infinitely. Detach from judging the way you get to where you go. We can choose to traverse life's adventure on a raft like Tom Sawyer, or ride in opulence and ease like Cleopatra. Release limitation about deserving or labeling what style of travel you choose. Be open. Have what you want. What you do gain will be the awareness of knowing how you chose to respond to what you created. The results simply reflect the outcome of the laws of cause and effect that were steered on the river by your own awareness combined with the higher knowing of Spirit within. You can always create anew.

Barbara Striesand in *Funny Girl* as Fanny Brice, was asked by Flo Zigfeld if she could roller skate. She answered "Sure I can." Never having skated before, she knew she would only get the job if she agreed to skate. Of course when put up or shut up time came, she performed miserably. Her act was so funny that it stole the show and made it an instant Broadway hit. I once got a job as a summer life guard before I knew how to swim! I used the two months before the job began to take Red Cross swimming lessons and passed all the tests in time. I wanted the job. Where else could an eighteen-year-old get tan, hang out with all the girls, and be paid all at the same time? I understand Fanny Brice's moxy and her faith in trusting herself and in journeying into the unknown. Trust Spirit within yourself as your absolute guide in every situation. It will increase your knowing and ability to utilize what you have learned.

Many times I agreed to painting commissions that involved painting in a style or medium that was new to me. In the process I would practice the skills until I got it right. Over the years, I became good at painting a diversity of styles and subjects as a result and I maintained a successful life as a free-lance artist. There is a great deal to be said for winging it! Have faith in life and your self, and trust that God will show up when you reach that place of knowingness where miracles are required to move forward.

We expand into greater acceptance of our desires, increase our faith and trust when as step into action of what we believe can be.

Speak Your Word

I am one with Infinite courage and Infinite creativity. I am one the that which knows all and is all. Nothing can shake the All-ness and power of Spirit. Where I am, God is. In this place all is well. I am shown what I need to know to feel confident and safe. I give thanks that my courage and patience are unshakable. I give thanks for absolute trust in the Divine. I am protected, supported and loved by Spirit. I accept perfect knowing and protection at all times from within and all around me in all ways.

Knowing this puts me in a place where I can call on the creative power within me. I am One with the spontaneous knowing of Divine Intelligence. The Prime Creator and I have a co-creative partnership that guides me in right knowing at all times. Because It is within me to know, I create what is best for me and accept the Divine Results that come. I give thanks that all is complete, whole and well in my creation as I freely draw to me the desires of my heart. I am One with the One Creative Mind of the Universe. I am thankful that I am One with the Prime Creator and know it, and therefore am myself a very powerful creator. I accept this in faith, as the truth, and I walk in strength and sleep in peace accepting all the good I can. And So It Is!

CHAPTER FOUR

The Journey And The Destination Are One

Things seemed strangely unusual. Everyone was speaking in whispers and treating little Paulie in a different way than he had ever experienced before. This morning was not routine. Ordinarily most days were quiet, with all members of the family attending to the daytime chores of operating the small town movie theatre. From his vantage of thirty-six inches off the floor, his perspective seemed freer and clearer. His ability to observe the truth in what was happening and remain neutral was uniquely detached from that of the adults who towered around him. He was just four and small for his age, but he knew he was not like the others.

The theatrical moderne design of the spacious apartment, one floor over the auditorium, provided ample space for the rooms that now filled with strangers. Their coming and goings today marked a dramatic shift that signaled he would soon begin a new era of his life. Over the coming years, it would reveal to him just how his unique awareness contrasted with the farmer mentality of the residents of the small Mid-Western, Iowa populace.

On a normal evening, the family came to life, working together in unison. It was a time of adventure for little Paul as his family went to work running the movie theatre below. Each night was full of magic and life, both on the screen an off. At the intermission of the feature, he would be ushered up the long, steep, stairs to bed. Silently dreading the time alone in the dark, he would lie awake almost in secret, listening to the muffled voices of the feature playing itself out below. He remained that way until, hearing the doors close for the last time and seeing the lights go off for the night, he could finally relax and surrender his small frame to sleep. He felt at peace and was secure and comfortable in what had been his sister's room before she left home. But it was still important to know that Mom, Dad and big brother were in their rooms. And even more important to him that it was safe to close his eyes. As a crib-baby, he had been placed in his older brother's room for the night. It was not his brother's choice to have him there. Paul could feel his brother's disdain for his presence in his room....and he blocked out memories of the teenager taking liberties with him as an innocent, defenseless infant.

The night before had begun like any other, with all members of the family on hand to run the theatre. Mom was selling tickets in the booth out front, and Dad was stationed on a stool at the rich, velvet, curtained door to the inner lobby, taking tickets. Big brother would be up in the projection room, taking care to splice the reels of film just right. His big sister had sold candy and popcorn until she married and gone off to live on an army base far away with her husband. Just turned four, little Paul would oversee the entire theatre operation. He roved from out front, where the sidewalk was lit by a colorful, neon glow, through the double open doors to where the smell and sound of fresh, popping popcorn was always present. Into the darkness of the auditorium, he would find a perfect front row seat always available. If the feature was a comedy, usually staring favorites like Jerry Lewis, Marilyn Monroe or Lucille Ball, the front seats were most advantageous. He could be in one of his favorite spots when the big, velvet curtain went up, revealing the fantasy and intrigue of far away places, mystery and romance. It was all in an evening of fun. Should the feature be the *Blob That Ate Philadelphia, The Creature From The Black Lagoon* or his dreaded but favorite, *House on Haunted Hill*, the back row offered quick refuge by dodging behind the curtained door to the interior lobby. Here he found a safe haven that allowed him to steal a peak at the spooky, gory details.

Impending Change

This one evening, the childhood of the little Paul I was changed forever. I was forced by circumstance into growing up overnight. That night my direction took the first significant turn in life that would ultimately lead me onto the path of being an author and teacher of metaphysics.

I recall seeing my father, usually energetic, sitting on a stool in the corner by the velvet curtain, my mother telling me not to bother him. She said that he didn't feel well, and that he was going upstairs early to lie down. What transpired after that I do not know, except that I remember going into his room in apparent response to a noise that had awakened me. Men in white jackets were all around him. A bulky, red, respirator on big wheels stood at the foot of the bed. A long hose led to a mask attached to his mouth. As I grew up, I became aware that his death was due to a massive heart attack. Later that evening, a neighbor lady, came over and took my hand saying, "Come on, Paulie you will spend the night at my house." I thought why? It seemed strange, since I had never stayed with her before, but complied when my mother agreed. Being a good Christian, the compassionate neighbor told me that my father had gone away to live with Jesus.

Her explanation of my father's sudden death only served to perplex and complicate my limited assessment of the situation. I would spend the rest of my childhood sleeping with a light on, lest the dreaded image of Jesus coming closer in the night would take me away. As a four-year-old, I had not learned the accepted finality of death, loss or panic, nor had I known grieving. Unfamiliar with the concepts, I simply observed my father's death. It was not until I saw my sister crying, the one person I related to on an emotional level, that I felt or began to understand what loss is about.

This day, marked by the return of big sister Gloria and her husband, was the beginning of a new era for me. As they enter, I am filled with the excitement and love for her. I always waited for her letters and cards and proudly displayed them in my room. I knew I could trust her and she would give me attention that my mother was not capable of. A night of confusion I had spent at the neighbor's apartment over the drug store next door is past now. Now that Dede is here, all will be fine. Or will it?

I remember those moments with perfect clarity. I can still see my sister coming through the door from the living room into the big central hall. Her eyes filled were with tears as she looked down at me. I recall being aware of how she leaned into her husband, Allen, and how she depended upon his strength to support her. They had driven all night to get to Iowa from Louisiana. As they entered the apartment, my memory of a strange and unique childhood began to unfold. As they made their way through the rooms above the theatre filled will caring small town friends and neighbors, I watched my adult life begin at age four. From that day forward, I have pain-filled, memories of a struggle between wanting to be a child and being told that from now on, I had to be an adult, and not really knowing how I was expected to act. For years I floundered in confusion as to who I was. Since I was ignored or passed over when I attempted to express the truth as I saw it to adults, I turned to silence, creating my own mental world I drew on paper. I stayed that way until my teenage years when the magic of blooming youth could no longer be stilled.

The Subconscious Video Recorder

Punctuated moments that stand out over the course of our lives as being particularly significant are the ones we consciously recall and return to in emotional contact. Our subconscious mind records everything we see, do and say, whether we remember them consciously or not. The four-year-old in me recalls those scenes clearly; my father slouched in the corner on the stool, the red respirator, the neighbor taking me home, and my sister coming in, leaning heavily on the arm of her husband, who was dressed in a khaki army uniform. Those childhood impressions have accompanied me my whole life through. They remain vivid and distinct as the day they happened and act as key clues to my own heritage and history. I remember experiencing them as a neutral observer. Much like an auto accident I experienced in my twenties, where I observed myself going through it in slow motion, from an almost out-of-body-like feeling of separation or with over-view.

I have some memories of my father, following him around, being with him in his shop while he worked. He was creative and liked to work with his hands, two characteristics I inherited. I understand that he was doting as any late-in-life parent could be. I do recall how he liked to jingle change in his pockets as he walked. I wanted to be like him. In response, one afternoon I found a way to empty all the change from the cash register downstairs into my pockets. I recall the confusion, desperation and urgency in the house when the family realized that the till was empty. As I followed Dad through the alley and around the block to the store fronts I jingled my full pockets, giving me away as the culprit. I do not recall being punished, although perhaps I was. My mother was always detached from giving me attention and affection. There is a great deal of evidence to the fact that she would rather not have had another child, since the other two were grown when I came along.

Re-birth

Jump forward forty years to November 1993. I have made a quick car trip from the city to Malibu to collect some things from the home I enjoyed sharing for several months following the sale of my own house. Currently, I am temporarily house-sitting at the home of another friend who lives in nearby Santa Monica. I have been entrusted to hold down the fort with his two teenagers while he travels to Nepal on a two-month, spiritual trek. Upon his return, I plan to go back to Malibu to collect my things, and seek a new residence of my own. All of my furnishings, clothing, and paintings are stored in the sea-view, bluff-perched, luxury home.

Today, I have returned with the intention of loading my truck with a few possessions, because there are wild brush fires, out of control not too far away. The day is tinted brown. Gold and reddish hues of sunlight penetrate the smoke cloud from time to time, casting an eerie, foreboding, glow onto the sky. I think it prudent to take more, but probably unnecessary so I grab only a couple favorite things. Looking back at my paintings, too large to fit into my truck, I wonder about options. Should I stack them in the drive and cover them with a tarp? Cut them out of the frames and roll them? Nothing seems right. As I drive up the long drive a voice in my head says; "there is plenty room for more, how about going back for more?" I hesitate, thinking about my sound system and paintings and continue on to the city. "Whatever I have, is what I need. This is only a precaution. Even though the fire is out of control, it is miles away." Little did I know that the next day would mark another significant era of change for me.

The fires came and went. Along with them so did all of my furnishings, clothes and paintings. Twenty years of history of my life and work as a California artist was incinerated in the minutes it took for the house to burn. The firemen, exhausted and out of water, were forced to abandon the blazing hillside in what should have been the darkest of hours of night. They had no choice but to escape a three-hundred foot wall of flame as it raced down the mountain slope in thirty seconds' time, consuming everything in it's path as it illumined it's prey.

I returned the day after the firestorm had run its course and began to poke around in the ashes with a stick. Virtually nothing was left with the exception of my grandmother's porcelain bowls, which I cherish to this day. A quarter-acre-wide swath of flame had rushed down the mountainside to the sea. Every home, tree and every bit of the lush foliage that had graced the mountain slope was completely incinerated. Only charred boulders broke the landscape. Remaining alongside them were the ghost-like chimneys of fireplaces that only days before had warmed the multitude of opulent, architectural, ocean view homes on foggy, ocean nights.

I was greeted by CNN. I was the first person of the day to be interviewed and seen global-wide. When asked for my response to what I found, I replied and laughed without thinking; "The sky is blue, it is a beautiful, new day. It's only stuff, I'm here, I'm healthy and alive." and I laughed. If they wanted tears in the ashes they were not going to get it from me. The night before, I had surrendered the outcome to God, not knowing what it would be. In doing so, I left myself completely open with a blank canvas and nothing but a total opportunity to create a whole new life. My spirit wanted change.

Life Is Subject To Change Without Notice

We continue to see massive flooding, wild fires and other disasters. We can observe the people on the news as if they are in shellshock, struck and confounded by their loss of housing and income. This is their time of challenge. However devastating a loss it seems at the moment, (and it is), it is a tremendous opportunity to begin anew. Once the smoke clears, the water recedes, we rebuild and settle into a normal sense of life again, we can begin to live, perhaps, in better ways than before. It is our human nature to desire to re-establish a sense of security and comfort as quickly as possible. In the U.S., our government is swift to respond in assisting. In other parts of the world, there are those who as not so fortunate. These natural disasters are telling us not to put our stock in the material. We are not our house, our car, relationship, profession or family. These things are a part of the out-picturing of who we are, but they are not the *essence* of who we are.

The so-called disasters, are wake-up calls pointing us within. Historically, man seems to wait until he has no options, or until he is out on a limb to call upon God. It is only when he is ripped from the very seams of his dreams, that he suddenly believes and takes the time to get on his knees....to ask for guidance and to listen to what he is being told on the inside.

It is best not to wait until you are in trouble to suddenly find God. Better to have a day-to-day, working relationship with the Creator within. The old idea of seeking help on your knees from a power outside yourself when the chips are down works, but it is going about things the hard way. If the intimate relationship had been there in the first place the need for the knees may never have come along! It is never to late.

The story of three atheists and St. Peter

Three atheists were surprised when they found themselves at heaven's gate. They had lived their lives with total abandon, never expecting or believing in the afterlife or in God. St. Peter was at the gate to explain that God is very forgiving and that if they could answer one question they would be allowed to enter. Hoping for a shot at eternity each complied to do his best. None had ever attended church or studied religion.

St. Peter asked them this question; "What is the meaning of Easter?" The first replied; "Why it is the day in November where we families gather and celebrate by eating turkey." St. Peter shook his head and rolled his eyes. Turning to the second he asked; "Care to give it a shot?" The second atheist, appearing uncertain, began "Easter is the day in December when everyone gets together and celebrates the birth of Jesus," he confidently replied, winking at the third guy. St. Peter, once again turned his head from side to side, "Sorry, wrong again." He turned to the third and posed the question again. "What is the meaning of Easter?" The third atheist was certain he knew the answer. "On Good Friday, Jesus Christ was crucified. His disciples took his body from the cross and placed it in a cave. They sealed the cave entrance with a large boulder to hide it from the Romans. Every Easter, Jesus is resurrected from the dead. He rolls back the boulder and comes out into the light. If he sees his shadow, he goes back into the cave and we have six more weeks of lent."

The chief, vital difference between Jesus and you and me is that He knew without a doubt that the Spirit of God is always available to him. Our heavenly parent is always supporting and loving us, and has answers, ways and means to replenish, support and provide sustenance and love. We just need to turn within to connect and develop a working relationship with it. It depends on nothing outside of ourselves. When we connect, all outward things are provided as well as inner peace. If we are One with the source then we are not shaken from life by the dramas of the world around us. In these times of change, I have often observed that those who experience disaster and who have a relationship with God seem to be able to adapt the right attitude and sense of gratitude to start anew. When these things happen, we can only let go and trust God.

Circumstance, forced me to let go of many of the things I felt burdened by and many others I enjoyed. However, in the process it simultaneously created new windows of opportunity that pointed me towards a surprising new career, of that as an author. Along with new stories to share, I gained an incentive and desire to make further change. I wanted to be able to write my first book *No Boundaries*. To do so, I required a fresh perspective. I became willing and able to make a choice to live differently, free from the need to support a lifestyle based on the financing of real estate. As a benefit of the release from financial responsibility, I was blessed with the time and freedom to write, detached from a painful struggle of making a living in a sagging economy. The fire included many blessings. I had asked for release, and I got it.

Whether it be earth changes, natural disaster, divorce, or the death of a loved one, no loss or injury is too great for Spirit to handle and heal. Each is an opportunity to grow, to expand, to create, and to live life anew. You can learn to choose to live detached from the importance of things. There are always more

things to support you, and for you to enjoy. There are new people
to love, places to go and fresh interests to carry you forward.

Speak Your Word For Clarity

There is One Infinite Intelligence. It is the power of Spirit
knowing Itself within me. The absolute all-knowingness of the One
Divine Mind resides within me and is available to me at all times.
I take the time to renew my relationship with higher knowing on
a daily basis. I expect to know what I need to know at all times. I
trust my own judgment and accept a greater sense of confidence.

Spirit is unencumbered by the limits or constraints of the
past, therefore I am free to be myself and make new choices. Since
I am One with pure Intelligent Spirit, I accept my knowingness
and support from life around me. I am clear thinking, knowing and
acting in all ways. I have gratitude for this greater trust of self and
life. I am supported by life and one with the greater flow of good as
a result. I am thankful that Divine Awareness flows through me,
and into my experience. I accept this as truth. And So It Is!

CHAPTER FIVE

The Little Darkroom Where Negatives Are Developed

"This message will self destruct in 30 seconds." Anyone who watched television during the nineteen-sixties in America would have been familiar with these words; "Should you choose to accept this mission - and for any reason you are unable to complete it, knowledge of your identity will be disavowed." The audience would next see a poof of smoke coming from the tape player as the tape self-incinerated and totally obliterated any trace of incriminating evidence. This popular, adventure series, titled *Mission Impossible* portrayed secretive and dangerous assignments of glamorous, world class, spies of the cold-war era. Each elaborate mission was carefully staged to depict a clandestine and complex spy effort designed to undermine ruthless and oppressive dictatorships around the globe. At the opening of each weekly episode, the same recorded voice instructed the agent, a *Mr. Phelps*, of the details of the next exciting and intriguing mystery assignment. Convolution and cover-up were the essence of the plots. Each story well reflected the mistrust that dominated the international political scene around the globe at the time. Lack of trust between the United States and The now former Soviet Union had bred a military build-up of a nuclear arsenal on both sides big enough to destroy all life on the planet several times over.

By the early nineteen-seventies the world watched as President Richard Nixon voluntarily stepped down from the Oval office to avoid impeachment for his involvement in the Watergate cover-up. The age of truth was beginning to make its debut on the world scene. By the 1980's America was watching all kinds of talk shows themed around the healing of relationships through the bringing of truth to light. Nearly fifty years after the fact, in 1997, the United States Air force released its official report of The 1948 Roswell Incident reporting the crash of a space craft from outer space in the New Mexico desert. The 1997 version was titled *Case Closed* ignoring the obvious fact the government had obviously exhausted its list of cover-ups and excuses for the unexplainable. However, it was a small step in their liberation, backing off from decades of a policy of convolution and secrecy. This official position fit nicely with which the military had taken a stance on homosexuals in their ranks of the *don't ask don't tell* policy. In 1998, the Clinton/Lewinsky scandal emerged in full force dominating our media and once again changed our views on Washington and affected what we think about our private lives and conduct. All of these incidents were just steps in the ongoing awakening coming as a result of our world embarking into the age of truth.

All of the cover-ups, the untruths told, and the malevolent dictatorships on the planet were spawned out of an atmosphere that was ripe for their presence. Because there was sufficient fear in the belief system of the culture, fear could take hold, perpetuate itself and thrive. Without fear, a dictator is powerless, a cover-up cannot survive in the light of truth, and life is a whole lot simpler for everyone. Joy and ease become the thrust for living.

Fear and Doubt

You and I are special agents on the quest for spiritual truth. I believe that our highest mission in life right now is to become who we came here to be. To emancipate ourselves from the limits that were historically imposed upon us is the surest way to begin to activate the seeds of awareness that live within our soul and were imprinted upon our genetic blueprint in our creation.

Along freedom's path we sooner or later discover that the ruthless dictators to overthrow are our own Commander Fear and his side-kick.... Colonel Doubt. **Working in tandem, fear and doubt cleverly create a side show constructed out of a lace of shadow and illusion designed to engage our attention.** They want us to let go of our goals and conform. They will stoop to any level in order to rob us of our power and steal our peace. They hope to gain stripes of achievement for converting us to fearful weak beings by tricking us into believing that we do not deserve peace of mind, success or happiness. Where you find one, you always will find the other.

Fear and doubt are easy to recognize in that they always make you believe that there are no options. Their chief mission is to suck the life and energy from our dreams. They will do anything in an effort to convince you that you are not enough. They want you to believe that conditions as they are will not support you.

Both Commander Fear and Colonel Doubt are false gods of a sort to the degree that we allow them be, in that what we give our attention to, we give power to. Doubts and fears are best dealt with by looking them squarely in the eye and dismissing them. We must replace the attention we have given them by turning it to the place where there is always power and peace; Spirit within. We must retrain the subconscious to believe that God is brighter, lighter and smarter than the old, dark and suspicious beliefs.

Doubts present themselves to us as counter agents who challenge our belief in ourselves. They reflect areas of need in our own consciousness where we need to bolster our faith.

"Your Doubts are your traitors." Shakespeare

Fear is a ruthless dictator who oppresses our dreams. He is easily recognized by the ways he manipulates your attention by making what appear to be no-option demands. **Commander Fear creates distractions by magnifying your own doubts in order to engage you in a game of distraction. The purpose of his tactics is to draw your attention from light into shadow. Once you doubt your own power, he has the advantage of deceit over you.** He knows that in the light of truth he cannot survive. He works in a little darkroom that doubt has prepared for him in the center of our consciousness. There he develops limited gray illusions of who he would like us to believe we are.

Neither fear nor doubt can exist for long in the light of Spiritual awareness. When we wake up to self-emancipation, we begin to recognize what a false god fear has been. Doubt, just along for the ride, is the whipping boy of fear. Both are fakes. **When we allow ourselves to bow to fear and doubt, we are self destructing our own rightful good by putting false gods before the Real and One Creative Presence within.**

You and God are the commanders in chief of your life's agenda. Every answer, every ounce of energy, and every measure of support including financial is available to us when we work in spirit. Mother Tereasa wanted to start a nursery. When asked what she had to offer, she answered, "Three cents and a prayer to God." She was told that she had no business opening a nursery. She agreed that she on her own was not enough. What she did state was that herself, three cents and a prayer to God was more than enough. And it was! She made a decision, held the vision, made the commitment and was detached from conditions as to how her vision would unfold, and allowed Spirit to fulfill her dream. Today there are many nurseries in her name. Despite enormous uncertainty and a tremendous challenge of poverty she chose to live at the level of love trusting the light.

We owe it to ourselves to live in the light as the light.

Light always overcomes darkness. When we step into a darkened room, we think nothing of switching on the lights. It is a fact that darkness cannot exist in light. Flip on the lights and the darkness automatically disappears. Even though many of us were born and trained to believe in the illusions and bounds of materiality and illusions of darkness, we have the option to choose freedom.

If we are going to change our experience we must begin first by stepping out in faith beyond the fears and doubts we may have. Know that they were born and harbored in the illusions of darkness. Peace is always available to us because it lives in God, within us. However, we must first choose to go to the place where we can experience it. Within the peaceful space of Pure Spirit lies the power to liberate the self from all limits.

You and I are comprised of pure energy. The energy that arranges itself into our bodies stems from the energy that also gives our spirit its life. Our primary spiritual and scientific genetic make-up is that of Pure Spirit. Since all energy comes out of the light of God, within that light is the power to transform. You and I have free giving us the ability to choose Oneness with the light and claim emancipation. There may be obstacles to overcome but with a conscious choice to go with the light, comes the power to activate change. In making that choice we have made a stand to be responsible for ourselves and gained assistance from God/power to discipline ourselves in disassociating from the things that we know will limit or cripple us. God-power is especially effective in dealing with those things, which are unlike the energy of light and peace. The basic vibration is completely different. Darkness cannot find a home in the peaceful light of Spirit. It cannot exist there!

There is no program, power or addiction greater than that of God. **The access to total emancipation only lies within the self.**

We are naturally challenged by the seduction and junk that life tosses our way. That stuff represents the random race-mind thinking that we were born into. It was historically created by the world for reasons that are no longer valid for you and me because we are expanding spiritually. When Hernan Cortez returned to the New World, he burned his ships upon landing! It may not always be wise to burn our ships, but in order to move past the historic, preconceived limits we must switch on the lights to the same kind of confidence in Spirit within our own consciousness. Should you feel powerless in turning on the lights then ask for help. Spirit will provide angels to teach you how to do it for yourself.

You and I are a God/Goddess ordained being, with the light, love and creativity of our Divine Parent residing within. How much of it we put to use will determine the quality of our experience. **We are a direct off-spring of the Infinite One, designed in the image and likeness with all of the seeds of Godhood necessary for wholeness innate within our genetic and spiritual blueprint.**

Because humanity has lived in darkness, we have operated on the false belief that we are powerless and destined to be helpless victims of circumstance. In agreement on the collective level, lambs will follow the lead sheep or whatever the consciousness of the herd is, generally accepting or believing at the time. If the lead sheep goes to slaughter, the group will follow automatically.

The collective belief of the race mind of the people of earth has been in agreement to limits for thousands of years. The limits were so deeply instilled that when Jesus spoke words of wisdom they fell on deaf ears or were rejected. They could be understood only at a level of belief that was acceptable to the times. Since they could not assimilate what he taught, He was condemned. From before that time, humanity slept in a semi-conscious state and experienced the limits of density and form as a result of it's limited beliefs. Now it is waking up to a greater lighter Reality and the Truth.

As we turn the millennium we begin to see beyond the limits and have little choice left but to live the simple truths that Jesus spoke. He came as a living example of how to utilize them. Once you practice the cosmic laws and gain understanding, you will have a new handle on life that will reveal answers to you as they come through you.

The Universal principles; **Our thoughts and Words are powerful tools of creation. Whatever energy we choose to project, is automatically returned to us in equal measure. Whatever we accept and believe to be true will determine the outcome of our experience. You and I have the power to heal ourselves and others. These aspects of God live within all of us. They are truth, love, light, peace, beauty, joy,**

awareness, creation and success. Use your own words of peace
and light to overcome anything less and purge the old beliefs and
doubts.

The Affirmative Power of No!

We have great power at our disposal as Divine Beings as
well. Our word holds the potential to create healing and change. It
is a vibration which states our intention in the creation of
conditions. What we are willing to accept and not is defined by our
word. It establishes in form what we desire and feel from our
deepest commitment within. You and I have free will to use as we
please. If conditions are coming towards us that are unacceptable,
we may use the power of saying *No* to stop them before they
manifest in our face. We are the thinker, not the thoughts. We may
say No to negative thoughts before they become manifest in
experience.

**Use your Word power to say no to fear. Replace it with
Love.**

At age sixteen, I was entrusted with a family car to drive
alone across the state to visit my cousins for Thanksgiving. The
highways in Iowa were built in the nineteen-thirties and were
narrow, with only two lanes, and with a curved, cement curb on
each side designed to keep the rich, black, Midwestern farm soil off
the roadway. I had been driving with adults on a learner's permit
for two years before getting my license. The summer before I had
done all of the driving on a family trip from Iowa to Texas and
back, so I felt confident alone. As I was coming over a railroad
blind over-pass, I was confronted by a car, passing a truck, in the
lane headed right for me. There was no apparent way for anyone
to move over. I shouted out loud, "No, No, God, No!" Immediately
the truck being overtaken braked and slowed sharply, allowing the
passing car to jump in front of him at the last minute. It all
happened in a split moment, so there was little time nor way for
me to respond. It was the first time I remember using the power of
saying *no* to a negative situation in order to correct it.

**We may divert tragedy by putting to use the Power
of No, whenever necessary. Use your Word Power to correct
imbalance. When you say no to what you do not want, you
automatically give clear space for what you do desire to be
instead. Say yes to what you do want and impel and
prepare for it to move into your life.**

Choose to say no up front, when confronted with a negative experience, or when something is offered that you know is not appropriate. "I'll pass," or "None for me thanks." Works just fine. The same is true of a task or assignment that you know you would detest carrying out. Taking it on only harbors resentment and does not accomplish a successful completion of the job. Better to be truthful by asking for an assignment instead that you would enjoy or be good at completing, rather than reluctantly accepting one that you know you would not like.

It is a healthy choice to "just say no" whenever necessary. You have the right to use you power for negation when appropriate.

The Serpent and the Pussy Cat

When I first moved to Sedona, I spent my first three days unpacking and settling in to my new house. One of the first things I wanted to do as soon as I was free, was to set up my easel and paint. My deck with it's panoramic vista of Sedona's red rocks, offered the perfect space. Shaded from the direct heat and light of the sun, it cantilevered outward over a pinon pine-filled ravine, with a majestic position of command high above the town.

I had anticipated painting amidst the splendor of Sedona for some time, so I quickly became involved in the joy of creating my first painting. It was truly a pleasure to be at home at last in my own perfect space, doing one of the things that most nourishes my soul. After some time I began to hear the swooshing of a nearby sprinkler. I had previously owned property in Topanga Canyon that was irrigated with aboveground, Rainbird, sprinklers. The familiar sound of water shushing back and forth enhanced the placid calm.

After about forty minutes, I began to think about the sprinkler. It suddenly dawned on me; "I don't recall seeing a sprinkler system anywhere on the property. Could it be so loud that I would hear it all the way from my neighbor's lot?" It jolted me out of the almost trance-like painting state I was enjoying. I decided to find out where the sound was coming from. I put down my brush and walked to the edge of the deck and peered over the side. I was shocked when I discovered that the source of the noise was not a sprinkler as I expected, but an enormous, green, rattlesnake. About a foot away from it, was our house cat! There Ayla and the snake sat on a railroad tie below, face to face with the rattler. She nonchalantly groomed her paws while the snake continued to rattle it's steady warnings!

This was my first experience living with a cat. In fact, I was skeptical and not too thrilled about the idea of having one in the house at all. I had traditionally been a dog-person and any cats that were around had lived out-of-doors. Up till now, I had thought that I would not have been too disappointed if she chose to wonder off on her own accord. I had been stubbornly attached to the idea that a cat might cause problems with guests who were allergic etc. In the past, I had experienced some minor, allergic reactions to them myself, so my fears were genuine.

As soon as I saw the snake facing the cat, I felt as though my heart had leapt into my mouth. I whispered in firm but pleading tones, "Oh no God, not this way." My heart could not accept this kind of tragedy. I spoke; "Ayla, you had better get away from there." I was rigid, afraid to make any sudden moves for fear of startling the snake I clutched the rail of the deck. The serpent was coiled. He continued to shake his rattler to warn Ayla. Later, I was told that when a snake is coiled, they are demonstrating their readiness to strike.

Ayla looked up at me and stood up on all fours. She turned around most casually and stretched a long, drawn out stretch. My jaw dropped in awe as she sharpened her front claws on the rough wood of a railroad tie and wiggled her rump right in the face of the menacing viper! As she quietly strolled away, and I breathed a sigh of relief. I could hardly believe what I had just seen. I wished I had a video camera. It was truly amazing.

I called 911 for the fire department to come and retrieve the snake. I was certain that there would be a better home for it elsewhere. The city sent a guy who was a snake specialist. Obviously thrilled at the prospect of capturing a live rattler, he was alive with a delicious, wide-eyed, look of excitement. He could not wait to get started. I gladly moved aside. He and a companion made short work of capturing the viper. Putting it in an old pillowcase we gave them, they planned to release it way out in the desert. According to them it was a Green, Mohave Rattlesnake, known to be the most poisonous of all rattlers! This one however, was an older, grandfather snake who had the wisdom of knowing that Ayla would not make a gracious, nor delicate lunch. She would have been too large to be a comfortable prey. I believe that she was not in the vibration of fear, and therefore not threatening. The snake was just telling her to keep her distance. She had grown up with garden snakes in California and had not been programmed to be fearful of encountering a snake as you and I might have been.

The incident was the turning point for me in learning to love the cat. I realized that the Universe in it's Infinite, Loving Wisdom knew exactly how I would respond to her plight. With my feelings of wanting to protect the cat, came the activation of the beginning of affection within me for her. In that moment I began to feel a real love for the cat for the first time. As I continued to live with her in the weeks to come, I discovered what a sensitive, and intelligent creature, the little snake charmer is. I became the champion for Ayla, and found that to have her on my lap, while reading on a chilly, winter night in front of the fire, was indeed very comforting for both of us. Dogs have a way of being present in a room and connect with their masters in various ways. Cats like to be where they can connect when they are in the mood. In the past, I had mistakenly associated their aloofness for disdain.

My saga of cat and the serpent reminds me of symbology of the Lion laying down with the Lamb. I found it significant to my circumstance. In that first week of residency in my new home, I could see that a new era of peace in my life was truly beginning. Perhaps this was a greater symbol for the world as well. In order to live in harmony in my home, I had to detach from my own unwillingness to accept Ayla's presence and love her for who she was. She became a great teacher for me as I overcame the challenge and opened to the love she had been trying to offer me all along. Animals naturally perpetuate love. They are great living examples of unconditional love in action. It is up to us to follow their lead. The Infinite in all It's Knowing, had put before me this wonderful opportunity to utilize the power of love in overcoming fear. In all of her Infinite Wisdom, Spirit acting through Ayla, had given me the perfect opportunity to use my Word power and to trust it in defusing this fearful situation.

"There is a single magic, a single power, a single salvation, and a single happiness, and that is called loving." Herman Hess.

Speak Your Word

There is an Infinite Intelligence in the Universe. It knows all because It is all, and It lives at the core of my being. The Creative, All-Knowing Mind of God within me is the answer to all. I accept the awareness of Spirit to flow within my consciousness, and I am a unique out-picturing of individualized God/Consciousness in action. Because I am aware of it in myself and others I am able to follow a path of success. I invite Divine correction into my experience, and I choose to go with the flow in flexibility.

I am one with right thinking, right knowing and right action. I cannot fail, for there is no failure in Spiritual action. Even that which appears to be wrong contains the yin and yang of Divine Intelligence. Therefore I choose to call my life good. By calling it good, I call forth the good into my experience. I choose to see it, focus upon it and increase it's flow as a result. I celebrate the good that is. I choose to participate in successful knowing, successful thinking, speaking and acting. I know I am One with Divine Success. I release anything that is not in accordance with my higher good and I give thanks for invite divine correction into my experience. I move forward positively in peace, and in right action. I thank God that I am one with my higher truth from this moment forward and I am clear as to what it is. And So It Is!

CHAPTER SIX

Reflections

When I travel and pass through crowded airports, I often marvel at the fact that there really are no two of us who look the same on the whole planet! It is really no surprise since I know that Spirit within our collective soul is multiplying Its, I, you, me, we diversity each time another child is born. Each of us is alike in many ways, yet we are uniquely different in many others. However, at the center of each of us lives the same Divine Spark of Intelligent Life that creates this uniqueness. Our mission while here is to discover it and build a loving and working relationship with our God/Individuality.

Buried deep in our own cellular and subconscious memory are the keys to knowing whatever our personal mission is. Vis-à-vis our own revelation of our real identity, or true purpose is linked to discovering our Divinity or oneness with Spirit.

We often connect with master teachers who assist us in reaching the place within that is complete peace and knowing. In helping to uncover our own truths, a master's guidance serves to prompt or prod us in claiming our mastery and to accept Oneness with Spirit. Often these master teachers are disguised in the faces of people we know and love, and sometimes in those who challenge us. It is said that when the student is ready the teacher appears. Life sends us exactly the lessons we need when we are ready, but not before we are capable of handling them.

Wherever we go, there we are....reflecting ourselves.

There are many gifts in life awaiting our discovery. Some are wonderful, and others not so wonderful. In any case the end result and a knowing of what we have learned with each is what we take with us and is that which holds a lasting importance. People in our experience who act as challenges are actually great gifts of awareness mirrored to us in disguise.

Those who challenge us will be in our face until we discover what it is in our own consciousness that is equal to what they are showing us. They are great gifts in disguise. Bless them as you release them, and give thanks for the awareness they bring.

As a result of encounters with the people we ultimately must choose to release and forgive, we may begin to emancipate ourselves from our own limits. They force us to examine uncomfortable or painful issues that we may have previously avoided. The highest thing in any situation we can do is to surrender our *own stuff* to Spirit. The act of blessing and releasing those who challenge us helps us begin to let go of the judgment about ourselves that has kept us in bondage. The challenges these people present us with cause us to get busy and work on ourselves.

The Gift

Several years ago I presented a retreat attended by a small, but dynamic group that included an individual whom I shall present as anonymous in name and gender. I will just call this person the *gift*. Although fun, loving and obviously on a spiritual path of growth, the gift had strong issues of control that manifested as the need to dominate any group activity. This individual challenged me as the leader by taking every opportunity to take charge of the group. The other participants informed me that when I was absent from the group, the gift would attempt to sabotage my leadership by speaking in discrediting terms about me. I had done my best throughout to accommodate the participant as lovingly as possible, ignoring the frequent challenges and lack of support, or by making light of them.

At the end of the retreat our friend, the gift, was the first to depart for the journey home. If ever you attend a gathering and have given others something controversial to talk about, you can be sure that at some point after you leave the conversation will be about you! Our need to process was born out of frustration and exasperation. Those of us remaining went out for coffee to work through with the desire to find some kind of healthy closure on our interaction with our friend. We were all baffled and confused by the energy and disruption caused by the gift.

As a group, we quickly discovered that our friend had reflected and brought to the light each of our own individual issues of control to be examined. The gift's unwillingness to surrender to the higher good of the group reflected a lack of trust that God was in charge. I, being the leader, should have been firmer in my leadership, and would be from now on. The individual seemed to view any discussion as a reproach and would immediately turn it around in attack. So I concluded it would not have been wise under the circumstances (to taking aside in counsel). I had enough to do leading the retreat without additional distraction. We made a collective agreement to turn it over to Spirit. I led an affirmative prayer for a loving healing for the gift, and for our completion with the challenge. "Where two or more gather in my name, I am present." We accepted and expected healing for all through consciousness.

The Stillest Reflections of a pond are suddenly changed into waves when the smallest of pebbles is dropped in to it. Love is the same. When introduced into a solitary, lonely soul, the beginnings of a wave of love are be created. Its eventual consequence is to flow outward seeking to fulfill itself.

A year later, the gift showed up for another retreat showing strong signs of a major clearing and healing. A dynamic, remarkable change was apparent. The individual was more fun to be with, non- challenging, and seemed to accept my leadership with ease. There were still moments when the gift would point out to me when I was demonstrating control. Some valid, others I knew to be the gift's own stuff reflecting back to me. It is always the leader's role to be in charge and make decisions based on the higher good of the group, as guided from within. There is a subtle difference between being in charge and being in control.

Trust spirit, and surrender outcome to the higher good. What you need to know will be revealed through you at the right time.

A couple of years later the gift attended yet another retreat, pouncing on me the first day when I lovingly encouraged an extra shy individual to lean into a group photo. I noticed that this new participant required extra confidence to join in. It was my way of extending love and bolstering his feeling of being part of the group. I may be guilty of the mother-hen syndrome when it comes to my retreats, in that I desire for all participants to get as much enjoyment, growth and love out of the experience as they can. However, the gift's ensuing comments pushed my own control buttons. Trying to explain it to the gift only fueled the fire, exuding further argumentative, words between us about control issues. I let it go and managed to stay clear of conflict the rest of the weekend, focusing on my job of guiding the group through events.

Finally, I began to quiet myself and simply observe what was happening around me. I carefully listened and watched for my own reactions and to those of everyone present. As I did, I began to hear my mother's dominance and judgment coming out in my own voice. I mentally began to thank the gift for showing me, however subtle, that I had a tendency to call on the old, manipulative tactics and judgments I learned in childhood. When I questioned the other participants if they had observed control in me, they stated they did not. However, each of the other participants, one by one, unsolicited by me, commented on how controlling the gift was, and how they were affected negatively by it on at least one occasion during the weekend. This brought me a new awareness as an observer. **The need to control and dominate in anyone reflects a genuine lack of trust of spirit and of the self, and a fear of going with the flow.**

Nonetheless we enjoyed an incredibly beautiful setting and perfect weekend. Everyone had a good time and all got the guidance and inspiration that they came for. I could call it a successful retreat. However, because of the distraction of the gift, there were times when it had been difficult for me to get the group into a spiritual mode. I was disappointed that as a result, I had to abandon several meditations and processes that I know would lead the group deep into a bountiful, spiritual experience. I let go and surrendered to the relaxed, party atmosphere weekend. Later, as I confided and expressed my disappointment and concern to a couple of participants, they felt that everyone got what they needed anyway.

However, I knew that a deeper and richer experience was possible. I saw that it as a sign for me to shift my intention in clarity and to establish more of a syllabus up front for my retreats, and let it be known in the advertising that guided spiritual process would be part of the seminar weekend, in addition to hiking and play. Spiritual Adventures in Nature would take on a new format. I had been beginning see signs that the original five-year-old process was in need of revamping. This was clarification. I gratefully thanked the gift for waking me up to it.

As a result of the presence of the gift participant, I set out on a new path of healing and releasing even deeper layers of my own learned control devices. I blessed, released and thanked our gift. We all have similar challenges from time to time, either in one form or another. Sometimes it is the one we occasionally see in the mirror. Trust that God is in others, yourself, and your experience. Let go of control. Infinite Intelligence knows the way to bring the perfect healing in and through you. Invite it to do so.

The release of dominant control is an essential part of our world's healing. As the truth and ease of God permeate the planet and all its cultures, families, and religions, we will experience the heaven on earth that only detachment from conditions and control brings. **As we observe dictatorships crumble, armies** dissolved, people living in freedom, we see the beginnings of a world housed, fed and self-expressed.

The need to dominate is a fear of surrender, fear of losing control, and above all it reflects a lack of trust in God.... and in the Self. Unfortunately, humankind has been taught to accept fear from the very beginning of childhood, rather than to accept the fact that the love of God stands strong and fierce before the face of any fear. Fear is not truth. Its only purpose is to control. Disassociate yourself from fear and express your own truth. It is the truth of God speaking within yourself. Truth stands on its own and requires no defense.

The Wisdom Of Inner Knowing

There is a place of awareness within every human being that knows when it is time for change. Our subconscious will nudge us when we need to shift or to grow. What can begin as a subtle urge for a new experience, can evolve into a passionate quest that leads to dramatic change. When we follow our hearts and intuition, the places we are led to will fulfill our deepest lifetime desires.

Speak Your Word To Be Free

The Infinite Love and Wisdom of Spirit is within me. It's power and knowingness go before me to clear the way in release. I choose to release the past and accept a new present and a new future - one that is based on speaking and acting on my own truth. I accept ease in knowing that I can trust Spirit within myself to lead me forward on my rightful path of expansion.

What I desire and accept for myself, I accept and graciously give to others. It is my rightful path to expect the best. I am One with the best in every situation. I surrender to free-flow and allow the love and essence of Spirit to reveal Itself through every experience. I freely let go of the past and walk with trust and confidence into each new day. I give thanks that I am released from the prison of past limited thinking or judgment. I claim freedom and walk with joyous courage in truth. I am One with the Light. I give thanks to Spirit for Divine support, courage and love. Divine Love leads me forward in Ease. And So It Is!

CHAPTER SEVEN

Manifesto

The Hubble Space Telescope, noted as an immensely significant achievement for humanity, took many years and hundreds of millions of dollars to design and build. As it was launched into space, the scientific community anxiously awaited the dawn of a new era of stargazing. Hubble's position outside of the earth's atmosphere, promised a further understanding of the inner workings of the Universe. Immediately, it proved its worth by opening a door of infinite opportunities for viewing the far reaches of space never before seen by human eyes.

Because of the Hubble, closer observation is now possible of stars, planets and unique clusters of young, celestial bodies in various stages of formation. Astronomers are now able to gather profound new information that adds clarity and confirms what they had earlier only surmised. My favorite of the celestial conditions as shown on PBS, is comprised of enormous clouds of energy that display colorful gaseous cloud formations. Existing in distant space, each is the size of an entire solar system. These phenomena, called Super Novas, act as a nursery for the birthing and hatching of new stars. Their purpose is to transform of the pure potential of energy into matter.

Our inherent connection to Creation lies with the Infinite, God Mind of the Universe. It's All-Knowing, sea of intelligence holds all the keys to Creation and the secrets to life. **Everything that has ever been created and formed is birthed out of the Super-Conscious God Mind.** This God-energy, storehouse of life awareness, performs functions of Creation like a vast star hatchery of ideas. Our Creator who formed the entire manifest Universe, is the force and energy that breathes life into our own ideas and dreams.

Every act of mental creation, as it is impressed upon and through the Super-Conscious God Mind, will unfailingly manifest perfect, appropriate results. Our mental pictures, words, thoughts and feelings, are constantly being transmitting through the cosmic Creator whether we are conscious of it or not. **We can count on knowing that the tendency of our thinking and established beliefs will correlate an equivalent energy into our experience.**

The Superconscious Mind accommodates a vast ocean of

fluid energy potential. **The vibration of our thought transmits ideas into the sea of God-Mind awareness.** Its purpose is for creation and expansion of Itself through all life. However, it can only return an equal measure of what we put into It as a thinker and a Co-creator. If our habit is to hold limited concepts of fear and lack (not having enough), or if we think in negative ways, we will be certain to experience the same. In other words, God can only give to us what we are capable of receiving and nothing more. **If you and I wish to experience a greater good and abundant flow, an equal measure of expanded vision and thinking is required on our part.**

Focus on what you desire. Your focus is like tuning the Hubble space telescope to study a particular star. It brings what you desire into clearer view and sharpens your awareness and magnetizes to you it. Combine your focus with the element of non-attachment as to how your desires can come, and you will see how the magnetic law of attraction is sharpened in your favor. It is as though an invisible beam or spiritual tether magnificently draws to you what you think about creating. **The power of Spirit does its thing best, when we remain focused on the end result, but let go of controlling the ways and means to completion.**

Spiritual Shopping
Manifesting

The law of attraction works in perfect synchronization when applied freely and naturally. When one is in the flow of it, all required elements to create what we desire fall easily into place. Everything that comes is in Divine timing, order and design. I learned it in my own experience when I rented a small guest house and required necessities. Acquiring furniture became a bountiful exercise in learning how to manifest.

Birds, Bees, and The Beach

It was privilege to live in the cottage so closely with the ancient, stout, avocado tree that provided shelter for squirrels, birds, cats and opossum alike. Not only did it shade my door from the Western, Pacific afternoon sun, but it provided happy, robust, eating. All who visited enjoyed a generous supply of the healthy fruit. Life was good in Santa Monica with the old tree's branches waving the wind of the ocean right into my door. I enjoyed its comfort and energy for over two years after losing my possessions and home to the fire in Malibu. I brought with me only a chest of drawers and a couple of patio chairs that had survived because I had previously lent them to a friend. That first night, I slept on a foam mattress from my camping supplies on the floor next to the dresser. It felt good to put my clothes in my own familiar drawers after months of wandering the world with a backpack. It did not exactly feel like home, but it was a beginning in constructing a new nest. I drifted off to sleep feeling secure at last.

Several weeks before moving into this space, I had awakened several times during the night with a terrible sensation that I was not alone. Sleeping in the open loft of my best friend's town-house with his teenage daughters coming and going at all hours of the night, had wreaked havoc with my sleep patterns. More than once, in the middle of the night, I felt a very black, kind of foreign energy drawing closer and closer to me, as if through the walls, it slowly approached to invade or commandeer my energy. I did not perceive it to be good. When I sensed its presence, I would jump up and throw on the light. Finally, in bold tones meant to feign off aggression I spoke, announcing to it that it did not have my permission to come to me, and that I would not allow it to. I called in the protection of God and angels, and I insisted that it leave and never to return to me. This was serious business. I commanded it firmly....and it was the final straw in alerting me that it was time to do something about my living predicament. I had hung loose for a while thinking I would be guided to a new living situation. I had not. My active decision was required.

I asked God for guidance and immediate help. Then it came to me to write a bold note, read it out loud, and to leave it in plain sight next to my bed. It was emphatic; *"My dear angels of right residence, Please help me immediately to find the right place to live where I can sleep in peace."* The next morning, I got a call from my friend Gail who asked me to house sit for two months while she traveled. I moved in immediately. While there, I repaired some earthquake damage and did some painting. Her friend and neighbor saw my work and offered me the cottage behind her mother's vacant house to live in for awhile in exchange for similar earthquake repair work. So moving to it was a blessing for all involved.

I had not started from scratch in furnishing a home since college, so when I required kitchen supplies I was not sure where to begin. My friend Leslie insisted she accompany me to a bargain store called Pic'N Save. Although well known to Southern Californians as the creme de la creme of discount stores, I had never shopped it. Always opting for higher-priced, big name stores had been a long-time habit begun in Minnesota when I was an employee of Dayton's department store. Like many baby boomers, I had been primed to shop high-end. Due to the temporary nature of my new home and my commitment to a simpler lifestyle, I committed myself to not to investing extensively in furnishing it. In the past, when I was making big bucks, I always shopped at the best stores. When I needed something I would go out the door fully loaded with checkbook and credit cards burning in hand. This time it was different.

Leslie has a sweet, convincing way that has proved a valuable entree into all sorts of wonderful situations, so I agreed to go. I was surprised by an abundance of great closeout specials and amazed that I could get everything I needed for what would have added up to hundreds of dollars more in the famous-name places. It was fun buying everything new all at once. By the time we left, I understood the literal meaning of *shop till you drop*.

The cottage was attached to a garage at the back of the lot behind another larger house. Since the front house was vacant, I enjoyed security parking in the garage for the first year, and entered via the alley. Every week, I discovered new treasures sitting next to trash cans in that alley behind the affluent homes of the area. If what appeared was an item I could revive with paint or cleaning, I grabbed it. The art of scavenging became a discreet and intriguing new adventure in furnishing my nest as well as new experience in exploring the path of least resistance.

In the days and weeks that followed, as I realized a need for an item, it would show up in the alley. The day I thought about getting a tea pot someone discarded a nearly new one. Later, I noticed the same designer version I had found in the alley selling in a store for eighty dollars! When I had an inclination to build a platform frame for my foam mattress, a pre-cut, plywood frame in the right dimensions appeared in the same way. By then, I more than suspected that I was perfecting the art of manifesting. When I discovered that a friend of mine was without transportation, a bicycle appeared. I gave it to him. He rode it all over town until he was able to buy a car for himself. I was on a roll.

When I needed kitchen items beyond the basics I had purchased new, I would find them at neighborhood garage sales for ten cents on the dollar. I came to anticipate my Saturday morning adventures in garage sale excursions, buying only the best quality and items I really liked. Whenever I desired something, it would show up, either in the alley or at a sale. The residents of that gentrified neighborhood are young, upwardly mobile families who have a habit of shopping at upscale stores. They freely circulate their goods by releasing and making room for more. Because they buy well in style and quality, it made my selection particularly fruitful. The best part for me was that at the end of each shopping spree, I still retained an abundance of cash for groceries and pleasures like entertainment and frequent travel. I began to know that whatever I required or desired would appear. It was fun seeing how having a vision of an item I desired and how being detached as to how it would come would always put it directly in front of me.

I attribute my ease in manifesting to knowing my oneness with Spirit and depending on God to meet every need.

I discovered the following to be true: **What you focus your attention on is automatically drawn to you. Know that God is your source for everything. Live as in constant prayer with gratitude. Your degree of acceptance of what you desire, and your ability to detach from having to have it, along with a willingness to let it be revealed to you in Divine timing and knowing, brings it into perfect experience.**

Whatever it is that you desire, its arrival in your life will reflect the consciousness of where you are at the time. If you require something better than what comes, you have the power of choice to say no to it and put in an order for another selection.

Manifesting A Vision

Eventually I thought it was time to have a television. A break of three years without one had felt really healthy. I enjoy movies and missed seeing a couple of favorites shows, so I thought it would be fun to have a big screen. Since I grew up in a household that owned and operated movie theaters, I am all for big screen entertainment. Big-Picture-Viewing and the smell of fresh popcorn is in my blood. So I went shopping and priced several models.

In previous weeks, I was gradually talking myself into the idea of having a television again. Each time I passed by the chest at the foot of my bed, I would envision a set on it. I would sit in bed and imagine and visualize how I would enjoy watching movies. I wondered how big a screen would fit the space. However, I hesitated in spending nearly a thousand dollars for space-eating, heavy, electronic equipment. After all, I did not know how long my life would keep me residing in the guest house....or in California.

I decided to sleep on the decision since it would be a larger investment that any I had made in furnishing my temporary home.

The next day I got a call from a friend who asked if I had purchased a television yet. He had a medium sized that he seldom used and he offered it to me. I gladly accepted. When I got it in the room it was obvious that a larger one would have not fit the space. Once again, Spirit proved to me that it always delivers the goods in the right time and way. Our part is to form a mental picture, and establish a feeling of gratitude of having what we desire - and be unconcerned as to how and when.

Many other items came to me just as I required them. A garage sale provided an arm chair and ottoman for hypnotherapy clients. They were upholstered in a fabric that matched cushions I already had. I found a contemporary, floor lamp, with an artistic band of neon attached to it for fifteen dollars. It replaced an identical one I had paid over four hundred dollars for in my life before the fire. A couple of weeks prior to that, I was missing some of the neat things that burned. I thought about how I would enjoy having that lamp again. I could visualize it in the corner. So I checked the lighting stores and found that it was no longer being manufactured. I had released the idea of replacing it, but was particularly charged by the knowingness of Spirit when I discovered it on the garage sale circuit! **You can make your vision and intent work for you by the power of focus and non-attachment.**

All of these things came to me in easy, inexpensive ways, showing me that knowing and accepting a oneness with the Law of Supply increases the power to manifest anything, without limits. Whatever Spirit brings to you will be personalized to your style, requirements and income. It was fun finding bargains. I had thought of garage sales as tacky before I experienced them. But shopping them taught me a great deal about lightening up. They were an exercise in non-judgment and non-attachment that made it easy for me to have what I wanted. At the same time I was able to maintain an abundance of cash and learned to be a powerful manifestor. I know that wealthy people always find ways to maximize and increase their investments and maintain liquid capital. The more money one saves by purchasing wisely, the more one has for other pleasures and investments.

Speak Your Word To Manifest

I am One with all the Power of Creation. The Creator Itself is who I am at my core. I enjoy knowing this truth. I live in Spirit, because God lives within me. All I require for the best of life expressing who I truly am is available to support and nurture me.

The perfect presence of spiritual creation impresses upon me It's higher will. My will in alignment with the will of God. I accept and surrender to that peace that passes all understanding and give thanks that It reigns supreme in all I do. Everything I could require already lives within God, therefore it all exists in me. I accept that which I require and surrender to God all that I desire, and I accept perfect manifestation here and now in divine timing.

I give thanks that I have perfect patience, timing and awareness to receive that which Spirit provides and sends. Perfect health, perfect love, life, home and work. I am the creative avenue of Spirit individualized as me. Therefore, I am one with the Creator. I accept the fruits of my oneness in all areas. God is my source. We are one. There is no lack. All is well. And So It is!

CHAPTER EIGHT

Destiny

We know from the study of Science that everything in our world at its root is formed by a particular vibration and arrangement of molecular energy. Deepak Chopra, a well-known doctor of medicine, author, and lecturer on metaphysics and quantum physics elaborates on the subject. He tells us that we may observe energy as it changes form, from the simple stream of energetic possibilities into something definite and tangible. When atoms are collided at very high rates of speed they become a non-localized energy. When the attention of observation is placed upon the experiment, a change is recorded that notes the energy changing form. Until the attention of an observer was added to the experiment, the energy remained constant. I was very excited to hear of this because now we have physical proof of thought creating form. This proves to the scientific community as well that thought, attention and decision create a change in the flow of energy!

At all times, your thoughts and mine are acting upon the Universal Divine Energy. It is merely a stream of possibilities until our thoughts or words cause it to become something definite by our action upon it. We create everything in our experience by our subconscious and conscious thought vibrations and the power of our spoken word, whether we knew it or not. What we think and speak about is crucial to our experience.

As we become consciously aware that we are in co-creation with Spirit, we increase the speed, sureness and accuracy of every manifestation and come to trust Its Intelligent, absolute knowing.

No Separation

Instant manifestation occurs when *you know that you know* that the Infinite Abundance of the Universe will provide for every requirement. Trust yourself to such a degree that you surrender and relax into the arms of Spirit. When you do, your dreams will flow to you. It is the false belief that we are separate from our Creator (and Creative Principle) that cuts us off from the good that we naturally have the ability to manifest.

**If we desire a better life tomorrow
it becomes necessary to upgrade our thinking today.**

As a child of a Divine Parent, it is your birthright to have all you require to be supported in ease. Every human being is One with Spirit. Judge not others by appearances; True wealth is not always measured in outer effects. If we feel undeserving or condemn others for having or not having wealth, our belief will keep us from manifesting what we desire. The law of mental attraction can only reciprocate with an equal measure of what we feel we deserve and what we focus on. To conquer self-condemning feelings of lack it is necessary to work on our consciousness of deserving. You deserve what you want because you are here! Dream and consciously visualize what you desire. It is a powerful magnetic process!

If you were not limited by a lack in any area: health, money or any other condition right now, how would you live your life? What would you choose to create? What is stopping you right now from moving into your vision?

Thought and word create form. We create in the same way as our Divine Parent, by knowing, believing and speaking things into being. What we give out comes back to us in equal measure in one way or another. If the world knew these simple mechanical working facts of the Universe, everyone would be knocking himself out to give freedom, joy, appreciation support one another. The world would be a very different place. Courtesy might become contagious!

Change Your Mind and Change Your Experience

When things seem to be going poorly, one of the chief causes is often negative thinking. When that happens it is essential to re-program your subconscious beliefs. If you make a home for the thought *I am not going to make it*, why would you be surprised when you do not?

For anything to come to you there must be a fertile ground of receptivity for it in your subconscious mind. It is essential to act and feel as though what you desire is already established in your experience whether you see it or not! The subconscious mind must be willing to believe and trust that what you desire is possible. Create affirmations that support your ideas to establish a receptive soil to receive what you desire within yourself. At the same time, be detached from having to have what you want, as if it never comes to you it would be okay. **Non-attachment to outcome is the key element that is the secret power to all manifestation.**

> **"For he who has not, It shall be taken away.**
> **For he who has shall be added unto."**
> Jesus, referring to the law consciousness

Here are examples of creative affirmations you may utilize to correct limited thinking; "I am One with Spirit, and I am One with Unlimited Supply, I deserve to experience all the good that God has for me because I am here and require support. I am a loved child of a rich, loving heavenly Father. God provides. I am free of my past and its hold on me. I let go of the limited thinking of the past, I choose a new success!" Design your own affirmations to support your prayers for desires made manifest. It may be necessary to change your subconscious beliefs to accept what you want. See *No Boundaries* chapters eleven through twenty-one, for more specific and detailed understanding of techniques you can easily apply.

You Activate the manifestation of your desires.

Our thoughts are the magnet that draws to us what we think about. Focus magnifies an out-picturing of thought into experience. We need only show up with the right attitude in order to claim our desires. There is nothing miraculous or unique about manifesting. It is the way of Creation and always has been. A confident manifestor knows without a doubt that Oneness with Spirit is all-inclusive. When we consciously create in Spirit, no part will be left out. What comes to us is whole and completely satisfying. Should something be removed from our experience then it is a sign that a higher good is coming in its place, and that it will require the space to exist in your experience.

Speak Your Word To Manifest

"I and I as One with my Creator and no one else, is responsible for who and what is in my life. I have the power to cause change now and always." Use this affirmation to invite and activate change and to bless and increase the flow of good into your life. Use it consistently and you will see it will work wonders. You and I are one with the magnificence of that which creates all universal good.

Divine Distribution

Writing and publishing a book can be a formidable task. All aspects of book writing from its beginning to the actual physical placement on bookstore shelves can be challenging for the novice. I feel blessed because the creative part of writing comes easily and naturally through me. After all, Spirit within already knows what I am to write. However, learning about publishing was an immense job for me. Acquiring distribution is another aspect of the complexity of the experience. For me, the process was like walking through a corridor lined with doors. As I progressed I would try each one. If they were locked or my entry was bared, I would move on to the next and so on. If a door of opportunity opened I took it as a welcome sign from the Universe and would proceed forward.

This testing of doors fit into my theory of following the path of least resistance. A locked door reflected resistance and signals that another choice would be better. To engage in struggle does not support our highest interests. I learned to let go of wasting my energy forcing doors that did not open easily. I began to see and trust that only the right and highest places would welcome my work.

A West Coast metaphysical distributor had been supportive after I submitted my first finished manuscript. The firm offered to pick up distribution of the published book right off the press. When it came time to seek nation-wide distribution for it in the chain stores, I began my search by sending copies and letters of promotion to several of them. Ultimately a well-known, prestigious house answered me by stating that it liked the book well enough to order twenty-five copies for their New York stores. I was pleased to fill their order and a send letter of inquiry to several of the distributors and wholesalers they recommended, since their policies required purchase through those routes. Sometime later, I heard from another firm offering me a contract that included an offer to provide not only warehousing, but shipping and billing as well! I was thrilled at the prospect. It was an answer to my prayers.

There was only one problem; the contract they offered was exclusive. Since I already had nonexclusive agreements with East and West coast metaphysical distributors, I would not be able to sign on. Needless to say I was disappointed.

I was preparing to leave for a camping retreat I was

leading at Joshua Tree the next day so my time and mind were occupied. I decided to let go of concern and instead continue to give thanks for Divine distribution on a daily basis. I made an agreement with myself not to worry. God would provide the ways and means in right timing. One month later upon returning from another journey, I received a letter from the second distributor. The letter asked me to call right away. When we spoke, I was told that it had decided to make an exception for me, and would take me on a non-exclusive basis with the first year's contract! Once again my prayers were answered! One author friend said to me; "God must love you very much. This is what we all pray for but never get!" I only know that my being detached from outcome and accepting Divine Distribution with gratitude brought the perfect results.

The clincher was that I had also been waiting for a reply from another large well-known distribution house. But I could not wait any longer. The second distributor had a deadline for entry into the market. When I inquired as to when it was, I discovered that it was that very afternoon! We quickly faxed the signed contracts back and forth in order to meet the deadline. It all took place in a morning's time. After lunch, I began to wonder if I had done the right thing. After all, it happened so fast. I wondered about the prestigious national distributor that I had not heard from. Was I limiting my options, or just feeling something like buyers remorse? I decided to forget about it and check the mail.

In the box, I found a letter from the big distribution house I had been waiting to hear from, declining to take me on because they felt I was too unknown to bother with. The irony is that my wholesaler, got me onto the roster of the well-known distributor anyway, and agreed to handle any and all business with them for me. I had been warned by other writers that this particular well-known firm is notorious for their ruthless treatment of authors. However, they have a good rapport with book retailer so more order through them than not. Since *No Boundaries* was written addressing the issues facing today's challenging and changing culture I wanted to reach the potential of the mass market. I am grateful for the Divine Distribution set up for me by Spirit.

You too, can experience perfect Divine results in your life by accepting in gratitude that which you desire now. Speak your Word daily in thanksgiving for completeness of your ideas, without being attached to conditions or as to the ways and means they will come to fruition. By doing so, those *things* will come to you in easier wonderful ways. Think of them as gifts from a loving Divine parent. See and feel the completed desires as you give thanks. I

guarantee that you will be happy with the results. *Trust yourself*
**to make the right decisions. Spirit within knows what It is
doing.**

Speak Your Word In Manifestation

**I give thanks that I have the Knowingness of
Supreme, Divine Intelligence within me. I recognize that
Divine Intelligence is The One Creator of all. My Oneness
with Spirit is complete unto Itself. God in me knows
everything about me, my world and everyone in it. I accept
that the Conscious Knowing within is manifesting the
desires of my heart. I accept Divine guidance and Divine
Timing in all my ways and in everything I do. The Absolute
Knowing of the One Mind of Creation fulfills the space in
my consciousness for completeness. I accept_____
as my desire fulfilled.**

**I surrender it to the higher will of Spirit to bring it
in the right, perfect way and time. I prepare my self to
receive, accept, and know the gifts of wholeness and
completeness right here and now. I give thanks for the
totality of Spiritual knowing that brings me to my vision
and it to me. I detach from having to direct the ways and
means. Thanks to Infinite Spirit for Divine completion in
this area, I am an Emanation of Perfect Pure Potentiality in
action. I accept Divine results in gratitude. And So It is.**

Socks in the Dryer

It is said that nothing is ever really lost. When the fire in
Malibu consumed my clothes and furnishings, I quickly adopted
the attitude that I was finally free of the baggage I had been
carting from house to house. All through the eighties, I moved
frequently as I bought, renovated, and sold homes for profit. Each
time I would sell and call the movers, I would hear them in the
background shouting; "it's Seagram, the guy with the heavy marble
tables!" I had not traveled lightly. For the first time in twenty
years, I now enjoyed a new freedom of responsibility from paying
on a mortgage.

With the new lightness and with the book writing process
well underway, I returned to guest speaking and seminar
presentation. I had trained for it extensively but been too laden
with business obligations to do it. In 1996, I gave a guest lecture
at the Santa Barbara Lighthouse Church of Religious Science. The

night before when I was planning my talk I spoke with God and asked for humor to flow through me to enliven the lecture. The next morning as I gave the talk, I told briefly of my experience of loss in the fire. The audience was full of empathy. I relayed the fact that all twenty, large, contemporary paintings, the best of my collection I was holding for a collective show of my work, had also burned. The congregation gasped. "But you know," I said, "I still remember them in every detail. I figure that when I leave this earth and go into the tunnel of white light, I will see them floating out there in the cosmos just waiting for me to collect....along with all the socks that have disappeared in the dryer." They roared with laughter and so did I. God has a great sense of humor. I did not plan it that way, but from God's lips to mine, out it came. At the conclusion of the talk someone in the audience suggested I name my next book *Socks in the Dryer*. When Spirit speaks, I listen.

Manifestation and Money

Money, a necessary aspect of our world, is no different than transportation, electricity, food or clothing. It is an essential commodity we all require. Having an abundance of money provides options and expands choices as well as enhances the enjoyment of our living experiment.

For one to be a successful manifestor of money it is necessary to detach from ideas of lack. Poor thinking is the root of all evil, not money. However, the worship of money is putting a false god before you. Money is simply a symbol and tool of energy that is required for exchange of goods and services in this world. It is one form of the energy and ideas of God within our experience for us to use while we are here. If you have issues with money being Spiritual or not, it might be helpful to develop a healthier relationship with it by thinking of it as spiritual substance.

What would you do if you had all the money you could use and enjoy? How would your experience and attitude change?

Money Love!

Money is a spiritual substance that represents the energy of Spirit in your life. To attract more money, it is **necessary** to develop a love affair with it by enjoying it. To handle it and watch it play and expand in your life is an art. Learn to care for this delicate and expansive substance well. It requires healthy nurturing, and your loving attention for it to come to you. Just like a rose on a bush, by cutting the flower and taking it inside to enjoy nurtures the blooming of more on the bush. Having it for use creates options and flow. The more you spend, enjoy and share of your money and wealth, the more will come to you. As you freely enjoy and circulate your wealth, more of it will circulate around to you.

The enjoyment of wealth magnifies and increases wealth.

Be a wise steward and you will learn to enjoy and master money. I think of it only as a commodity for use like gasoline, telephone calls or food, and at the same time it is a sacred substance from God. Like the fruit on the trees, there is plenty of it around. Why not make use of it, and enjoy it while here?

Circulation Is The Key!

To develop a healthy, playful attitude about money you must spend it, circulate it, and give it away! If you are short of funds, then it is definitely time to circulate what little you have. Put it out and watch it come back. My absolute key to having an abundance of money is to tithe ten percent of what I receive on a consistent basis back to the places and people where I am fed spiritually. Tithing activates the law of increase and the law of ten-fold return.

Learn to celebrate the enjoyment of money. If you condemn cash, you will never have enough to support yourself well. Poor thinking brings poor results. Just as thoughts of disease bring illness, fear-filled thoughts, like I won't have enough, invite and perpetuate exactly the same, limited experience. Do the opposite. Celebrate your money flow, by enjoying what it does for you and be grateful in acknowledging your Source. Universal Supply is God money available to you at all times. It is a spiritual substance.

Your powerful subconscious is your direct line to the Creator of all supply. As you work with Universal Infinite Supply and acknowledge that it comes from God by tithing, the Divine Absolute Knowing of Universal God-Mind pays attention to your focus. It responds to your requirements for change. Focus on increase rather than lack. As you tithe, its loving knowing will bring necessary adjustments in awareness that you require to expand. The awareness that comes will be fine-tuned to the level of where you are at the time. Trust your guidance and intuition. I wrote *No Boundaries* in order to assist others in changing limited, subconscious beliefs. **It is impossible to change a limited experience without changing your thoughts about it and what you desire to experience. As you create a loving, healthy, generous attitude about money, respect it and share it, you will observe it's flow through you. It must flow outward if it is going to flow inward. Circulation is the key!**

Money Affirmations:

Create and use positive affirmations to support a fresh, abundant and healthy attitude about money. Example: "I am wealthy with the wealth of God. I am One with Divine, universal supply. God is my source. God is within me, and God is All. Therefore, I am whole, perfect and complete. Because Spirit dwells within me, I deserve the best and to be supported richly in all my ways. Spirit in me knows the completeness of my desire and assists me in knowing everything I need to know to accept it. I have everything I require. Money is good, I enjoy more than enough of it. I give freely and joyously, and receive graciously with an attitude of gratitude. I am supported and loved. I love myself." These affirmations will get you home. Use them consistently to change your awareness and to prime it for success. When you do, the higher part of you, your God-self recognizes a call to that part of Itself within you, and responds by rising your awareness. In the process you shift your vibration to the higher rate on all levels of your life, and you will be on your way to being a master manifestor.

The Money Formula

An abundant flow of money to use and enjoy is created by tithing ten percent of all income to the places and people where spiritual food is received. As we acknowledge God as our source, at the channels where we are fed spiritually its flow is increased measurably for us. I see a tithe as seed money that activates flow and is gratitude for what I have received and for what I expect to receive. To do it keeps me in the flow of all good. See *No Boundaries, Let Go Of Limits And Create Success* for detailed understanding and instructions on tithing. I want everyone to prosper in living heaven on earth now, fully supported and to be free of anxiety! This is the secret answer to always having all the money you require, and enjoying it more!

The Infinite Mind of God within us is capable of creating

unlimited ways and means to fulfill any desire, including great wealth, if that is what is required to complete a picture. What the world calls wealth, may or may not be part of your picture. **"Your relationship with Universal Supply is your wealth and it reveals the ways and means to produce anything you require at any given time!"** (*No Boundaries* pp 140).

Our degree of oneness with our Creator, and our relationship with Infinite Supply determines the quality, quantity and speed at which we manifest the things into our life that we require and enjoy. The more attention we give to the conscious awareness of Spirit within ourselves, the more It does for, with and through us.

"Seek Ye First the Kingdom of Heaven and All these things Will Be Added Unto You."

Choose to observe yourself as life hands you exactly what you are willing to receive. Be willing to grow into living your vision as well. If you do not yet know what that vision is, go window-shopping and play act and imagine owning it. Spend time visualizing your desire, as if it were already an established fact and be detached as to how it will come to you.

As we awaken to our Oneness with God, we will experience ease in manifesting desires.

Speak Your Word To Create Flow, Expansion And Increase

There is One Infinite Power in the universe. It is the joy, wholeness and magnificence of Divine Intelligence. I accept fully that the greater part of me is Spirit. Since Spirit is Infinite awareness knowing all, It *is* my *Greater Potential*. There is no lack in God, therefore I accept that God in me, knows how to expand my awareness so that I may live, move and breathe into the greater experience of my life path. I accept that my consciousness is one with the greater awareness of Infinite Spirit.

I choose to accept a larger picture of myself and a larger self-image. I allow God to move upon my subconscious awareness in ways that expand who and what I am, and what I believe myself to be capable of. This includes my ability to appreciate, and receive and to participate in wealth. Knowing that I am supported in all of my ways, I joyfully invite the conscious knowing of Spiritual expansion to move through me and focus upon the greater picture and plan for my life. Thank you God that I have increased awareness of health, wealth, and an expansive attitude about life.

I accept Divine intervention and correction of my life plan. Knowing it can only be for the better, I accept change and gladly release anything that is standing in my way of success. I establish a new attitude of expansive awareness and accept that I am always guided from within. Life supports me in every good way, including financially. I agree to expand. Thank you, Spirit within me, for my creative, open, non-attached expansive attitude. I am One with that which creates all. And So It Is!

CHAPTER NINE

Spirits and Angels

The narrow, tall, house mysteriously called to me. Its odd, shadowed position between two high rise apartment buildings wooed me to stop and look closer. It was if an unseen breath one would feel in a moonlit graveyard began to speak to my soul. It whispered spell-like tones of melancholy; "Let your eyes and heart rest here awhile. Dream a little with me." In the early September night air, no longer sticky from the humidity of the day, the darkened house looked so sweet and forlorn. Even with its paint blistered and window shades torn and sagging, there was a dignity about it. Looking upon the narrow, tall Victorian, I felt a comforting feeling, like the kind created by the sound of a fog horn cutting a thick mist, or the drone of trucks that lulled me to sleep as a child as they passed on a distant highway.

Looking closer I could see that it reminded me of another house I had seen in St. Paul on fashionable and historic Summit Avenue. It had been similar and smaller but equally good in style, and similarly faded from neglect and time. I had attempted to buy it a year earlier, with the idea of restoration. Before I had the opportunity to begin negotiations, the tenants intentionally set it afire, destroying it forever. I remembered now the phrase "good-bye, house." spray painted across the porch, and how sad I felt. As an architectural student and long time apartment dweller, I had been excited by the prospect of a home of my own to enjoy and restore.

Now, a year later, I was out walking after dinner one evening with my college roommate, Dean Hand, when we came upon this new find I stopped in my tracks. Lurking, dark and hidden, back from the street and camouflaged under big old elms, it appeared quite run down. With only one or two dimly lit, dirty panes of glass revealing a gossamer-like trace of light and life. The decrepit window coverings, and over-grown bushes completed the haunted house look. However, the grace and charm of the Victorian style gave it integrity and an element of hope.

Coming upon the old house in the dark awakened a sad, longing within my heart. It was like looking upon withered, yet carefully planted rose garden that had seen the glory of better days. Someone had put a lot of thought and care into the design. I could see that it had perfect symmetry, with two cantilevered, gargoyle-faced beams supporting a triple window on the second floor. Above each, was a smaller window of intricate stained glass design. I wondered who once lived there, and of the stories the rooms must hold.

"Dean!" I grabbed my friend's arm as my eyes focused in the dim light, "This is just the sort of house that I have always dreamed of living in!. Its like that one in St. Paul on Summit, I told you about." He squinted to see. "It looks pretty sad to me." As I began point out its architectural merits and tell him of what I would do to bring it back to life, he too began to fall under it's spell. I don't recall now how much time we spent under the streetlight before walking on to our destination, but I know I that dreamed about it off and on for the next few days. As school began I became busier with all the social activities of a nineteen-year-old college student, I forgot about it the little Victorian.

At the time, Dean and I shared an apartment originally designed as a one bedroom unit. We had converted the living room to a second bedroom, so we would each have more privacy and save on rent. The old, four-story, building housed an array of students and working singles, so an abundance of social life filled its broad halls and big rooms. Across the hall were two girls that Dean and I began to chum around with. They were always inviting us to parties and having us over for drinks, food, and conversation. They talked often about how they would like to share a big house with a couple of guys. Because of their carousing lifestyle we were not overly enthusiastic about joining and sharing a space with them. When they called and asked us to go looking, we would put them off or decline. One night they were particularly insistent about seeing another house they had found and had acquired keys to. They plied us with good hors d' oeuvres and a couple of drinks, so we went along for just the ride. I was overwhelmed when we pulled up in front of the same Victorian house I had spied while walking a few weeks earlier. I could hardly wait to see the inside.

The spooky interior looked even worse than I imagined. It was creaky, dingy, sagging and poorly lit. Obviously neglected for a long time, the floors were badly in need of refinishing. Many light fixtures were broken or missing, and wallpaper was ragged and stained. However there were fourteen interesting rooms. It had several pantries, fireplaces, tooled leather walls, and inlaid, exotic carved, woods abounded. All of the time we were inside, I had an eerie feeling that we were not alone. I mentioned to the others that this house felt haunted. The added mystique of possible ghosts heightened everybody's excitement and interest. Later that night Dean and I deliberated as to whether we would consider a successful co-habitation with these party girls in the strange old house with the name Stebbins skillfully carved in the front door.

I had obvious feelings for the house and Dean was always up for a new adventure, so by morning we obliged their demands for a prompt answer and agreed to take it. Feeling the house was big enough for all of us, we felt we could handle any compromises so we all moved in at the same time.

In a short time our concerns about the girls turned out to be right. Living with the two of them was not easy. One was an actress on stage in full drama most of the time. The other, bless her little heart, fit the stereotype of a dizzy blonde who had a nasty propensity for frequent and violent temper tantrums. Fortunately, within a couple of month's time, circumstances changed for both of them in their work situations and they could no longer afford the rent. We quickly found more copasetic male roommates who could pay their portion of the rent and we settled into a peaceful and productive life in the house.

The initial trouble with the girls was worth it. Were it not for them I might not have moved in to the grand old place. For the first time in my life, I lived in a real home. It was more than just a house. When one stepped into the lofty, two story entry, it was easy to imagine life as it was one hundred years before. It felt secure and in a world of its own, even though it was flanked on either side by two high-rise, apartment buildings. I had been led to the sweet Victorian in the dark of night in answer to a life-long dream for a real house of my own. Now I had one that provided a firm foundation and a rich backdrop for living. I quickly became a happy and productive art student. I enjoyed living in a home and in Minneapolis, a community rich in cultural heritage and alive with art and commerce.

Shortly after moving in I discovered that my original suspicions were real. The Stebbins House was haunted. Not with poltergeists, grinding chains, or dungeons containing skeletons, but by a lovely soul who had once lived there....and died there.

Research revealed that her name had been Vera Stebbins. Her father, an architect had built the house for his Scandinavian bride. It is a well-known fact that when an architect builds for himself, he puts an extra measure of thought and love into his work. Vera's architect father had given an attention to detail in unique ways. The Stebbins' had been *Spiritualists*. They built the house with the intention of it being a spiritual home as well as physical shelter. The front entry floor was a parquet comprised of several kinds of Oak and exotic walnut woods, featuring a large inlay design of a pentagram. Its points were open towards the front door, indicating that the house was open to all free spirits to come and go as they pleased. The Stebbins House lived up to its spiritualist heritage of being host to all who visited. We had many fantastic parties and guests. In the years I lived there, the house became a gathering point for close friends and strangers alike. It was one of the most comfortable and creative homes I have ever lived in. The Stebbins house certainly became my first real home. For many years after leaving it, I dreamed about moving back in. I fantasized buying it, sawing it into pieces and shipping it via rail to California! However, my bank account was never as big as the dream.

The Stebbins raised a large family there. They added on a spacious, unheated nursery on the rear that was used in the summer months. I used it as my art studio. Their family of nine children eventually outgrew the bedrooms and bathrooms so they added a second house at the rear of the property facing another street. This afforded a very large, wooded, private, back yard between the two houses. With a lake across the street from the rear house at Loring Park, it was a dream for the nature-loving artist in me.

As a child I had always known that I wanted to be an artist. While in school, I was happy to be working nearly full time in a creative job after class and on weekends that more than nurtured my soul and my bank account generously. With several roommates helping to pay for my large home, I lived well. Frequently on days and nights off, wonderful friends filled the gracious main floor rooms with good times and laughter. The sounds of joy resounded in the high-ceiling spaces with music and voices resonating off the parquet floors. The nursery/art studio served me well for all of my art projects. We called it the cold room. It was not for just the lack of heat, but because of the energy in the space as well. There was a chill, a feeling that made most people not want to spend time there. But for me it was great because I could get a lot of creative work done in it without interruption. A space heater in the winter helped it to be an acceptable workspace. I became comfortable at hanging out with spirit energies that visited me in the wee hours of the night.

Ghosts

The Stebbins house definitely had a life of its own. For the first few weeks of our residence, life felt unsettled and spooky at times. Doors would slam unexpectedly and we would hear whispers in the next room and sometimes I would feel strange, cold, bizarre feelings without reason or warning. The previous tenants, children of the sixties, had been hippies and used it as a commune. Over the years, many tenants had come and gone. As far as I could tell most of them had abused the grand old house in one way or another. My art studio had been used by the commune as a temple for some kind of occult ceremonies. Hearing of its history, I had good reason to bring in an occultist priest to come and do an exorcism and a blessing of all the rooms before we moved in. (It was the late sixties, after all.) As I began to refinish and restore parts of the house the unsettled feelings began to calm. By now I began to suspect that Vera was in charge. After all she had been born in the house and lived there for all of the ninety-nine years of her life. Wealthy and well-traveled, she lived with a companion but never married. It was clear she was still there. Stories from former tenants reported of seeing her glide down the stairs in the two-story front hall. I never did see her, but I felt her presence often. On one occasion I heard her voice.

It happened in the evening of the day that the grand piano was brought in. Dean, who is now in Spirit, was a wonderful pianist. He decided a couple of months after we moved in to get a piano. With Dean, everything had to be on a grand scale. That first night he sat down and began to play classical music. I was in my bedroom above. Lovely chords began to fill the rooms and echoed up the stairs. Our other two roommates were somewhere in the rear of the house, over the kitchen, in the former service quarters. The house was large and well built, too large for voices to carry from the front to the back, and up rear the stairs. It was not unusual for us to be sequestered in all of our rooms and not hear one another. After Dean played the first few bars I heard the sound of a lovely and mature, female voice sigh...."Ahhh." I raced down the stairs to the living room to report the experience to Dean. He had heard it too. His eyes were filled with tears as he continued to play Rachmaninoff. Just then, the other two roommates rushed in to share the news. We had all heard Vera's voice at the same time from different parts of the house. As the piano music resounded though the high-challenged rooms, it added a new feeling. Peace had been restored to the Stebbins house and come to Vera's domain once again.

In the months following, I continued to refinish, paint and polish, bringing the finery back to life, and the energy of love continued to flow from Vera. It was her love and my creativity that brought the proud old Victorian to new life and gave me the home I had always dreamed of.

Most of my friends and new roommates were comfortable with the other worldly presence. I shared the house with several sub- tenants over five years time. One or two could not handle the paranormal energies and, like the first two, moved out almost immediately. Most stayed on and loved the warm feelings that enveloped it. When I return to Minnesota, I always visit the house and Vera. It has been moved to a new location, just off Stephens Park across from the Minneapolis Art Institute. A location I think is appropriate. Most of the wings have been removed so it's not nearly as large as it had been when I called it home, but now it is preserved on the city's historic registry. There is a large sign in front telling a brief history. It has been converted to an office building. I visited the office of the psychotherapist who was renting there. She agreed that it is definitely haunted. We exchanged stories; mine about the loving memories, and hers about how the rocking chair starts moving every time she gets a patient who is agitated. I felt Vera's presence and a feeling of love and warmth as the feeling of Vera came to me on that first visit back. Her spirit still visits there.

Angels

One of my favorite people from Minnesota was a fun-loving, precocious sharp-witted gal named Debbie Garrett. I met her when she and Dean dated briefly. In no time, Debbie and I became the best of pals. We soon became the kind of friends that get into all types of outrageous adventures. There was seldom anything we would not try as long as it was crazy and fun. Somehow we managed to stay out of serious trouble. Debbie and I were very connected to one another, so much that I would think of her and the phone would ring and it would be her. Often her name would pop into my head just as I would walk to the window and see her coming to my door. She knew I always was ready to put down whatever I was involved in and have some fun. We traveled in most of the same places, so it would not be unusual to bump into each other while out and about in the city. It was always a good excuse to go have a drink, share food or take a walk in the park.

Over the course of the years, with Debbie in Minnesota and me in California, we lost contact with one another. A couple of years ago I heard through other friends in Minneapolis that she had died rather suddenly of a heart attack. Since we were the same age, I was stunned by the news and saddened that I had let our friendship fall by the wayside. She had gotten involved in some serious drugs after I left and had many psychological and physical problems as a result. Once or twice she had called me in California, awakening me from a deep sleep in the night. I was unable to respond to her requests to visit me in California. She wanted to stay with me and bring along her niece with two infant, fatherless children. Her slurred phrases and stoned words may have shrouded a deeper cry for help, but I knew I was unable to assist. She was involved in several recovery programs at the time but I was involved in my own struggle to maintain stability with changes in my own experience.

When I visit the Twin Cities I connect with Debbie's mother and share fond memories. As I travel to familiar places, it seems strange not to run into Debbie. Minneapolis is not the same without her. Nothing from the past ever is. Nonetheless, being there brings up memories of her fun-loving, willingness to laugh. In 1994 I visited Minneapolis for the first time in eighteen years. The few friends I had kept up communications with had repeatedly invited me to come and visit my old home. I had left the Midwest with almost a vengeance of never wanting to return to winter. Although I had fond memories of life in Minnesota, my childhood in Iowa had not blessed me with the same. I just wanted to put it all behind me. However, in the same year of losing my home and possessions in the Malibu fire, I felt a growing need to connect with the place that had provided my first happy home.

Fate brought Debbie's memory back to life when I was re-introduced to a friend of hers. I was a guest attending a party in Minneapolis at Jon Hampton's home. He had been my best friend during the years in Minnesota and of course had known Debbie. At the party I was introduced to a woman whom at first I remembered only by name. Someone that Debbie had often spoken of. In the early nineteen-seventies, I met Nancy P. on one occasion only briefly when she came to my house with Debbie. During the years that Debbie and I were playing in the singles scene, she was married and raising a family. Today she is a divorced, carefree, gregarious, young grandmother enjoying her freedom. Being the life of many frequent parties and dinners she attends, Nancy is a well-connected interior designer who seems to know all of the right, fun people in the Twin Cities. As far as I can tell, Nancy is in demand as *the* guest extraordinare for anyone who is entertaining. I know why she and Debbie were close friends. Debbie was always the life of the party. I can only imagine that the two of them must have been quite a pair.

One of my pet peeves is people who beat around the bush. Perhaps that is why Nancy and I get along so well. We share a fond love for Debbie's memory and enjoy spontaneous fun. Nancy makes no bones about calling the shots as she sees them. It is that quality that draws people to her. She is real and direct, getting right to the point. Her quick wit greases an expansive but slightly warped sense of humor. Without being crass or off color, she has a way of making comments that might ordinarily seem shocking into big laughs that anyone could appreciate. She comes up with statements that are precise and well delivered, hitting the mark right on the bulls eye. She's got her timing and delivery down to an art.

In the workplace as an interior designer, Nancy also is a master at connecting people and at getting things done. She sets her vision on her purpose and applies the powerful, secret keys to detached success. "Be in the flow of the moment without having to dominate how results will unfold." She knows that one creates the best results possible by being non-attached from the control of conditions. All of the right elements will come into alignment at the right time when one does. The highest good is accomplished for everyone involved.

It is not without enthusiasm and passion that Nancy delivers feats of achievements to her pleased and appreciative clients. Enthusiasm and passion are the other two essential and equally powerful ingredients of success. She recognizes that if one thing is not working, another will. She is flexible, shifting gears to easily make a different choice. Another high spiritual key. This willingness to not determine conditions is what allows the higher good to come from the field of unlimited knowingness where all created.

These keys to genius are available to everyone, not just Nancy and me. You too, participate in a process of spiritual creation, whether you know it or not, every time you make a choice or decision. Be detached and let the greater good work for you and come to you in wonderful new ways.

Since that first return trip to Minnesota in 1994, I continued to travel to my old home each spring. I would paint for Nancy's design clientele and many who were also former clients of mine. When a design would be proposed, I let Nancy know if it was something I would be able to execute. If what she or the client came up with was something that would be unrealistic to paint, or over budget, I would suggest alternatives. She is open enough to easily accept what will accomplish the job to the satisfaction of all. I enjoy creating a work of art, the clients are pleased with the efficiency and beauty, and I am paid well. Everybody wins - which is the end result of being committed to success, but detached as to how it must come into being.

One morning, as Nancy and I were driving together to

view a project, she told me about a girl friend she had counseled. Apparently The friend who was in the midst of a long, drawn out divorce, had phoned Nancy, all upset because her soon to be ex-husband had not come home the night before. She was distressed, wondering what could have happened to him. Since he had left the house dressed only in a tee shirt, jeans and cowboy boots, where could he be? Could he be injured or in the hospital? Apparently the gal had been lamenting to Nancy a few days before that she was wishing that the separation was complete. Nancy in her easy off-the-cuff way replied; "Wake up and smell the coffee, Sweety.... your soon to-be *ex*, was out getting laid! This is just what you've been wanting. This is perfect. Relax, you're tying to get rid of him anyway!" It is tough when the changes that divorce brings causes us pain and worry. Nancy is sensitive and knows this, but she knew that what her friend really needed most was some lightening up.

The friend expressed further concern. She was leaving for California on a trip that afternoon and she feared that he might not come home in time to take care of the children while she was away. Nancy had a quick reply for that one too. "You're not that lucky. He's just out sowing his wild oats! He'll be back in time. Lighten up." Nancy's comments got her to laugh and stop worrying. Nancy's words of wisdom were exactly what her girl friend needed to hear in order to relax, let go, and get prepared for her trip. The soon-to-be-ex did show up in plenty of time.

Nancy's humor is a great gift reminding us to let go of some of life's worries and to lighten up about the things we cannot change. She understands that being detached from the hows and the ways of problem solving is the best way to get results and she tells a great story!

Ninety Nine Percent Of The Things We Worry About Never Happen.

The shortest point between A and B is a straight line. Gandhi called it the path of non-resistance. Deepak Chopra refers to it as being in the gap of no time and space where all things are possible. By being detached from controlling conditions and open to the field of infinite possibilities one can create with newness and with apparent genius. I summarize it as the infinite power of detachment. My friend Nancy P. serves as an angel of light and is a great example of one who operates best in the infinite field of non-resistance and is open to the greatest good. She puts detachment into action while bringing the healing gift of humor into every day life as well as being a vessel of connection for many on her path.

Whenever I get stuck in problem solving I know the best answer will come to me when I practice surrender. Struggle is never the key to success. When we are trying to figure things out, we are coming from what we have learned in past experiences. Why not choose instead to create something new through effortless knowing? Let the ideas come to you in creation or problem solving. The leaves on the trees grow through effortlessness, the river flows by its own accord, and the planets move on their own as part of a divine scheme. "He maketh me to lie down in green pastures and walk by still waters," is the new paradigm. Detach, let go and let God reveal ways and means. There is tremendous power in doing so. Bring everything you require into Divine timing and order by allowing spirit to reveal it to you. It will come through you when you let it.

Angels On Assignment

I believe that angels do exist, and that they come in many different forms. You and I can be angels of assistance whether we know it or not. When Spirit puts someone before me who obviously requires an attitudinal healing, I get busy and call in angels. I know that I am not required to do the actual healing work myself, nor do I have to get directly involved with a person with a bad attitude who requires some obvious healing. I do not have to get directly involved or in their line of fire in order to be of assistance. There are many angelic beings we can call into assistance or to assignment to do the job for us. They are experts at it.

Each of us has the ability and the right to call for angels of help at any time, in any circumstance. They are waiting for just that to spring into action. These beings between God and Man joyously dive in to a situation to provide wonderful ways and experiences to facilitate change. We must be detached as to how they come or accomplish the healing.

Healing can come to anyone. If they are seeking it and working in Spirit, ways will always be presented to them. It is not up to us to determine how those means will come. Sometimes we may recognize the need for healing to be immediate, significant and essential, when those who require it do not. You or I may act as the instrument or messenger of healing who calls the light of change into the experience for them. If it is for the higher good of all involved then there is nothing wrong with employing a little

Divine intervention. The world will be a better place for us all as the light of spirit expands through those who are in need of it most.

Angelic Assistance

I became acutely aware of a need to do just that one day a couple of years ago. I was dining in a restaurant with a friend at the end of a particularly busy workday, and not in the mood to deal with the uncomfortable situation I was dealt.

I was caught completely by surprise by the abusive attitude of a woman seated near me. At first, I failed to understand the negative energy she was projecting. Yet I felt her overt hatred that was clearly directed towards me. It was a form of prejudice I had not seen nor experienced in liberal West Los Angeles ever before. This very large, overweight woman of a different ethnic background than I, began to speak in loud tones making reference to the differences between us. There was no question in that her comments were pointed at me. With my small, athletic frame and light complexion, I seemed to represent all she disliked. I found it difficult to enjoy my dinner in this unusual and uncomfortable circumstance. I returned home quite upset from the unprecedented, prejudicial attack. It gave me an idea of what she and others who are the victims of bigotry and hate crimes must feel and experience. l felt a disturbed sense of compassion and sorrow, yet I knew some deeper note had been struck within me.

It had been clear to me from the onslaught of the attack that her spirit recognized my light, and that the direct, surface abuse was a deep, desperate, inner cry for help. I spent a good deal of time pondering the situation. Still troubled by it, I went into meditation looking for answers to my own pain. Why me? Why must I be a target of attack? I do not mind being a light and a healer but I knew I must protect myself from this and other sorts of abuse, my spirit is sensitive. I have had my own ridicule issues from childhood to deal with. Yet I knew it was essential, but not enough alone to just let go of the situation by practicing forgiveness and release.

I called a friend for consultation. She is very sensitive to energy and suggested that I first provide a psychic energy shield to protect myself from further attack. I did as she instructed and surrounded myself with an energetic field of mirrors to deflect anything that she or anyone else would project. At home, I could still feel the attack. She was not going to let distance stop her, this woman was desperate for healing. She came to the right place.

Little did she know what she was in for. Or perhaps she did. Could the darkest of her fears and hatred have been uncontrollably drawn to the highest part of my energy? The light of spiritual love is easily seen as a torch leading to freedom when shined towards those living in an dark abyss of fear. She had spotted me from the moment I walked into the room. I feel that her Spirit recognized my light.

When people come to me for healing, I use everything I have. I call in all the ballistic missiles of Spirit if necessary. Healing is not a halfway business. If I am putting the good energy and investment of my time into it, then I expect definite results. Desperate cries for help call for desperate measures! I did not want the toxicity of her energy being poured into the race consciousness any longer. If it was too much for me who understood what was happening, I could not imagine how brutal it would be for others who did not.

It was time to call in the troops. I boldly spoke my words for special angels to be charged and assigned to her, to work her over in the highest way so that she would get her healing in the right and appropriate way that was best for her. It would be unique so that she would understand it, and get *cleared up* once and for all. Next in my mind it came to me to image and prepare a space in a box car on a freight train, way out in the desert. I energetically lined the interior of it with bronze mirrors and lit a single purple flame of healing in the center. I called for a special team of angels to be assigned to her to do the work. I energetically placed her in the car surrounded by the team of angels. I performed my own spiritual mind treatment prayer by speaking my Word for the highest healing for her, to be directed by God. I was on a roll, I began to feel better. Yet, I still needed to disconnect from the situation.

It was time to unhook myself from the train.... and the painful sting of her foul slurs. I envisioned my train car and engine uncoupling or detaching from pulling the train behind, completely letting go, detaching myself from the situation, and releasing and forgiving her. As I gave thanks at bedtime for her complete healing, I checked in. I could see the train parked way out in the desert. I saw brilliant, purple, flashes of light coming from the lone boxcar on the desolate tracks. The teams of angels were performing their psychic, spiritual, healing surgery on the woman so desperate and ready for release. I knew her negativity and energy could not be allowed to be spread throughout the world anymore. Perhaps something in me was healed that night as well. I had asked that any shred of prejudice within myself be revealed and healed shortly before the incident. That situation got me clear fast! Everyone of us are God's people. No matter what color, shape, size, or choice of activity we make.

In the morning I checked in on the boxcar once more. The scene looked and felt neutralized and quiet. I got a sense that the angelic team was sewing her up and preparing to put her back into the world. I sensed peace. I knew my work was complete with that one and that I had done what I was called to do.

It may be essential for you to do what I did by calling for angels of healing to intervene when necessary. You can remove yourself from harm's way when it rears its ugly face by using this method of healing in absentia, and detaching from the trouble. I believe that some situation in the physical world would coordinate in her life so that she understood the ramifications of her actions once and for all. Whatever it would be was not up to me but I know as a result she would be a changed soul.

"Judge Not ...."

Recently I met a fundamentalist Christian bus driver who chauffeurs tour groups throughout California. He told me that he had been hired to drive an all-Catholic group up the coast and had felt uncomfortable and judgmental about it. In answer to his prayers, God had spoken to him; "These, too, are my people," he heard in his mind as the group boarded. His attitude was changed forever. Who are we to label judge or blame others for their differences.

I grew up in Iowa in the fifties and sixties where anyone who differed from the norm was suspect or feared. I was a teen-age artist, with long hair living in a community of red neck farmers. My mother married one of them when I was twelve, giving me even greater challenge to rise above. Need I say more. I have spent plenty of time in therapy, in prayer and in forgiveness over my childhood. I still have no desire to return to Iowa for a visit. I am sure things are different there now, but why go there and push those buttons. When I left the Midwest it was with a complete sense of detachment; at the time it was the sooner and farther the better.

In downtown Los Angeles there is a Funicular railway, or tram called Angels Flight. It goes straight up a couple of blocks to what used to be a different neighborhood than the one at the bottom. For me, leaving Iowa and my past behind was my angel's flight to the freer pastures of the West! Sometimes we must rise above that old familiar territory to start fresh with a higher clearer view for our own lives to transform. Envision your own Angels Flight to create freedom and fresh air when you require it.

Recently I experienced another example of a need for angel work in L.A. traffic during an evening rush hour. I had just gotten off the freeway and had been attempting to get into the far, right- hand, turn lane for about a block in heavy traffic. I approached a red light where I intended to turn. I was the second car back from the light, so I turned on my signal again and cranked my wheel, as I began to inch into the empty right lane. A car came flying up blowing its horn and whizzed just past my right front fender. The driver slammed on his brakes stopping just inches away, turned and began to deliver the foulest obscenities I had heard in a long time. I could tell by the look on his face that he was one very angry young man. I'm not talking, just ticked off, I'm telling you he was ready to be really violent. I just sat and looked at him thinking "I'm not going to buy into this." I was able to smile, feeling happy to be past the point in my life where I might have dived into his pool of anger by responding on any level. It felt good. I realized that I had finally graduated from the ultimate traffic school. I still get angry when appropriate, but not at other drivers who just do not know what they are doing. Vengeful anger never resolves anything. To get revenge only pulls us down to a lower vibration and propagates negative energy in our culture.

This was another case for the angels. I called them when I got home and asked for them to be assigned to this young man to do their healing work for the highest good. I directed that his healing might come in a way that would be completely appropriate, loving and safe, while illuminating him to the laws of cause and effect. Perhaps he has not had the opportunity in his life to see that his attitude or actions have an effect on his experience. Perhaps he has not experienced love that is nurturing and self-sustaining. Or perhaps he was just having a bad day. When I speak with friends and they tell me they are having a bad day, I usually respond by reminding them that the sun is still shining, or that they have their health, they have food on their tables and that there is much to be grateful for. Even if the sun is not shining, it still is a day that God made. So what if something did not turn out the way they had planned? Be detached and enjoy the gifts and apparent mistakes.

Perhaps the mistakes are life's way of slowing you down to notice the good that is there. Who and what determines what your day is like, other than you? Does one incident affect the quality of the whole day? Does one bad apple make the whole bushel bad?

Remember you can call in angels to assist you in correcting

your experience and that of others. Just remain detached as to the hows, means and ways healing and know that change can come. Ask for Divine healing of the highest order, appropriate and right for the highest good of all involved. Then step aside to let it happen. Detach, just like I detached from the boxcar and the angry driver. I may never see either of those people again, But I know that their spirits called to me in an hour of need. God put them in my face to help awaken a greater good within them and myself. Our Word has the power to heal and change conditions. There is no stopping Spirit when it has a cause to fulfill its own completeness.

Victim or Volunteer?

You can be the vessel of healing, rather than a victim of circumstance. Choose to look at these situations we label bad and realize that you have an opportunity to make a difference in the lives of those in need and in the quality of your own experience as well. The ripple effect on the pool of our world will be tremendous as Spirit moves through you by means of your word permeating the pond with love. For each person you and I touch there are tens, hundreds, or even thousands that are ultimately affected. You are the gift of living light reading these words that can make the difference in healing our world.

Helen

One of my favorite angels and teachers was Reverend Helen Street. She was a great spiritual teacher with an incredible sense of humor. I could relate to it since we were both born Virgos. We have a label and compartment for everything. We cannot help but do it as we are born organizers. We love order and have a terrible need to judge. Helen used to say...."when I was born I came out of the womb wearing a black robe and a powdered wig. The doctor took one look at me and said *here come the judge!*" She may have been judgmental at one time but all I ever observed from Helen was an incredible flow of love. She had a way of getting an audience laughing so hard that you felt as though you might fall off the chair, and then hit you with the softest and sweetest, loving, whispers of truth, forever etching them into your heart.

Helen always walked her talk and eloquently expressed the gift of detachment in her teaching. She was unattached to politics and to formality. Just like Nancy, Helen did not give a hoot to what others thought of her. She died of a brain aneurysm a few years back. It was just like Helen to not be sick even for one minute. There are so many people leaving the planet these days. I am seldom surprised when I hear of another death. We just cannot know how another's life path fits into the grand scheme of things. If I know Helen, she is busy entertaining and teaching on the other side. In Religious Science she was called the Bette Midler of Metaphysics because of her great ability to make others laugh and her outrageous taste for flashy clothes. I'd bet a buck that she and my friend Debbie would really kick up a good time together. I guess I'll see em at the pass.

Speak Your Word

There is one Infinite power. It is All-Knowing God who prevails over every aspect of my being. I give thanks that I know who I am....a Divine Being. I give thanks for all of those in spirit who are my guides and guardians and that they assist me in clarity and purpose. They watch over me and protect me in health, travel, relationships, home, love and career. I am blessed to be so cared for. I love myself and know that in some way, they are a part of me and my life. For I am one with spirit and all that is good. Life is good. Praise God. And So It Is.

CHAPTER TEN

Speed Bumps

My street was a busy concourse. Its convenient location provided me with a center of operations five minutes from the beach and downtown Santa Monica in one direction, and quick freeway access leading to the busy Westside of Los Angeles in the other. Although a secondary thoroughfare, the avenue's geographic advantage offered rush-hour and airport commuters a convenient, short cut alternative to the congestion of primary arteries. However, it was a source of irritation for most of the residents in terms of traffic and noise, especially at peak times. My cottage in the rear faced a quiet, private, park-like garden and most of the traffic sounds were blocked by the houses and trees in the front.

A generous neighbor across the street offered his driveway for my use as safe-haven, overnighter for my car. Backing on to the busy thoroughfare in the morning was difficult enough, however dashing across on foot was downright dangerous. Cars sped along well above the posted limit all day long. On several occasions, residents' parked cars had been taken out by drunk drivers in the night coastal fog. For that reason alone I was committed to off-street secure parking. The raceway was intimidating and challenging for the local cat populace as well, adding several near-death experiences to their nine lives.

Ultimately, the city responded to the frequent complaints of the street's residents. When an interviewer came around asking for signatures from those in favor of installing speed bumps, I gladly signed. I anticipated the day when I could cross the street in safety and get to my car without having my own near-death experience. The day finally came when the city crews arrived to install the bumps. The task took most of the day. I had expected that they would install those short, stiff, obnoxious bumps one finds located propiatorily on the asphalt roadways of golf courses and gated communities. (Wouldn't we all just love to have a conversation with the man who dreamed them up?) The speed bumps installed on my street were a bit more graceful, (as a speed bump could be) extending about seven feet across, and rising fairly gently to a full five or six inches in the center. At each bump a sign was posted for fifteen miles per hour to signal and slow the careless down from the former fifty plus!

That evening's rush-hour brought quite a show. Since no public notice of the alteration had been posted that morning, none of the motorists expected such a dramatic and sudden change by afternoon.

The very first bump installed on our block was right in front of the house next door. The unsuspecting, preoccupied, commuter crowd was in for a rude awakening as it sped full on to the fresh black asphalt mounds. A chaotic scene of who-was-passing-who, played itself out like a hilarious black comedy. Those of us who park on the street during the daytime watched at a safe distance from our front porches and sidewalks, and quickly moved our cars to more secure locations. At five-thirty, an onslaught of unsuspecting commuters were the first to test the new bumps. Irate and furious drivers, they slammed full force with bumpers and tail pipes banging and flying as they hit. Anything not welded down or bolted on to the body of the cars was projected into space. It was highly entertaining for awhile. I considered bringing out some lawn chairs, passing out a round of drinks, and making a batch of popcorn for the neighbors!

Some of the more agitated drivers began to speed up and pass those to their right who had carefully slowed in advance. In mid flight over the fresh asphalt, middle fingers were slung into the air erect, and grimaces were directed to those who were observing the newly posted speed. The wild show reminded me of a demo-derby. They must have had too much coffee at work. In my cottage in the rear I heard the crashing of bumpers hitting the pavement and the chinking of small parts hitting the curb all evening long. I was grateful to be parked off the street, protected from the careening and crashing. I thought about getting up early and making a big pot of coffee and selling it to the morning drivers. I could pass it through the window as they slowed and would charge a buck a cup. I would call it *Zen coffee - with or without sugar bumps* and have a peaceful affirmation for the day written on the bottom of each cup. *Leaded or unleaded?* But then, I don't even know how to make the stuff, let alone drink it.

In the morning the saga continued. It became less noticeable day by day as people became accustomed to the monster mounds in the road. From time to time I would hear an occasional crash of a bumper hitting the pavement, and noticed bolts and small car parts littering the street on a regular basis. The bumps did the job they were supposed to do. People who live there can now back out of their drives and cross the street on foot without fear of being mowed down. The cats are living longer too. They now cross without the additional terror. One ruthless driver persisted in blasting his horn day and night when he was forced to slow for each of the bumps. I got the feeling it was one of those; "If I am going to suffer then everyone else will, too," kind of guys. I observed him gunning his engine and braking for the forth time at the speed light on the far end of the block. Apparently failing to see the futility in the action as he wastes energy, brakes, and gas in hyperactive vented anger. I remember those days.

Speed Bumps Of Life

We live our lives at a hectic pace, often rushing, going back and forth, round and round from place to place. In the morning the alarm rings, we dive for the shower, dress, run for the door, and lurch into traffic, coffee in hand. Jump started by the caffeine, we buzz into the morning's flurry of activity. Flying through lunch and into the afternoon, we seldom take time to realize why our stomachs are feeling uneasy. By the time we plow into bumper to bumper evening rush hour, (an oxymoron in itself) we arrive home feeling beat. Perhaps the day brought accomplishment. Perhaps just getting through it was accomplishment enough.

Throughout our day, we may encounter different kinds of speed bumps. Missing a light before it changes, an elevator before the door closes, or answering that ever-important phone call, all reflect homage to the addiction to a pace and technology we have created as an integral part of our culture. Just like the speed bumps in the road, those obstacles are where they are, as warning signs. They work to slow us to a safe and reasonable pace. The headache, the stomach cramp, and all the little aggravations throughout the day are effects of an attitude of struggle that our culture has come to accept as normal. All of the little struggles represent places where it would be wise to apply balance and order as they tell us when to adjust our pace. We could all use more grace in our lives.

The speed bumps on the road are there to save lives and maintain peace, as well as protect the security of communities. If we lived in balance and respect for one another, enjoying the time to travel in ease and comfort, arriving refreshed and composed, there would be no need for them at all. Yet we continue to create the necessity for their existence by choosing speed over common sense. In our workplace we have exchanged reasonable schedules and fair profits for a quick buck and the philosophy that who ever comes in first is the winner. What happened to *its not whether you win or lose, but how you play the game?* Does the thrill and satisfaction of life begin at sixty miles-per-hour? Is that where the action is? Does success begin in the fast lane, or is that where it ends?

It is proven that if we expend time rushing and conduct

our life with the idea that there is not enough time, our heart beats faster than normal and our nervous system is a bit hyperactive. As a result the body expires earlier that it might have and we fulfill our own destiny of "There's not enough time, or life is too short." We all know people who have expired early due to a stressful lifestyle, and others who received wake-up calls just in time to choose to live wiser, slower and to treat themselves and their loved ones in more loving ways.

The irony of the speed bump saga is that most of the drivers sped up as fast as they could between bumps, only to jam on the brakes before hitting the next one! I eventually discovered a way to cruise along, barely braking and accelerating at each one. When traveling the road of least resistance, it is necessary to detach from conditions whether they appear favorable or not in order to maintain a sense of peace. Remember that the peace of God is right where you are at all times. If you are spending time upset or angry your vibration is in a place that will cause you to feel non-synchronized. To have peace of mind you must first live and behave in a peaceful way.

Establish a peaceful state of mind by beginning each day in peace as a spiritual practice. Take time to meditate, pray and reflect before hitting the morning activities. Maintain the rhythm of it all day by breathing into it. Stay with it by making a commitment to practicing the presence of Spirit in all you do, especially when behind the wheel and other times when it may be challenging to do so. You will be the catalyst and stability when others are caving into chaos or loss. **Spiritually, there is never loss, only the opportunity to create.**

Spirit precludes all time and all space.

Obstacles in our experience act like speed bumps. They are only reminders telling us to slow down and establish peace of mind. All things are Divinely timed when we align with our Higher Power. When we take the time to *be here now* and flow with Peace, we will always be at the right place at the right time. Our Oneness with Spirit determines the flow and natural knowingness in our day and life. God will always lead us in the right direction and get us to where we need to be at the right Divine time. It will be in the highest order for all involved.

Perfect Speed, Perfect Timing

Recently I took a group to my secret, retreat place in Mexico. On the day of our scheduled return, I made certain to double-check all of the arrangements in advance. I was especially prudent in checking on the boat schedule that would take us to the city where we would catch a taxi to the airport. There were two scheduled water taxi departures that day; one at eight am., and one at two thirty p.m. Our plane was scheduled to depart at five so there was no need to leave in the early morning. I had the whole group assembled on the dock with luggage at just the right time to meet the boat. However, it was a half-hour late. When you are waiting for a ride to the airport, the last thing you want to be is late, or to feel anxious or rushed.

When the boat arrived, I commented to the driver that we did have a flight to catch. He assured me not to worry. Fifteen minutes into the cruise, he made an unscheduled stop to pick up additional passengers with cumbersome luggage that they swung and slammed onto the deck. As we made our way out to sea, one of the newly boarded passengers announced that he needed to get off at the next dock, making another unscheduled stop. I began to silently fume as he sat right in front of me, crowding the tiny boat and blocking my frontal view! Prior to picking up this last group, the driver had slowed to a stop to rearrange everyone further back in the small ponga in an effort to provide greater balance on the rough seas. Now this tipsy, sweating gentleman of considerable ballast was in my face, his full weight in the bow of the filled to capacity boat. I kept quiet, remembering that I am a spiritual being having a human experience. I worked at detaching from my own judgment and did my best to practice the Presence....somehow I managed to persevere, nonetheless gritting my teeth. Hey, I am human too!

The next unscheduled stop let off our unexpected passengers at a beautiful bay affording us a close up view of it. I began to feel calmer, as the stop proved to be a surprisingly quick side trip to an area I had previously wanted to check out. Again, we set out to sea. Now I felt less concerned about keeping to the schedule. I settled in and enjoyed the ride and stunning view. The spiritual pacing I had put myself through before when sharing the crowed seats on a rough sea, had primed me to appreciate this more relaxed state of mind. As I settled into a calm and began to enjoy the ride, I remembered that everything was in the hands of God.

I had done my prayer work that morning, so I accepted the

Divine timing and order of the day. I realized that even if we were late, and missed our plane, it would be for the higher good. A gift would be revealed and we could stay another night and take in the resort city and experience its gifts. I settled in, trusting the driver and God. They did not require my assistance to run the show. It is my philosophy that when I am getting a group of people from one place to another on a time schedule, it is important for me to maintain a relaxed, yet *in charge* attitude. It helps to have everything thought out or lined up in advance, including prayer work and spiritual mind treatment. Often, it is not possible to anticipate changes, so it is best to maintain an attitude that everything is Divinely taken care of whether it appears to be or not. It is anyway. (sometimes with the responsibility of taking care of the group even *I* forget that *God* is running the whole show, handling everything, even the smallest of details!).

The boat approached the dock and we prepared to land. Usually upon docking in this charming, busy, port city, we would walk about a block, carting our luggage to the local taxi stand. This day, a cab pulled up to drop off a passenger just as we collected our gear and headed from the pier! I hailed it and we tossed our bags into the trunk, piled in, and sped off for the Aereopuerto. We made great time to the terminal and were checked in efficiently and in record speed. At this point, we discovered that our flight was late in arriving, and that we would have an additional half-hour to peruse and shop the airport. Of course, Spirit had arranged everything in our favor. God knows nothing of rushing unless we program ourselves to operate that way.

The Hawaiians tell an old story about the difference between themselves and a *Hoale*. A non-Hawaiian Caucasian has an appointment in Honolulu. He rushes through the heat of the day to get there on time. He makes his meeting on time. He arrives hot and full of perspiration. The Hawaiian takes his time getting ready in advance. He strolls leisurely along and arrives when he arrives, cool, calm and collected. He knows that whatever time he gets there will be right. I think we have much to learn from the native cultures. Remember if you rush, possibly you are taking years off your life. Certainly running at hyper-speed depletes the body's natural energy that could be just as well used to enjoy a well-paced and graceful experience. Like the Hawaiian, to remain cool is to be cool. Just look to our role models and heroes that we consider to be cool. They are simply cruising along. Be cool with Spirit, where in all is well, on time and right on. You can probably tell what era I grew up in, but, hey, what can I say, man? I'm a child of the sixties.

Speak Your Word in Gratitude and Acceptance
For Success

The Divine Knowingness of All guides me in perfect Knowing at all times. I identify with this Higher part of my Being right here and now. I accept that Spirit guides me to my rightful success and provides everything for Divine fruition and acceptance within me. All is known in God. Since The Master Creator dwells within me, I trust It to reveal to me what I need to know to embody success.

I accept what I need to know from this moment forward to be the success I desire. I am Divinely supplied with right information and awareness to propel my life experience forward into a state of conscious love of life and into everything I do. I love what I do so much that I attract successful experiences, people, and support that fills me with motivation and energizes my vision. I thank God for Infinite Support. I am supplied with everything I require in health, wealth and Spirit. God is my Source, Substance and Supply, I can only prosper all the way. I Am One with the One Creative Power of the Universe. Thank God I Am Rich! And So It Is!

CHAPTER ELEVEN

The Shift

An Olympic swimmer becomes a champion by perfecting daily strokes and laps. A maestro of the piano too, must practice daily exercises to be celebrated. For you and I to become secure in the mastery of creating our own destiny it is essential to apply the principles of manifestation consistently. We build understanding upon them as we use them. At first we may find it easy to evoke certain things as we become trusting and agile at working with the law of supply. Becoming secure in knowing that the rent is always paid or that there is extra money for the movies, new clothing, a vacation or investments is good daily stuff. However, we may find in time that our greatest desires rarely come to us quickly. It because we have more of a vested interest in their being present in our lives to reflect or add to our own feelings of completeness. That perfect relationship, large sum of money, or something we have always wanted may seem somewhere outside of our reach. Sometimes they have not come because we are just not yet clear as to what we want, or it just is not yet the right time. More often it is that for one reason or another we feel unable to receive what we want.

The bottom line is this; Until one consciously practices spiritual creation feeling complete within the self, with or with out the desires in hand, one may not see them made manifest in form. Therefore, it is necessary to see and feel our desires as complete before we actually have them and it is necessary to prepare a place in our mental household for them to exist. When we are fully ready, the time will be right and it will also fit into the divine plan of our life.

Visualizing what we wish to create establishes a place for ownership of them in our consciousness. Living in the atmosphere of our desires in advance of receiving them is an essential part of the whole picture of creation. We become finely attuned to what we are visualizing when we begin to act upon our requirements and desires in conscious creation by breathing life into them. It is first essential to have the intention of accepting something definite in order to experience a specific result. Like the swimmer or the concert pianist, the more one exercises the art of manifesting, the better one becomes at being a master of it. **Preparation is seed for receivership!**

I enjoyed two comfortable years of living and working out of my rented cottage in Santa Monica. There were many times when I felt a desire to move forward to larger quarters. However, the ease of cheap rent afforded me great freedom to travel, and the cool, ocean breezes wafting through my door lured me into staying far longer than I had originally planned. Still, a deep yearning for the space of a real house with more rooms and doors that I could close for privacy began to eat at my heart. Finally, it was the crowding and confusion of running three businesses in one room that forced me to act out of necessity and prepare to move.

I inherited many humbling gifts as a result of living in a situation of compromise. They served to expand my understanding. I could see how people who, for one reason or another, must function within the confines of limited space. It forced me to economize on scale, become more organized and orderly, and be more creative in working within the constrictions of what I had available. So I have gratitude for the experience. Yet I knew that the pendulum of balance always returns full swing when the time is right. I was getting messages to move to a larger home more and more frequently.

Establishing Divine Order

From time to time, I entertained a friend from out of town who would spend the night sleeping on a mat I rolled out on the floor. The need to have more space was exacerbated when company was present. It became more obvious to me one evening when I was working with a letter of confirmation from my first bookstore chain, inviting me to sign on with them. One minute I had the letter in my hand, and the next I could not find it. Searching for it and looking around the room revealed a clearer picture of the state of my life. Clothing and dishes were on the bed, a pair of boots I was polishing and paperwork hung over the edges of the kitchen sink and counter. Stacks of paper filled every available space. I froze for a moment and looked at the reflection, and lack of organization around me. I suddenly realized the limits of my living situation. How could I possibly run a business like this? On top of it parking my car was still an on-going challenge. Because of nearby Santa Monica College and its parking restrictions, I had no choice but to move my car from one side of the street to the other, depending on what day and time it was. For security at night, I slid it into a neighbor's drive. Clearly, it was time to expand and move into a larger more complete home. I finally got the message. Hurray, at last! But where would it be?

I began my search by creating three, affirmative posters using a bold, black marker to inscribe empowering statements for use as sort of treasure map. I taped them to my refrigerator so I could see them all of the time. First I created one that read, "I can easily afford the home of my dreams." I had owned many homes, but experienced the strain of keeping up with mortgage payments. It was important to not re-create the stress I had worked so hard to release. I lived with the first affirmation for about a week before realizing the need for another. It read, "I am led to my dream home and my rightful location." I did not know where it would be, but I knew that Spirit within me would reveal it. So I placed it next to the first, bolstering my confidence and giving clarity to a dream that I could live in an area other than Santa Monica with its secure relationship to Los Angeles.

Spirit is a present-tense verb!

As I lived with the new affirmation for a couple of days, I recalled something I had overlooked: affirmations work best when put into the present tense. If I wanted to live in my new home by fall, it would be necessary to bolster my affirmations and engender the idea by painting a mental picture of it as being complete and established now. As a result, I created a third affirmation that emphatically announced, "I am living in my dream home now!" I placed it next to the other two, creating a triptych of powerful pledges I could not miss. Every time I approached the undeniable billboard my subconscious would get the message, insuring deep subconscious acceptance and eventual manifestation.

Altered States

When thinking about the upcoming move, It occurred to me that I had been stuck in this *where to live* scenario for some time. There were communities in Arizona, California, and Hawaii that seemed likely candidates, but as much as I wanted to, I could not seem to break free of Los Angeles. How could I be sure of the right direction for me to move? About the same time, a couple of friends who had been stuck with particular issues in their lives told me of a very special healer they had sessions with. I noticed obvious breakthroughs they seemed to be experiencing as a result of their working with her. I decided to call her and make an appointment for a session. I was overdue for a major change.

On the phone she seemed caring and extremely psychic. She immediately plugged into my issues without revealing much to her. I committed to a sitting. The actual session lasted for five hours and turned out to be one of the most unusually interesting and penetrating, life transformational experiences I have had to date.

We sat opposite one another on comfortable sofas, separated by a low, candle lit table. I felt an angelic presence and the love of Spirit fill the room as it flowed through her words and eyes and into my awareness. She began to speak of balancing my inner, right-brained male, with my left-brained feminine side. To be a well- aligned spiritual, human being, we all require a healthy balance of both male and female energies. She went on, telling me that I had deeply buried and smoothed over a tendency to be dominate and controlling, a characteristic that I inherited from my mother. I had lived quite successfully as a right-brained, male dominant soul and as a teacher of metaphysics. However, the feminine within, despite my being an artist, had never been allowed full expression or to come into full balance with the male counterpart. She was right. I had always ignored nurturing myself and did my best to gloss over or play down the complaints of others. Rather than express genuine caring, It was far safer and less intimate to intellectualize the problems of others rather than show true compassionate caring. It is one thing to talk about a principle and another to put it into action, especially within one's self.

There were other related issues. She noted that I had reached a ceiling of being able to function at the level I was at. My apparent inability to move away from Los Angeles had made me acutely aware of it myself. She continued to tell me that I could go no farther in my spiritual development without bringing this very important aspect of my own being fully alive. She stated that it would come into play in everything I did from now on. This may seem difficult to understand or to handle but stay with me here, I am going somewhere important with it.

As we got deeper into the session she never left her seated position across from me. At her instruction, I continued to stare into her eyes. She began to tell me that she was unplugging some of my father's DNA in the right side of my brain, that made both he and me passive enough to be controlled by a domineering wife and mother. As she spoke, I felt a tingling sensation in the right side of my brain. She continued to work on both sides, activating a more safe and loving, feminine aspect into harmony within my inner male counterpart. Again I was aware of a tingling sensation.

As we were deep into the mid-point of the session, I began to notice the room changing. I observed her aura illuminate, her face and her hairstyle changed several times. I knew we had gone to another level of awareness and perhaps into another dimension when I noticed the furniture and my body dissolve into a pale misty, yellow glow. However, all felt sacred. I sensed the presence of angels and guides. More than anything I felt trust for what was happening and the loving presence of Spirit. I wanted any healing God had for me, and indeed to bring to full life the power and glory of wholeness of Spirit in me and as me.

She continued; "Wow are you ready for this! I've never seen anyone so willing and ready to leap forward as you are now." Why live half when you know that you can live whole. I knew it was time for change. She announced that from now on, I would begin to think and act differently, and make different choices. A process of adjustment would take about three months for the nurturing, feminine aspect of my being to come to life, and that the first three weeks would be the most dynamic, and perhaps even tumultuous. It would be as though I had a new wife or partner within to consider. Another part of my own personality would come to life, and would have a say in taking its rightful role in my decision- making process. Before the male had dominated, making all the choices and not having to take anyone else into consideration. When I did consider the needs of others, it was related to how it would affect me. With exception of my spiritual practitioner and retreat work, she was right on all counts.

In hindsight, I wondered how others who need this kind of help are able to shift without assistance. As I thought about it, I became clear that each of us finds our rightful way. Most may not be this dramatic or dynamic, but I believe that our spirit always finds the appropriate outlet and guides when we are ready. We draw the right people to us and set up circumstances that push us towards change when the time is right. There is an intelligence at work in our lives whether we are aware of it or not. I believe that the path of life for each of us is moving just the way it is supposed to according to a Divine Design. Our Spirit or soul reaches out, like a magnet, creating just what we require when we are ready.

I returned home at midnight and fell into deep, secure sleep. In the days and weeks that followed, I did feel differently. A week later, I was scheduled to lead a retreat in a magnificent sequoia forest. It was a joyous weekend at Mineral King in the high Sierras of California. Still early spring in late June, there was plenty of snow run-off from the high, craggy peaks, causing wild flowers to bloom in great abundance. A fine time was had by all.

However, I was not having such a fine time as I began to hear myself speaking to the participants in the commanding

language I had learned from my mother. I immediately picked up
on similar verbiage in one of the participants. Hearing my own
words reflected so bluntly, made it difficult for me to stay in charge
as a leader and to be unconditionally loving at the same time. I felt
some confusion and disorientation as I attempted to be more open
to my own needs and to those of the group at the same time. I
managed through the weekend to remain calm and returned home
to rest and process the changes I was feeling within. In the weeks
to come I became more at ease as I enjoyed my new attitude,
honoring the gentler side of my being, and becoming open to where
it would lead me. Now the house hunt could continue.

The Next Phase

It was time to get serious about moving. I returned to
Malibu, got a paper, and began to scope out rentals. I happened to
stumble on a flashy sign, touting banners for the Malibu Beach
Club. It was posted on a handsome, older, Mediterranean, style
building, with massive stucco arches that framed a seaside
courtyard. I had admired it for years in passing. This time, freshly
painted a crisp white, and brought up to date, it was very
appealing. I decided to take a look.

The manager led me into an open courtyard, facing the
Western horizon of the bright, blue Pacific. The scene looked
Greek-island-like with a single palm tree at the center column of
two archways facing the ocean. The sea air blowing in felt cool and
uplifting. He led me to a magnificent, premier unit right on the
ocean. It was more like a townhome than an apartment. It was
fixed up exactly the way I would have done it with all new
windows, lighting, white carpets, paint, appliances and tile. It had
great architecture with high, beamed ceilings and large wrap-
around decks. Big sliding doors on three sides encased the room
with a magnificent energy of light and surf-facing views. The
building also included underground parking and a laundry. After
three years, I was really tired of taking the laundry out and
dealing with the challenge of parking. The unit was expensive, but
definitely worth it, since it included everything on my wish list,
especially it's strong integration with nature.

It is said in real estate that there are three things that
determine the value of property; *location, location, location!* I
returned home to sleep on it. However, not really sure I wanted to
spend that kind of money for rent since it would be comparable to
a house payment, I needed time to think. It would be good to treat
myself to some luxury after the cloistered living. I had given up

much to be able to afford to write and publish. It might be time for balance. That night, I could see myself living there. I mentally moved in, and planned how I would furnish it, the spiritual work I could do there, and of the joy of breathing in the fresh sea air with its empowering, negative ion charge. On the other hand, I debated as to whether I would feel comfortable writing out that hefty monthly rent check.

The next day, I took my friend Stella to Malibu for moral support and advice. On the way we stopped at a bookstore where I spied a beautiful blue and gold poster with inspiring horses rising from out the surf into solid form. I showed it to Stella. She suggested that the horses represented rising up and surging past one's fears. She went on to say that as the surf rises in power it falls in surrender to God at the shores of our desires. Her interpretation so moved me that I knew I had to buy it on the spot, and to go out and claim my apartment on the sea. It was just the answer I had been waiting for. We drove to the building and rang the manager's bell. Still frightened, but more excited I was ready to commit to a year's lease and the financial commitment that went with it. However, I decided to surrender the outcome to spirit and remain detached and accept that the highest good for me would reveal itself. If it were not the right place for me, something more appropriate would be provided in Divine Timing and Order.

I informed the manager of my decision. I was dumbfounded when he told me that the apartment rented late the night before. I felt a wave of disappointment, but was relieved at the same time. I returned home. I had no choice but to let it go and continue to work with my affirmations. I began to realize that there was a process of expansion taking place within my own consciousness. Spirit had clearly guided me to see the unit. When I asked God in guidance why I was shown it, the words "I took you there," came to me. As a result I could not help but think about it as I went to sleep, imagining the joy of breathing invigorating, sea wind. Hearing and seeing the surf from every room would have been incredibly inspiring for all my creative endeavors.

In the days that followed, I had a hard time getting the beach house out of my mind, yet I knew it was a lot of money to commit to every month and that it was gone for now. I must release it. Before I had been there, I had painted a painting of Greek island buildings with archways facing the sea. I hung it over my bed. Daily, I looked upon it and thought "There is a place I would like to be." My vision brought an equivalent experience to me. Spirit showed it to me for the purpose of expansion. I continued to surrender my desire daily, knowing that everything was in Divine Timing and order, and giving thanks for my perfect right residence in nature. When it did come it would be totally right, and would fit all of my needs including budget. I must remain passionate in my desire for a home, but non-attached as to where and when it would come.

A week later on Friday, I drove up the coast for the day to deliver some art to the Santa Barbara Inn. On the way back, I stopped by the building in Malibu once more, and walked around to the ocean side. On the sand, I ran into the manager again and he informed me that the prospective renter had backed out! I figured that this was my chance and immediately filled out an application. I was certain it was mine. He felt there would be no problem in my qualifying. I returned to the guest house and packed all weekend, making plans to move immediately. It would be a quick move as I was due in Minnesota on Thursday. I would move on Tuesday.

On Monday morning, I called the manager. I was stunned when he told me that my application had been denied. The owners of Beverly Hills Leasing refused my application because I am self-employed. He stated that they would prefer someone with a corporate check. How could they possibly refuse me? I became agitated and spent about half a day on the computer composing a letter to them to *prove* my integrity and value as a proposed tenant. I was in a huff. Writing helped me to let go of the situation as I realized that our vibrations did not match. It was a great building, but with management that lacked the kind of flexibility that I stand for.

Back to the trusty affirmations. I blessed Beverly Hills Management as I detached once again from the Malibu Beach Club. I knew that is absolutely necessary to release blame, or resentment if I were to progress and move forward in a positive way. However, I still felt crowded in my little house. Looking to my affirmations on the refrigerator, I decided to make them my light at the end of the tunnel.

The experience had served me well by expanding me in many ways. I was now be prepared to pay more rent and I continued to know that a Divine Unfoldment was taking place. Spirit would lead me to a situation that fit all the way around. On August first, I traveled to Minneapolis to paint a mural at Orchestra Hall for the famed Minnesota Symphony. The job was a great success and I was paid well. I came home with funds enough to make a comfortable change and upgrade in residence.

While in Minnesota, I enjoyed visits with old friends in my former home town. A few nights into the visit, I asked Spirit to reveal to me the reason for the denial in Malibu. That night, I dreamed one of those Technicolor, dreams that explain things in vivid detail. I saw beach houses falling into the ocean, and enormous, powerful waves overcoming the shoreline. I knew I was being protected from what was to come. Later, when I returned at the end of the month, I began to hear the first reports of the coming winter weather, predicting that the worst El Nino conditions ever in history would hit the California coast. I said to myself "Ah, once again God is taking care me."

Upon returning to California from Minneapolis, the search took up and again led me back to Malibu. This time to an old farm house located in the heart of Cross Creek, an exclusive, beautiful, rustic area, in a canyon situated within walking distance of the only river in Malibu. I had spent many afternoons hiking in the area over the course of many years and always longed to live there. The original ranch house for the entire valley was offered at the same rent as the beach apartment. However, close neighbors afforded little privacy and there was no heating system in the charming, but small rooms. I thought it over, and over, trying to make a fit. I came to the conclusion that there were just too many compromises with the fifties' vintage bathroom and kitchen. I had gone a long time without a dishwasher and other amenities. If I was going to change locations and pay more, I wanted it all. I detached and decided to let it go as well. I began to wonder, did God really have a place for me that would meet my requirements, including easy affordability? And what about those affirmations, were they really working?

When you decide to create something you really desire or require, remember this: to accept compromise is to short-change yourself and it is not believing that the Law of Attraction can work. It is essential to trust yourself and God and feel that you deserve what you desire. Be patient, Spirit will provide according to your acceptance. Work to bolster your levels of acceptance by using affirmations and maintaining an attitude of gratitude for the completed desires.

Let Go & Let God Do Her Thing.

I recalled the last time I home hunted and could not find satisfaction. Then and in fact on several occasions in the past, I had applied a formula that always brought results: Detach from the search, let it go, take a vacation, let it rest and come back to the hunt refreshed. I decided to apply it, and go to Arizona for a few days of touring. In past years I had taken groups to Sedona in

Northern Arizona on retreat and looked at property for a possible
future home for a retreat center, so I knew that I liked it.

It was the end of August and very hot. For some reason,
my air conditioning in the car began to fail. At the Arizona-
California border, I became exasperated with the intense desert
heat and pressure of the drive. I announced to my friend Joe who
was with me, that I was ready to turn back. He issued an
immediate and blunt request asking me to pull over. For the most
part, Joe is a pretty mellow guy. This time, he rose to the occasion
and gave me a much needed, attitude adjustment lecture, "If we
are going to continue on this journey, then you are going to be in
a good mood and enjoy it!" I immediately cleaned up my act and
thought cool thoughts all the way to Sedona. On arrival we found
a hotel with a pool and enjoyed the sunset with the inspiring views
and energy that Sedona is famous for. The cool, evening, mountain
air made the heat of the day seem as far behind as Malibu and the
smoggy, California coast.

The first day we took in Sedona, hiking to the spectacular
rock formations and electromagnetic vortices, did some sightseeing
and sampled wonderful restaurant cuisine. The people were warm
and exceptionally friendly, making the stay feel even more
inviting. On past visits I had hunted for retreat property with my
realtor Charley Thompson. I decided to call her and see if there
was anything available that made sense for me as a retreat home.
As far as I am concerned, Charley is *the* ace in the hole realtor in
Sedona. She is candid and makes no bones about what is what,
and what is not. I love that quality in anyone. In a Realtor it is
especially valuable. Charley has a solid friendliness and
sophisticated, discerning eye I trust. She gave me a rundown on
the market and showed us a few properties. Nothing had appeal,
so she referred me to Foothills Leasing for a possible rental. By
now, I was caught up in the idea and magic of living in Sedona.

The difference between Foothills and Beverly Hills
Leasing was like night and day. Foothills was professional in every
way. Friendly and helpful, they demonstrated a willing flexibility
to make things work. I asked the rental agent to show me property
that was large enough to utilize as a small retreat or Bed and
Breakfast. He complied with a list of addresses and a map, circling
potential sites that could serve that purpose.

The first home located on the creek turned out to be a
sixties cottage with numerous, poorly designed add-ons. It backed
up to a steep bluff on the West letting me know that it would get
dark early every afternoon, and that it would be especially cold in
the winter. Great for a summer cottage, but not for year-round

retreat. The next property was on a typical residential, tract-like street. Like the first property, it was locked, so we peered through windows to see what we could. It was large enough with four bedrooms, three baths and a deck, but it had no fireplace. It might work, or perhaps I could work with it, I thought. There are no bad views in Sedona, but this one was definitely very ordinary.

Not sure what we would do next, I consulted with Joe. He suggested looking at the last property circled on the map located in another part of town. It was near Cathedral Rock where we were planning to hike for the rest of the afternoon so we would drive past it on the way. Joe read the particulars out loud, noting that it was listed only as a two bedroom but with good views. It did not sound like it would fill the bill, but we decided to drive up and take a quick look at the view anyway.

Coming up the hill I commented to Joe on how inspiring the approach was. The road ran along state forest land of pine covered slopes, just at the base of a majestic, red rock, mountain. The neighborhood appeared to be peaceful and exclusive, with just a few, large homes sparsely intermixed. With lush, forested natural, terrain, it had a great feeling of exclusivity. The abundant nature and wonderful views all around the hilltop in every direction enhanced the feel.

The house looked contemporary yet rustic, and Frank Lloyd Wright-like, with its natural materials and long, sleek lines. We pulled into an empty carport built of sturdy, trusses, supported by substantial, earthy, adobe columns. A covered bridge-like walk led to a handsome, carved, front door with a simple brass knocker. The words "Peace to all who enter here" were inscribed on it. The doorknob gave a welcome turn in my hand. I always like the open door policy. To me, it spiritually symbolizes the path of least resistance. I see it as a sign from Spirit to move ahead. This was beginning to feeling good. "Oh yuk, it has blue carpet," I blurted. "But wow, what space, high ceilings, glass for days, and a knockout view!" The pale steel, blue of the carpet softened, as my eye balanced it with the piercing, red of the majestic, rock spires that expansively, back-dropped the big sheets of window glass. Rising high above the lush, pine carpet of desert floor the trees whispered to my soul "this is home."

I exclaimed a joyous yes! This is it! The architecture dramatic and clean, was accentuated by a sweeping openness, leading from room to room. I explored further, repeating the claim as I went into each inspiring light-filled space. I sensed an uplifting energy accompanied by a feeling of great peace, strength and serenity. There was an abundance of light and air, that I require wherever I am. Even though it was a hot day in the high nineties, the scent of lush pine rode in on cooling breezes, through all the open windows. Even in full August sun, the house was comfortable because of the shade afforded by its broad, sweeping overhangs.

Each room opened to an outdoor patio. Graceful twisted, ancient Juniper-pines, pressed up to the glass all around, giving one the feeling of living outdoors in a primordial forest. The trees in their totally natural state completed and complemented the strong, rustic architecture. It was if the forest and the house were one. This was the house I had dreamed of for the last five years. I had put off having a home far too long. By now it was five o-clock. In addition to the two bedrooms it had two bonus dens that would serve perfectly for the B and B. Too late to return to the leasing company. I knew that if this was what I had been waiting for, it would keep until morning.

When things shift, they happen all at once. I had spoken my word in prayer for the right new home for four years! I had made both a mental list, and one on paper that was very complete and included every requirement and joy I could think of for the perfect new home. These were the basic tenet: The first and most important was that it be located in opulent nature. I preferred a warm climate with clean air and water. It would be a place that felt inspirational, and be large enough to do group retreat work as well as serve my own creative needs. It would be in a place where I could hike daily, and easily commute to Los Angeles and other parts of the country. It would be located in a prosperous community that supported culture, the sale of my art, and my spiritual work as well. Sedona and that house as far as I could see, would more than fill the bill. I turned in all the necessary paperwork for rental.   By now I knew I had no choice but to detach and await results. Trusting that a higher good would prevail was the only thing to do. If it was right for me, it would work out if not, I would be back with the affirmations, looking somewhere else. It was now in the hands of God. (Was it ever not?) I went for a hike and gave thanks for the highest results. At noon, I checked back with the agent and received an answer. He gave me the high sign. I breathed a sigh of relief and thanked God for the long awaited yes. I would return in two weeks to begin my lease. Since the house was on the market, Foothills agreed to a month to month agreement. From the start, I saw it as mine, owning it free and clear, fully paid for, and having the cash to add on an art studio over the carport.

On the return drive to California, I was exhausted so Joe

drove and I stretched out in the back of the truck and fell into a
deep sleep. I awakened with the thought; "What have I just done?
I have just signed away several thousand dollars in deposits for
rent on a house for sale in a small town, in another state. Am I out
of my mind?" I though to myself. "Yes I am out of my mind. My
spirit is making this decision. This is a higher choice." Just then I
opened my eyes as we were coming into Phoenix. We passed under
a huge, multi-level freeway ramp under construction, I knew I had
make the right decision. Twenty years of living with mega-
freeways the symbol of smog, congestion and L.A. is what made me
do it. I deserved a better life. It was time to leave the concrete and
fast lane behind.

      Spirit knows our needs and all desires and Spirit knows
how to deliver. I had made my choice to finish writing my first
book was the higher priority before acquiring a home. When it was
done and on the market, I moved on my long awaited mental
desire. God poured in the blessing that correlated to my mental
picture and desire that had been building over the years. We do get
exactly what we want when we practice spiritual manifesting.

Co-create Divine Destiny.

      Opportunities come to us for a reason, I had been praying
and asking for the right home for a long time. I believe that spirit
offered me a window of opportunity to leave Los Angles and to
move to a better place for me to live the next part of my life. Had
I not jumped on it, the window may have closed and not availed
itself until another blessed moment. Meanwhile I would have to
wait and pay the consequences by staying longer in Los Angeles.
I barely took the time to ask if this was the right decision. My
spirit governing every part of me knew that the time was right and
that I had found exactly the home my soul had been seeking and
awaiting.

      I could not have maintained the vision without my trusty
three P's. The consistent practice of prayer, patience and
persistence add up to strengthened faith and prove that
maintaining a vision brings absolute results. Getting what you
want may take time, but if you stick with it, mental and spiritual
work always pays off. It must, for it is a cosmic law. *What we think
about and plan for, we create.* Be focused on what you want, be
detached as to the ways and means of delivery that your desires
can come. And above all trust God and your own power to decide,
and stay grateful.

Hollywood Moment

When I was twenty-two and new to Los Angeles, the Universe offered me another window of opportunity. It was a hot and smoggy August day. I had walked to a nearby bank, and was waiting at the corner stoplight. Typical L.A. sounds and sights of traffic filled the intersection. Cars were dashing to make the light in order to avoid another long wait, sitting with air-conditioning blasting away in the heat. I was wearing short, cutoff, jeans naturally fringed around the thighs that all youth wore in the seventies. A dated, Cadillac limousine pulled up to the light. I thought to myself, "How odd this long, old black car looks, I wonder who is in the back seat?" Not wanting to be an obnoxious star-seeker, I casually turned and glanced at the driver. Here was a gentleman as unique as the car. The gray-haired driver was wearing horn-rimmed wing style eyeglasses of another era and an official chauffeur's cap. Now I was really curious. Dare I chance be obvious and look to see what mystery star was sitting in the back?

I thought to myself; "perhaps it's Natalie Wood or Warren Beaty, or someone like that." I decided to steal a fast look at whoever might be in the limo I thought to still be behind me. Meanwhile, I failed to notice that the driver had quietly rolled it forward into position directly at my left thigh. In a bold move to satisfy my curiosity, expecting to look back, I spun quickly on my heels and leaned down towards the curb. I found myself staring nose to nose with an infamous Hollywood legend. I froze. It felt like I was looking into the face of a ghost, as I peered eye to eye, nose to nose with the famous face I had always wanted to meet. No more than five inches away, batting her huge, thickly painted, false black eye lashes *at me*, was Mae West! I realized that she was flirting with me, By now I was completely numbed to any movement. It appeared that she was attempting to entice me to join her in afternoon delight. I could think of nothing but her familiar words; "Why don't you come up and see me sometime."

I am sure that the color drained from my innocent, young face. It seemed like an eternity, but the light finally changed and the car slid slowly and sleekly into the intersection, turned the corner, and floated silently away.

I will never forget that Hollywood moment and my one, big missed opportunity to meet Mae West. She was one of those people I had seen so often in my parents' movie theatre and on television. I had often stated I thought it would be a hoot to meet her. It was indeed, and it was my window of opportunity to have spoken to her. I was too stunned and naive to know how to respond. I doubt that I would have been interested in what she might have had in mind, yet I would have loved to have shared a conversation. You have to be quick when spirit presents those opportunities. Unlike the Mae West episode, when the house of my dreams came along, I did not hesitate for one moment to dive right in. **My spirit knew what I wanted.**

Know Your Vision As Real.
Be Willing And Prepared To Claim It When It Comes Along.

Speak your word in creation of your vision.

There is one Infinite Presence. It is the Intelligence that lives within me. It knows everything about me, my desires and my highest purpose in this life. I give thanks that Spirit guides me in all my ways including my knowing. My Spirit knows all that is right for me and my highest good at all times. I accept that the Divine within me knows exactly how to bring my good to me and me to it in conscious awareness and acceptance. I am one with the desires of my heart. I remain steadfast in my trust that God is in charge.

I release the past and anything that does not support my rightful demonstration of peace, abundant prosperity, joyous love, right home and work. That higher vision from God which I choose to align myself with comes to me now. I accept the changes that support it, and I let go gracefully as I surrender to God's will within myself and all around me. I accept the perfect right Divine _____ for me in this sacred moment. I praise God that this idea is complete and whole unto itself. Because it comes from the highest place, intention and surrender, my demonstration is complete in the Mind of God - my source. I thank and praise God. I accept the best of all Spirit has to give. It is my honor and privilege to receive and enjoy what comes to me and through me. And So It Is!

CHAPTER TWELVE

Get Real, Get A Heart Tin Man.

I was the very last of forty applicants to be examined at the end of a long day. As I entered the windowless room, I noticed how unusually dark it was. A single, long table was placed in the center of the room. Three examiners that comprised the panel were seated across from an old, steel government-issue armchair. It felt like I was entering an interrogation chamber from a movie scene. Only a small gooseneck, desk lamp shed a dim illumination on the barren-looking brown, masonite folding table. With its harsh bulb blaring into the shadows into the room, light was eerily cast in dramatic shadows, the way it would have be in a Humphry Bogart spy drama. Coming in from the golden sunset outside, my eyes adjusted slowly to the contrasting scene before me. The severity in the difference from light to dark intensified the mysterious, shadowy atmosphere I was now becoming a part of.

I took my seat expecting a cordial yet pertinent interview. "We feel you are here to cause trouble," the woman in charge of the panel barked. My head reeled as if I had been slapped in the face. As I staggered to answer a barrage of questions that followed, I became confused by the angry banter, having nothing to do with the material I had so lovingly turned in heart and mind. The golden carpet of comfort and confidence I had come to trust as support over the years, suddenly was pulled out from under me. I was grilled, fried, flipped and burned by the ruthless, Gestapo-like examiner. My class had been prepared by teachers and ministers all week long to expect a loving and supportive interview. Instead, I had walked into what turned out to be a baited interrogation. Later, in retrospect, I suspect that the chief examiner had been coached to ask me a unique set of questions.

For nearly ten years of my life, I had put all my faith and trust into thinking only the highest of this organization and its leaders. They had taught me much, with openness and love, or so I believed. Now they were teaching me something quite different. It seemed like first degree betrayal. I wondered, had it been my mistake to accept them as family in exchange for the early passing of my own?

When I had trained to become a Spiritual Mind Practitioner in Los Angeles, I had not been discouraged by official *rules* established by the parent corporation that dictates rules to the branch churches stating that one had to be officially licensed before assisting others in spiritual healing. I gained confidence in my own abilities while still a student by assisting my friends in healing various problems by utilizing Spiritual Mind Treatment, a scientific, and extremely effective form of prayer. As a result, I became an expert practitioner long before it was time for me to be "officially" licensed. During one summer off from ministry training, I completed Edwene Gaines' Master of Prosperity Teacher Training held on Lookout Mountain in Alabama. That same summer, I flew to Hawaii, acquired a state of Hawaii minister's license, and performed my first wedding ceremony. While there, I presented prosperity seminars in several churches on different islands, and taught a seven-week course in the Honolulu Church of Religious Science. I reveled in growing while learning. As I shared the principles of metaphysics taught by Ernest Holmes, Mary Baker Eddy, and Emerson, the founders of New Thought, I became adept at putting them into action. **In the process, I confirmed for myself that to activate a principle, we must step into it's action.**

I had been busy loving the work. It felt as though I was flying on the wings of angels. Without a doubt, for the first time, I could see outer results of what I already knew on the inside. I felt as though the breath and blood of God were flowing through me. This ministerial exam was the last step, and I was more than ready to be finished with classes after five years of study. I felt confident to be let out into the world to seek my own rightful ministry, whatever it was. I was already teaching classes assisting the ninety-seven year-old, master teacher, Dr. Robert Bitzer in my own local, branch church. However, as heir apparent to the Hollywood Church of Religious Science, however, I was not certain that I wanted the role and responsibility of a traditional ministry. I had always loved retreats and the kind of closeness and breakthroughs that people share and experience as a result of participating in them.

I had passed all the years of ministerial study and written exams with flying colors, so it was part of the natural course for me to complete the program and become licensed as well. I had been at ease and fully prepared, feeling confident and comfortable with the material. That morning, something had not felt right in my stomach, almost like the feeling that one gets from the rumble of s distant thunder telling of a coming storm. I spoke an affirmative prayer calling for the truth to be revealed to me.

The next question was asked; "Why did you use these three ministers' names as your personal references?" I fumbled for words of truth, "Because I consider them to be my friends, as well as my mentors and teachers." Hello? Sometimes, I hang out with my spiritual teachers. Consciousness attracts like. Several weeks after the exams, I discovered that two of the three friends I had submitted as references were being politically blackballed by the *hierarchy* of the organization. Apparently, they had expressed disappointment at the way things were being run at the time and were considering breaking away. The third was unpopular with the ministers because she was an independent. However all three of my friends were extremely popular with the lay people of the church. I had begun to see why although politics and organized religion do not mix well, they usually go hand in hand. Often they act to defeat the freedom and openness the original designers of a liberating movement set out to establish.

The examiners concluded the session by handing me a crudely sketched diagram on a scrap of paper that was supposed to represent a well-known triangular graphic. One that illustrates how our conscious mind, subconscious mind, and superconscious Mind of God works within our minds. It was so poorly sketched that I had difficulty recognizing this familiar symbol. I had used it often in my own classroom, carefully drawing it on the blackboard, so as to make its purpose clear to my students. To an artist, this version was about as unprofessional as anything could possibly be. It was certainly was no way to make a clear presentation. I left the room feeling complete disgust, and sick to my stomach.

I had been very clear as to who I was and what I represented. I was committed to serving in a spiritual capacity, long before I walked into that room. My purpose is to walk and talk in love and light, with freedom from any controlling or structured limitation. Above all integrity is what I stand for. I had presented a written statement to the committee, (required upon applying for the exam) concluded with "I am most drawn to this teaching because it promotes "staying open at the top!" A direct quote from the founder of the movement Ernest Holmes, who had urged its followers to be prudent in remaining *open at the top*. The committee with their ego-based fears were anything but open. As far as I could tell, they had been more leaning the other direction.

By now, I was on automatic pilot operating solely from a deep levels of absolute spiritual, gut knowing. I was aware that it was time to arm myself from further attack. Like a sentry poised on lookout, my third eye was now wide open, alert and sharpened to the truth of what was happening around me. I was relieved to get up and move towards the door. However, I felt even more vindicated at the next thing I saw.

As I crossed the darkened room, I noticed the president of the parent international church organization that presents the testing and licensing, (since stepped down) seated in the shadows of the darkest corner next to the door. It appeared as if this individual was on hand to oversee the exorcism. Just one year before, the two of us had spent an entire afternoon walking through the forest, deep in spiritual conversation. At the end of that day, I had politely shunned overt moves to engage in physical intimacy. With this clear picture of who I was dealing with, I escaped from the vengeful witch hunt into the light of the golden sunset and sea mist. Breathing the brisk, liberating, mind-clearing ocean breeze, I suspected I had been set up and would never be the same.

Whatever form it takes, real truth in action takes into account the higher good of all involved.

Perhaps I am a rebel. At least one who is opposed to any kind of structure that controls and limits one from expressing one's true nature or in seeking a rightful path. In hindsight, I saw why my minister friends were considered rebels as well. They are free-spirited, open and loving, freely accepting truth whatever the source....and not controlling. People with vision always easily recognize and see through binding limits. They automatically know what requires releasing. Truth can only flow when all are served not just for those who fit a format. It is a privilege to be a rebel for the free-flow of Spirit. I can wear the "cloth" on Sundays when I guest speak, but I know that I prefer not to sustain the role on a daily basis or to spend my time in an office.

I had been urged by my teachers and members of the committee to consider the road of convention provided by the church as the only way to go. I had forgotten my original purpose of remaining independent in order to serve many on a more universal level.

In the interview, I saw the effects first hand of what control and convolution can do. I went in with an open heart and was harpooned by judgment, incrimination and fear. The rigid energy of a dictatorship, by its suspicious nature recognizes light and sees its sails of freedom coming into view as a pirate-like threat to its very existence. It fears that it might lose its hold and power. When it gets to that point, the fear destroys the best of what it sought to create and project in the first place. The principles of spiritual freedom and expansion cannot flow when tight controls are in place. It was right action for me to see the light, claim my light and go a different way from the crowd. I was not alone. Of the students who were interviewed that day, the most obvious, dynamic potential leaders, were failed. It is the manner in which the deed was carried out that I address here, not a question of whether the students passed or failed based on ability, sincerity, or intent but the matter of justice as to why.

I returned home and immediately experienced a horrific flu, the first and last in about fifteen years. Louise Hay in her book *"You can heal your life,"* says that flu is mentally related to an attack on your personality. I felt betrayed beyond measure. All the unconditional love and acceptance I had worked long to understand and trust was now up for re-evaluation. I practiced forgiveness for many months afterward to just let it go and I was so infuriated that I quietly left the movement. My integrity meant more to me than any membership or license. After all, I had been to school, finished all the courses and bought the tee shirt!

God within me had well chosen as my friends and mentors the perfect renegades to help shake up the system. Of those who were being blackballed, one and formed a new organization based on openness and loving support for its member churches.

I am told that the original organization has healed itself. The principles of the teaching of the Science of Mind, when practiced with an open, sincere attitude of non-attachment as they most often work for the higher good of all. In this case, a few key individuals had veered off the course of non-attachment. In attempting to exercise their will and personal agenda through politics, they were unable let the highest good to flow. I waited and deliberated long as to whether to share this story openly or not. I do so now because I believe it has value for all of us.

In our world, we observe and experience injustice on a daily basis. When it happens in our own experience we must practice forgiveness in order to move forward in a healthy way. You must accept the release that forgiveness provides even if your story never comes to light, for vengeance, blame and guilt create disease and stagnation. Release frees one to move forward. I could have gone home with my tail between my legs and retired from being a spiritual leader. Instead, I was propelled to be independent, free of any single organization, leading retreats for many, and to become an author sharing the vision with a much larger audience. And what the heck, pinning the tail back on the donkey once in awhile feels pretty good!.

Choose To Be Your Own Master

Keep a watchful but relaxed eye on the politics. Those who volunteer to serve organizations must be detached from personal agendas and be willing to flow with the higher good of the group. Watch out for controlling domination of the egos of a committee consciousness. Egos are myopic and do not necessarily place the higher needs of the whole community as a priority. At the same time, appreciate your spiritual teachers and masters. They give much of themselves and dedicate personal time and energy into giving you their best.

"Keep the high watch." Emma Curtis Hopkins

Many of us came to this world to be energy busters. Know that often **we are born into limitation so that we will learn it's limits first-hand from the inside out**. As we rise above limitation and awaken in knowing, we can change our lives and help others to recognize and activate higher truths by instilling them into our culture. We came to help reveal injustice, break it apart, and pave the way for a new freedom for the spirit of humanity. Our commitment to living true to ourselves free from constricting limits will be the living cornerstone anchoring a healed, healthy and love-filled world!

The stone that the builder rejects, will become the cornerstone. Psalms 118, vs. 22

The energy, power and majesty of God lives in everyone. For centuries, this Universal truth long hidden and denied from our world, now is revealing itself within every being on the planet with an enormous energy and momentum that cannot be denied. All of life including plant and animal, and every bit of humanity is holy, not just the priests and sages. Our thoughts and words are powerful tools of creation. Humankind has within itself the power to heal and change conditions. Where would history be, if Jesus, Martin Luther, Abraham Lincoln, Martin Luther King, Gandhi, Mother Tereasa and Princess Di had not come along? They were all energy busters. Elvis and The Beatles completely revolutionized music. In the beginning, they were all condemned for being different and for instigating change. **Let your light and talent shine. It will overcome anything less than its own glow.**

Whenever a new paradigm is about to emerge, or a shift is

about to take place, we observe the old demi-gods rising up in an effort to maintain control. Something in them knows their reign of power is soon coming to a close. False gods are based in fear. Love and light always overcome fear. Despite the obvious opposition we see, planet earth is moving into a new paradigm based in love. Those who are willing to walk in the light of truth and freedom will prosper because they know that to go with the flow requires taking into consideration the higher good of the whole. In doing so, the life of abundance and enlightened ease will be established. We are now being called upon to let go all we have held on to historically that is born out of fear. The old culprit, fear, will no long support anything in the light and a truthful age centered in Spiritual Knowing.

When That Which Is Perfect Is Come, That Which Is Imperfect Shall Pass.

Boldly Living Your Bliss

Of the time you and I spend on this earth, we may feel like we have experienced several unique, incarnate lifetimes within the span of this one life. Our wisdom and awareness expands as we grow through each relationship, marriage and change of profession or home. Along our road of life we acquire experiential knowing.

However, a deeper spiritual knowing precedes all experience. Understanding is essential first in order for us to be able to know that we are having an experience. When we come to a *knowing that we know* we are attuned to spirit, which knows all, we automatically gain additional clarity without having to see all aspects of the larger picture. In this place of peace we are able to override any sabotage of self-doubt and come into concert with the greater aspects and gifts that a spiritual life offers. Increased awareness allows us to examine where we are and where we are going with a greater discernment than in the past.

The secret key to change lies within our own attitude.

As one awakens spiritually, it becomes clear that it is no longer necessary, wise or fruitful to repeat mistakes, or to create new ones. Take the time daily to establish a right mental attitude of knowing and trusting of spirit within before leaving the house. Throughout your day stay *open at the top* by maintaining an attitude of non-attachment to having to control conditions or judge either the self or others. With this greater sense of ease established, you will create a renewed life that imbues the soul with a self-trust and Oneness with Spirit. It is a place of unlimited choice and creation and where there are no mistakes and no real loss.

Non attached, co-creative partnership with Spirit is the key to Knowing Oneness with Divine Wisdom. Become the observer in your personal, experimental lab of life and see where your choices lead. As you do, life will become less trial and error for you, and more succinct. Struggle is released, and ease is embodied as life flows.

God is in every situation and person we encounter. Whatever or whomever comes into our experience has the potential to offer a unique adventure. With the realization that Spirit is all there is in all of It's many forms, comes expansion of our capacity to love ourselves and a greater compassion for others. When we live from that place we can rarely feel failure. The gifts in each encounter reveal the presence of Spirit. No matter what happens to us, how much or how little money we make, this realization of true wealth brings peace of mind. We find satisfaction in knowing that we have done our best to reach an end result in our efforts. It is easy to see that our inner focus on Spirit has brought joy and a flow of creativity into each endeavor. Divine timing and order have prevailed in all we do, and if we tithed by giving what we expect to receive, we enjoy in financial security as well.

Every part of what you have done in the past contributes to the whole of what you are doing today and what you desire next.

Opening a retreat home from scratch in Sedona was a rich experience for me. Each day brought many gifts. Every guest came with gifts that enhanced my own awareness. The multitude of things I did throughout my twenty-three years prior to that in California as an artist, retreat leader/author added up to a wealth of life experience I applied daily. In the process, I saw that every facet of my working career always supported me being right where I am now. In addition to travel nature retreats, being in Sedona doing my work, gave me more experience in moving towards my vision of a larger experience.

"I Am What God Is Doing Right Now."

Few people discover their life's work when they begin their first real job. It may be rare when it happens, yet some do find career satisfaction right off the bat. If they stay with the job long enough to become proficient, they inevitably rise up the ladder of success. We know that in America anyone with a natural ability or interest in his or her chosen fields has the opportunity to achieve great rewards. It may take some longer to find work that they enjoy, and others may work at a job a whole lifetime without feeling the kind of pleasure that doing what you love brings. The obvious key is to do what you love, or love what you do.

As a college art student in Minnesota, I found my perfect work right away. I was able to pay my rent and enjoy an abundance of spending money because I worked at a job that I loved. Fresh from the cornfields of Iowa, at eighteen, I was moved by my family into a dreary Men's Y. located in downtown St. Paul. So as not to be there as much as possible, I experienced new adventures by spending my after-school hours strolling and exploring downtown. One of my first discoveries was Dayton's department store. There I marveled at opulent, creative displays that depicted arts and crafts from countries all over the globe. I had not seen anything like it in Iowa. Determined to get a job there, but not knowing what I would do, I filled out an application for employment. When called in for an interview in the creative exhibition department, I felt right at home with all of the art supplies and props. I was hired by the director on the spot. With a handsome income for an art student, I immediately went out and rented my first apartment.

Spirit in me knew where to take me to where my highest interests could unfold. Not only did I live well, but I enjoyed a professional workshop, stocked with the finest of materials to complete my school projects. By constructing professional-like models and works of sculpture and paint, I easily dazzled my professors, and, even more important acquired on the job working artist, skills.

The learn by doing technique has always proved successful for me. As a teen, I trained at home, building and painting projects in a basement workshop. I spent endless hours down there constructing models of buildings and assembling scale-model cars. The skill and experience in working with my hands, paid off at Dayton's, in art and architecture school, and later in California buying, remodeling, and selling real estate and in publishing books!

From the time I was twelve until I graduated from high school, my mother and I lived in the house of a despotic, ill-mannered step-father. Whether it was an effort to paint the steps leading to the basement or explore and clean the attic, he never failed to answer my requests with a perfunctory and predictable "No". Despite his lack of support, I learned to take the negation as a challenge and go forward on my own to excel at completing a project anyway. Eventually, I stopped asking his permission altogether. The lack of encouragement served to instill in me a strong will to succeed and a deep and brazen courage within, especially when dealing with circumstances of injustice. Later in life that courage served me well. I relied upon being bold enough to promote my retreats by standing outside of auditoriums to hand out flyers. My stepfather's earlier denials and criticism only served to propel me forward in becoming-self motivated, courageous and determined to succeed.

Know that when life hands you situations of challenge, the way in which you meet them may determine your future. Persistence, usually applied with wisdom and tact, can create openings and windows of opportunity. *Take time to go within and seek guidance before acting or dealing with uncomfortable situations....it helps.*

You Qualify Yourself For Mastery

Speak your word to emancipate yourself from limits.

There is a Great Knowingness within myself. It is the all-knowingness of Spirit within me. It guides, directs and beautifully choreographs all activities in my life. I accept this highest self-knowing of Oneness within myself as peace, confidence and right knowing in all I do. Divine Intelligence flows in every activity of my life here and now and everywhere simultaneously.

I move in the ways of Spirit. I accept that God is in, through and all around me all of the time. God is never wrong, but always right on. I let go of a need to judge what others choose do for themselves. Whatever they choose is right for them. What I accept for myself reflects the highest outcome for all involved because I accept spiritual clarity and act accordingly. My actions are based on inner guidance and integrity, even if I would have preferred another answer. I realize that all others are God expressions in my experience. I make the right choices for myself and choose not to judge others for what they do or believe no matter what I perceive that to be.

The Divine Presence is in charge of my whole experience. Therefore, I let go and let God run the show. I detach from control or having a need to run the show. It is God's show. I accept Divine results, whatever they are, and whomever is involved. My life is an expression of the One Mind loving itself. I know that the results will be for the highest good of all involved and that what I desire and require is delivered to me as I accept it in Divine timing. I release these words in gratitude, expecting the best. I am the best and one with the unconditional love of God. I give thanks for the best of Spirit in my entire experience. And So It Is.

CHAPTER THIRTEEN

Attitude

"Lights, camera, action, we've got speed," the movie cameras are rolling in Hollywood. Before the stage supervisor barks out "roll'em" to the crew, the director describes to the actors how he envisions a scene to be played. If the performance does not come out just right, or a prop fails on the set, the actors have the opportunity to do retakes.....as many as it takes to get it right.

I was once interviewed by Eyewitness News in El Paso, Texas where I was painting several large murals at the airport. During the taping, a carpenter walked through the background and dropped a heavy board on the floor. The falling wood made a bit of noise and sent up a huge cloud of dust flying in the background. The interviewer asked me if I could repeat word for word, and gesture by gesture the descriptive comment I had just made. At first I declined. Repeating it would have been impossible because what I said was completely spontaneous. My TV host quickly reminded me, "You can do it." "You are from Hollywood!" He struck of chord I could resonate with. "Yeah, why not?" "He's right, its true I am from Hollywood" I complied, and from that moment forward, I have been completely comfortable in front of television cameras. I just needed the right cue to reach my *potential*.

Some days I feel like we are all acting in a movie with pre-written scenes. It makes me feel more certain that we can and do create our identities and choose the roles we play in life. When it is time to begin to act out a new movie, we make choices that cause us to begin to set the stage for a new set of circumstances. Whether those choices are pre-destined or if at the time we are consciously aware of them, career changes, moves to new locations, or the budding of romantic relationships often cause us to alter the way we do things. Sometimes before we can give ourselves the green light to a fresh experience, we must first correct our thinking if we do not wish to repeat past mistakes. It was our thoughts and beliefs that led us to the red lights and dead ends.

**" Blessed are the flexible,
for they get not bent out of shape."**

When I find myself limited or repressed by challenge, I know that it is most essential to take charge and be the director of my movie. If I wish to neutralize the so-called problem, I must redescribe the situation to my subconscious, creative computer by changing how I think, speak, and act about it. If I do not wish to repeat an error it becomes prudent to choose a new attitude and design of how I would like to see my experience manifested....and maintain it. Affirmations work for me to delete negative thinking from my mental computer and correct my speech to affirm the positive desired state. You too, can create personal retakes and get things right the next time around. Choose to label the next movie a success in advance. Know that there is no real loss when you accept the joy held in the potential for re-creation and retakes! Experiences that causes us to learn are of great value.

In *No Boundaries*, I tell about hanging upside down off the edge of my deck and examining my garden (and my circumstances) from a unique perspective. By becoming a neutral observer, I saw that what formerly had appeared to be a problem of considerable worry, was in fact, no thing to worry about at all. I was able to release the charge of fear by practicing non-attachment and becoming an observer. I doing so, I was able to see myself removed from the torturous, mental soap opera that I had created. We have a tendency to automatically label a challenge as a problem. When we do, it is easy to become involved in our own personal drama. Since we cannot sell movie tickets to these movie dramas, we might as well decide to look past them by seeing them differently. In making the choice to move beyond a false appearance and the drama, we gain a neutral perspective and gain power and advantage to begin fresh. We can now create and experience the movie story of life with greater clarity and illumination.

F. E. A. R. - is False Experience Appearing Real.

Of the things that go bump in the night and frighten us, most are harmless. They come from fear-based false thinking that we were trained to buy into from day one. We were taught by our world not to trust ourselves, life or God. So when a threat or danger comes along, the possibility of loss appears to be very real. When in the constricted energy of fear, we are automatically robbed of our true God-Power, and our freedom to see and act clearly. A mask of fear blinds one to seeing options and blocks out the vision and clarity that choosing to stay in the light would normally bring in crystallize awareness through us.

Some obstacles that seem too painful to deal with are often opportunities that contain real growth for the soul. However, it can be tough to discern a knowing of when to stick it out and when not to. To struggle with activities that do not nourish our spirit is neither wise nor healthy. We always have the power to exercise our free will. Those old patterns and habits may resist change, and friends or family may advise us to remain rigid. But you and I have the power to create a re-take and make a change at any time. If we are going to bring peace to our hearts and minds and move forward in success we must use our God-given abilities. We may even decide not to continue at all and surrender that unwanted job, dreaded task, dying relationship or to continue to live in a community that no longer supports you in a positive way. I believe that to release what we do not enjoy and go in an entirely different direction can be a higher choice that opens doors to our rightful success.

To not exercise choice and power is to remain stuck!

Our higher soul knows the difference and when it is time for change, and when it is not. If the urges are coming again and again, them it is time to make a move! When we surrender to our spiritual power and make the decision to release fear, we move forward in trust of God's knowing within the self. Just as an actor would call upon his talent to bring out the perfect character, with a retake and change of terminology, our outside performance will conform to a new inner design and vision. Give it time, patience and God's love.

Change Your Mind To Change Your Experience

You and I are the painters of the canvases of our lives and the directors of our movies. Since we have this power of choice, we may change our thinking and direct our experience into another direction whenever we choose. If we desire peace, we must remove our attention from that which causes us pain or unrest and establish a peaceful attitude. *God-potential* for balance is present at all times in all situations. Take time to connect with the *Source of all peace and the knowingness* that resides within you. When in that place of Oneness, all of the answers that come will be Divine Solutions and therefore perfect in nature, timing and order.

Surrender What Does Not Serve You

Painting commissioned murals has supported me well for many years. My career has been rewarding in many ways and provided a wealth of diversity, satisfaction and extensive travel.

About ten years ago, things began to shift. My work provided generous time off and sometimes presented handsome windfalls, yet I remained stuck with the feeling and belief that life might always be a tough, uphill struggle. In 1992, A sudden and brutal economic recession hit California. Its unprecedented length made it difficult for me to keep up with my expenses. I was not alone. Many Californians were long accustomed to having an abundance of work and money. Like the others, I had no choice but to put in longer and longer hours. I began to take on work that normally I would have turned down. I rarely took time for lunches or breaks. Too often, I found myself precariously dangling from high scaffolding on noisy, dirty construction sites for hours upon end, just to bring home enough bucks to get by.

For twenty years, I had worked with wonderfully appreciative clients and designers. As the economic recession deepened, I became stressed with people who were unnecessarily rude, self-centered, unappreciative or verbally abusive. I had put in my time in college and was wealthy in terms of on-the-job experience training. Yet the benefits were no longer reflected in my life. At the end of the day, I would return home exhausted, only to face mounting debts in the struggling economy. My business that had previously and easily supported a comfortable and exciting lifestyle now seemed to offer no way out. The harder I worked the more insurmountable and unending the situation seemed. I knew that something had to give.

One day, as I accompanied a friend to the Broadway Department Store in Century City, we passed through the men's underwear department. When I saw the Calvin Klein's and the Jockeys shorts, I froze in my tracks and was jolted into remembering when I could easily buy whatever I needed. Every pair of socks or underwear in my drawers now was full of holes. "I remember these!" The fresh packages of underwear reminded me that I had long since put my personal needs behind the duty of making payments on mortgages, investments and renovation loans. Seeing the freshly wrapped selection awakened me to the fact that if I deserved a better way of life tomorrow, I would have to release the things that were holding me down today.

"You won't find a new haven in the woods, if you are unwilling to leave the old familiar trail." Anonymous

I began to focus and pray for ways to eliminate the burdens. My home was located in an area that had been increasing in value when I bought it, but by now it was valued at far less than what I had paid. I had acquired, renovated and sold numerous properties by borrowing the necessary funds on credit cards to prepare for resale in a formerly robust market. Now the market had suffered a severe downslide. I wanted with all my heart to let go of the struggle of making high interest mortgage payments and the painful work it took to keep them up. I set out to create different thinking. I began by designing and using positive affirmations that led me to a creative way to sell my house. It worked. Once I was free of it, I focused on the elimination of debt. A year after selling my house for less than what it would take to cover the debt, the gentleman who bought it, walked away from it. I had no choice but to submit it to a bankruptcy in order to clear the balance of the construction loans and the high interest mortgage. Even though I had made all payments on time, I knew I could no longer continue to drag a dead horse behind me. When I added it up, I had paid back the original principle amounts and was committed to many future years of interest. So, I felt justified to file when the bankers I spoke to told me that they actually make money on bankruptcies as they encouraged me to free myself to move forward.

It doesn't matter how fast you are running with the football, if you are running in the wrong direction.

Once relieved from overwhelming financial pressure, my life began to turn around. Even though the equity and future down payment I had built up over a thirteen year period was now lost, I relaxed enough to feel peace. I would have to trust God to provide the ways and means to have a home again. Gradually, I found more gracious and loving clients to work with, but only after I started turning down the work that did not nurture my spirit. I prayed for a way to serve in a spiritual way by teaching and writing.

"Nature demands change in order to grow."
Ernest Holmes.

Now I was able to have the time and mental space to begin to write and expand into my training as a teacher of mental-physics. In hindsight, I see that choosing that experience required a colossal attitude adjustment on my part. I formed a new awareness that grew out of the process of letting go. One that took place over the five-year period as I wrote and published my first book. By staying committed to its completion, *No Boundaries, Let*

Go of Limits and Create Success revealed to me a new energy. All along, I worked on myself as consciously in the light as I possibly could. I had my dark nights. More so in the beginning, and especially right after my temporary home burned, as I didn't have a permanent place to live. As time went on, I felt more and more confident and began to understand what real joy is about. It comes when we are able to live free in a detached state of emancipation.

The spiritual lesson is this; **There always is a way.** If you have a mission or feel impassioned with an idea, know that it has been given to you for a reason. By making your goal your prime object of focus, you will be able to fly with it. Spirit put the spark into you so that you could soar in heavenly bliss to your vision while here on earth.

True Real Estate Is The Real Estate Of God, It Lives Within Us.

As to the ownership of real estate. My lessons of release revealed to me that I do not have to own the estate on the hill to be lord of my manor. I learned to love myself more as a result of the three years I spent living as a tenant in my small guest house in Santa Monica than when I owned the grand luxe homes. Complete freedom from debt, utility bills, mortgages and higher income taxes all contributed to the quality of my writing, publishing, retreat work and life. I became more fully aware that to live in Spirit every minute of every day is the only way to experience perfect peace, serenity, security and permanent supply. After all, we never really own anything. As the Native American people believe, **we are only stewards while here on earth.**

The Culprits and Saboteurs: Fear and Doubt

Commander Doubt and Colonel Fear were often present, looking over my shoulder. They appeared often to shadow my liberation. Yet, they served a higher purpose in reflecting my own doubts back to me. **Doubt and fear can only be present if we have a place in our consciousness that is equal to what they represent.** In order to be free, I had to act as if I was emancipated. I told myself that things were all right even when there were ample reasons to cause me worry. Sometimes, shadows of fear would bump me in the night, but I denied them a permanent home in my consciousness by casting them out. I continually affirmed and told myself that life would get better. Eventually, it did. I practiced my affirmations daily and sometimes hourly as needed. I designed them in my own words to represent freedom. Maintaining that state of mind of feeling free is what turned the tide. You have the power to do the same when needed. In fact you must. Only changing your mind, surrendering to spirit, and being willing to act upon guidance can change the tide.

Our attitude is our real boss!
It determines how far we will go.
It sets the quality of our experience along the way.

Sometimes we just have to keep on dancing even when the music has stopped. That is how I felt most of the time. I was not without health challenges. I had to adjust my diet as well as my attitude of stressful living in order to clean my liver that had been polluted from the years of breathing construction fumes and toxic paints. It became necessary to eliminate being around the chemical, paints by turning down any work that involved the use of them. By consulting with professional, holistic consultants I discovered natural ways of cleansing by consuming only organic vegetables, fruits, grains and free-range fowl.

Because I persisted in staying with my spiritual commitment to practice the Presence and trust Spirit, I am a new man. Before, I was a good teacher of metaphysics because I resonated with and understood the principles at an intellectual level. Now I can speak on them from the heart because I know there is no other way for me, but to live from that place.

Walking Our Talk.

The Universe always provides what each of us require when we get clear and committed in our willingness to accept change and heal. Sometimes we must begin by saying no to what we know does not serve our higher good. Spirit in its infinite knowingness, will naturally replace the limited experience with that which is right for our highest growth in order for us to a receive greater good. Be willing to detach from the negative - accepting and trusting that improvement will come whether you know what its form is or not. The Superconscious Intelligence of Spirit is within you and your experience. Accept that It Knows everything about you to provide appropriately and accordingly the changes for you.

To Experience success, it is essential to keep your attitude in line with what you desire.

Acting the Part.

I admire people who are genuinely committed to working on their own mastery of spirituality and metaphysics. Bill Cady is a friend who definitely puts God first and honors his own needs as being equally important. One day, I asked him how he was doing and he said that he felt terrible because he had not heard from a potential employer he wanted to go to work for. "Stop right there," I commanded, "if you expect to be a spiritual master and teacher as you intend, you had better improve your attitude. Get over this self-pity party. You are not your job." I went on. "The Infinite Intelligence of the Universe has the perfect right employment for you, it just has not arrived yet! You are still here, you have perfect health, your rent is paid, there is food on the table, you have money in your pocket, what are you complaining about? If you are going to be a master teacher, then it is essential to begin right now to live from your center, and not by outward appearances. If you let conditions rule you then you will continue to be a victim and not get to your goal." I was tough on him. I knew he could take it.

A few days later we spoke, all was well. He had yet to hear from the firm he wanted to work for, but he had experienced an attitude adjustment. He was happy! Why not? There was food on the table etc and he had his freedom to devote his time to his spiritual studies. Which by the way, was what he asked for. The next time we spoke, he was thrilled to be working at what he said was the perfect job! One far better than the original one.

At the human level, we think we know it all. Instead of preparing to receive what we are creating, we may choose to treat ourselves poorly by complaining. We waste what could be productive joy-time, lamenting that what we desire is not yet become visible. **Capitalize on the good that is, have gratitude for what you desire and observe conditions conform to your attitude.**

**Forgiveness releases the negative of the past.
It creates new windows of opportunities.**

"It is a fact that a man or woman who faithfully accepts an idea on the inner plane, will one day see it made manifest in the outer." Ernest Holmes. It is essential to live mentally, accepting what we desire, in advance of experiencing it in form. Add the element of being detached from outcome and you will be assured of that whatever comes along will be the highest and best for you and all involved.

Speak your Word: Release the Past and Clear the Way.

There is One Infinite Power. I am one with The Divine Creator. It knows everything about me, including how to release what I need to let go of in order to leap forward easily and joyously in my life experience. I trust Spirit, knowing that as I let go, I clear the space to receive my greatest desires on a life path of success.

I release and let go once and for all - _____. Spirit in me and my experience knows exactly how to do it. Therefore I surrender my stuff to God. Letting go of all issues concerning ____ I accept my freedom, permanently from this limitation. I willingly let go, I willingly forgive, and I invite and allow Spirit to flow through me in release. I give thanks that there is nothing more for me to figure out. Spirit takes care of everything. I let go and let God handle it. I am free. I choose to act accordingly, treating myself to the freedom, abundance and joy. I release all others and any condemnation, guilt or fear that I may have chosen in the past.

I accept perfect Divine Results. Spirit in me knows the highest and best and is the best. I welcome the best new experience. I accept that it contains all the elements to support my expansion into greater joy than I have ever known before. Spirit is Clarity. I Am One with Spirit, therefore I Am clarity. I am alive with purpose, filled with vision and have the motivation and everything necessary to carry out my mission in life. I am clear as to what it is. I Am supported by Spirit within me and all around me. Thank God I Am free.

I move forward with ease, confidence and lightness, knowing these truths and I accept divine order and timing. Knowing that I Am One with the One in charge, I live detached from the past, ready to claim my good. I give thanks that I know that I am One with love, light power and truth. And so it is!

CHAPTER FOURTEEN

REAL ESTATE

We all encounter challenge from time to time. But, let's face it, when we are in the midst of our troubles, it can be difficult to maintain an overview or have a clear perspective of what the bigger picture is. Later, when we look back and see what we have learned, we remember most the highs and the lows of each situation. I find solace in knowing that every stepping stone I've trod gifted me with essential growth and added to what makes me who I am today.

For those of us who have lived in northern climes, we know all too well that winter can be tough to bear. I spent six years in Minnesota where the weather can be extra brutal. The temperature can drop in a few short hours to forty and sixty below zero, and may sit there for days on end. It is not uncommon for snow to fall from late September and appear in early May. Despite the cold, I enjoyed my college years in the Twin Cities of Minneapolis and St. Paul. However unlike many of the region's residents, I did not share their love for the winter months. Even though I ski, enjoy skating and hockey, I have difficulty feeling hearty and jovial when dealing with extreme temperatures that make me sweat profusely under layers of thick clothing and frost bite my breath, nose, eyes and ears at the same time. I tease my friends who are die hard residents, "If you don't like the weather in Minnesota, just wait....it's bound to get worse."

I admit to having a genuine disdain for the cold so, for the first two years after completing art school in Minnesota, I traveled in January to the great Southwestern, Arizona desert. It was an annual pilgrimage to escape the lengthy, harsh, season. In mid-June after my second sojourn, I realized that it was time to permanently migrate West. Within two weeks of the decision, I closed my business and sold everything but what I could fit into my Cougar convertible. Top down, I heeded the call; "Go West young man." I decided to locate in Scottsdale with it's booming growth and sophisticated blend of culture and nature.

When it came time to procure housing, I spied a modest home for sale. It had a tidy swimming pool in the back with a beautiful view of prestigious, Camelback Mountain. I found a way to raise a small down payment and bought it directly from a retired woman who planned to move to Florida. Since neither of us was represented by a broker, I took on all the tasks of handling the sale that a real estate agent and a mortgage broker would have normally handled. In the process, I earned a hands-on education in real estate purchasing and investment that provided a strong foundation of working knowledge that proved useful in later California during the hot real estate, boom of the eighties.

There Are Infinite Ways To Accomplish What You Desire.

There are God's laws and there are the laws of man. Most of man's laws serve us well. God's laws are the unchanging principles we are all subject to in this world. The laws of gravity and cause and effect dictate the fixed relationships between man and nature. However, there is a great deal of gray territory that is not so definite, even when it appears to be. Here is where choice and freewill come into play.

Sometimes, it is favorable to read between the lines or to bend the rules a bit for the higher good. I learned first-hand in my first real estate dealings with the purchase of that little house in Scottsdale that man's rules are usually negotiable and are often flexible. Initially, when I turned in my application for a mortgage to the lending banker he stated that my debt-to-income ratio did not show adequate income for qualification. I knew that I could easily afford the home and was obviously disappointed.

This wise and generous man must have seen the remorse in my face. He slipped me a fresh application and scratched some quick figures on another sheet of paper. As he handed them to me he looked me squarely in the eye and said; "Go home and rework your figures. This is what I need to show in order for you to qualify!" He taught me a grand lesson in business that day. The lesson: man's rules are sometimes negotiable and occasionally may be circumvented for the higher good. It was a reasonable deal. I had the money, was a solid buyer and the bank wanted to finance the property. It was a win/win situation for all involved.

I commuted to that house after moving to California and used it as a vacation home and as a place to do business in Arizona for over three years. Later, I traded my equity in it towards my full ownership of a primary residence in Los Angeles. I never forgot the real estate lesson. In business, everything is negotiable. When we let go of trying to figure out a way to success and move into surrender and trust of Spirit, the answers, and ways and means to get us there will come. Like I stated earlier, there always is a way. God knows what it is. Let Go and Let Spirit Reveal it to you. You will know what to do when the time comes.

Speak your word to live in the free-flow of spirit.

God is all there is. The Infinite Presence lives within me. It lives within everyone and exists in all things. I choose to live the Kingdom of Heaven on Earth where I am, right here and now.

I choose to live peace and plenty on Earth beginning today. I accept it in my heart and mind from this moment forward. I choose to see all others as living expressions in the Kingdom all around me. I accept my stewardship of all that comes to me and all that is in my experience. My home and body are my living temples of Spirit. I reside in them as a wise and loving steward, taking care of what God has given me. I enjoy being One with the Presence in all its wonderful forms and ways. I acknowledge God in all I do in all my ways. I put my Spiritual needs first.

I give thanks that Spirit goes before me and lights my path with illumination, safety, health and abundance. I see that the real estate of God is where I live in consciousness. My real estate is blessed because it is what the Infinite Intelligence has given me to take care of and enjoy. I praise the Infinite Universal Love of Life flowing through me and every experience. I release holding on to anything that is not for my higher good and I accept the innate Divine results in every area of my life. I give thanks that my life is the life of God individualized as me expressing the Kingdom of Heaven on Earth today! And So It Is.

Make Spirit The Chairman Of Your Board!

Do not try to bargain with Spirit. Besieging God on our knees to bring a desire rarely works. "If you'll give me what I want, I promise to be good" rarely brings the kind of lasting results or satisfaction that we seek. I know because I have tested and tried it. Asking for trade-offs or bargaining for deals with God does not bring the desires of our heart to us. It is far better to hang out with Spirit as our best friend and daily companion, and have our needs met as we move through each day.

"Seek ye first the Kingdom, and all of these things will be added unto ye." To seek the Kingdom is to live heaven on earth by keeping Spirit in your heart and mind's eye, first before all things, and in all ways. "All of these things" represent what we require to sustain us, as well as the things that provide comfort, joy, and fulfill our highest desires.

Divine Dealing

God looks down over Italy. He sees a street thief standing on a corner. The man is spinning a gold chain around his finger. God speaks to the man, "I've got something for you." The man asks, Cuenta Cuesta?" (How much is it?) God replies; "It's free, its a Commandment." "Give it to me," The man demands. "Thou shalt not steal," God replies. "Get out of here," the thief answers, "Without stealing I have nothing!"

God moves on to cast his gaze over Paris. At a sidewalk cafe, he sees another man sipping wine. God says to him, "I have a commandment for you." The man asks, "How much is it? "Sans L'argnt?" (It's free) God replies. "Donnez-moi un," (Give me one) the man demands. God complies, "Thou shalt not commit adultery." "Get out of here," the man answers. "without adultery, I would not be here!"

God goes on to Moses, knowing he will not be disappointed in the answer he gets. He says to Moses, "I have got something for you." "What is it?" "It's a commandment." "How much is it?" Moses asks. "Its free," God answers." "I'll take ten," Moses retorts.

Ease Is The Name Of The Game.

When we try to force the creation of something that is not for our highest good, it may come to us, perhaps easily, but usually not. If and when it does, it may not remain. When conditions or timing are not right, our creation may disintegrate before our eyes. Trying to hold on to it may cause us further stress. It might blow up in our face anyway, or we may feel as if the rug is pulled out from under us. Forcing these situations in any way wastes far more energy than any time we have invested in trying to create them. I believe that if something is not right for us, or the timing is wrong, it simply will not come. Affirm Divine Timing and Order when speaking your Word in Creation. When circumstances and timing are right, all is right and things will automatically fall into place.

In accepting an easier way of life, it is absolutely essential to choose a path of non-resistance. It is always the natural way to the richest fulfillment in any situation. Maintaining confidence while remaining impassioned about your desire is essential. However, it is being in a detached attitude about the outcome or way it may come to you that gives a breath and lightness that is required for the fruition of it. All things work in concert with one another for the higher good of everyone involved when we are in spiritual alignment. The act of creation works best when we take our attention off the ways and means. Conscious Creation through spirit with an attitude of non-attachment to outcome always brings best results. When we are alive with our whole and complete vision of success, everything falls into place in a natural order. Gratitude for the desire as already complete quickens and seals it to us.

A certain amount of footwork and vigilance to the vision may still be required to bring the desire to fruition. Had that first little house in Scottsdale not been right for me, the deal would have fallen through and another more appropriate home would have appeared. Should you find yourself pushing to force something to happen, you may get the results you want but they won't last. It is impossible to push a river. Better to go with the natural flow.

For every action, there is an equivalent reaction.

Observe Hitler and Sadam Hussein as big time examples of "how not to act." The results of their lives paint a strong and obvious picture of the futility and negative results of getting back in equal measure what one creates or puts out to others. They have been great teachers in our world, demonstrating how cause and effect works when power is misused.

It is easy to observe a controlling friend or family member who acts to force a personal agenda over the good of the whole. Attempting to manipulate or control others into doing things serves only their personal satisfaction, not necessarily the higher good of all involved. People who engage in acts of petty theft or telling untruths wonder why their lives do not work in their favor. The effects of what happens as a result are a living proof of acting on wrong thinking. Forcing an agenda, stealing, or telling lies do not work. The law of Karma is always creating balance. What goes around, comes around.

If man's laws fail to get the crooks, then God's surely will. In the late 1960's Georgia's state governor George Wallace ran for President. He had made a few mistakes. One of his biggest ones was by taking a stand against racial integration. He boldly declared; "Segregation forever!" In that same year he was shot by a would-be assassin. His wounds left him paralyzed from the waist down and confined to a wheel chair for the rest of his life. Recently, he admitted that he had learned his lesson. Apparently, after thirty years of confinement leaving him "in the back of the bus for life," he had plenty of time to live with the consequence of his negative words and opposition to a basic human equality.

No Man (or Woman) Is An Island.

Some people think that success and financial security are what life is all about. Although one may function well for a long time operating from our heads, real satisfaction and peace comes to us when we are able to integrate our hearts with our minds. In our culture, especially in business, many receive honors and riches from use of their business acumen. Still, they may search endlessly to fill the empty spaces in their souls and hearts. All the money in the world does not serve one who lives totally in the head.

My friend Diane told me that until she discovered how to unconditionally love herself and her fellow humans, she had laid waste to many a suitor. By land mining the way to her heart as a means of protection, she was able to maintain control and keep herself safe from intimacy. If a man got to close, she found ways to blow him up emotionally! You and I require close and personal relationships to prosper. It is in our cellular make-up to be interactive and dependent upon one another. If we were meant to be alone we would each have our own planet.

**Every time we love or open ourselves to it,
we move into a greater flow of trust....and expansion.**

Reggie

Reggie is a talented and loving man who at one time owned a successful hair salon in Honolulu. With a number of employees and a strong following of patrons, he quickly achieved success in the high style, high-ticket business. Reggie prospered in the ways of the world. He told me that he drove a Porsche, lived in a Honolulu penthouse apartment, and sported expensive diamond jewelry. He had collected all the stuff that people think are important outer signs of success. Yet he was unhappy. When I asked he why, he said that what he had not learned was to fuse his heart with his mind.

For recreation and personal challenge, Reggie trained on a bicycle for the Iron Man Decathlon held annually in Hawaii. Every day he would bike several miles. By checking his stop-watch along the way, he would know which stoplight he should be at, by what time. In order to keep within his work schedule, and to synchronize his life in perfect timing, his entire day relied on the schedule, down to the minute. There was no extra time for people if they did not conform to the schedule. Nor was there time for

Reggie to feel his own emptiness.

Everything was right on schedule. One morning he pulled up to a light on his bike and prepared to make a left-hand turn. The schedule was suddenly broken when car came speeding up behind him and blasted into him, throwing him sixty feet into the air. As he was flying, he had two thoughts; "Now I'm running behind on my schedule I wonder what's going to happen to my bike!" He said that he knew in that moment that there was something wrong with his life. Instead of being concerned about being injured, his focus was on the schedule.

Reggie told me that hitting the pavement felt like touching ice. "It is so cold that it feels good, yet it burns and hurts at the same time." People were running towards him. As he attempted to get up, the pain was too unbearable to move, and he realized that he was not going to make his first appointment. He continued, "I felt like I needed to call my receptionist before anything else could take place!" The schedule was clearly falling apart.

Then he heard a voice. "Are you okay?" "I looked up into beautiful, blue eyes staring at me." Reggie went on; "A complete stranger was looking into the window of my soul with such deep care and compassion. At that moment, I realized what life was really about." It was that level of communication with another spirit that for the first time brought a deeper focus into his view. For the next three days in the hospital, teams of specialists were coming and going from his room. His fourth, fifth, and sixth vertebrae were crushed. His lower lumbar discs were chipped. He had interior hemorrhaging and suffered from post-traumatic brain damage. Reggie told me that he knew he was in serious trouble when he reached to pour a glass of water from a pitcher at his bedside, and he dropped both. Reggie began to pray daily.

In the seven years since the accident, life has been one challenge after another, but it has also been a very special life of recovery. I find his attitude to be remarkable. Reggie is a loving, compassionate, caring man. He is able to walk normally, still with challenge and sometimes pain, but he is doing well. He rarely complains. His quiet, appreciative nature shines. When friends ask why he is so quiet, he states that he is doing his best to absorb the essence of his friends and the environment that he is in. This is a man that who tells me that he went out of his way to cover his heart up. Now the gentleness of it is as apparent as that of the tin man from *The Wizard of Oz*.

"We are all connected. To live without the awareness that we are, feels completely lonely like there is no

connection at all. To be aware that we are, makes me live
more in the moment. It stops me in my tracks and helps me
to be more awake to what life is about. Living is not about
yesterday or tomorrow. With this new awareness, now I
stop and notice how I am observing, how I feel, and to take
time to appreciate people and places, no matter where they
are or what I think about them." Reggie 1998.

Reggie told me that the accident was the key turning point
in his life, one that totally changed the direction of his spiritual
walk. Without it, he would have gone on living unaware that we
are all part of one another. He had no choice but to detach from
living as a solitary man. The biggest lesson for our planet at this
time is that we are all One. We are One life form, breathing One
Spirit, alive in God, each as an individualized idea of our Creator
as a human. When we begin to live it and care for one another, we
will experience the gifts of heaven on earth. The first step for the
individual who feels alone is to release the belief that to be a
solitary being is the natural way of life. We must reach out to one
another, communicate and give love in order to receive it.

Speak Your Word To Realize Ease And Knowing

There is One Perfect Intelligence in all of the Universe.
The Divine Awareness of the Creator is within me. I accept my
Oneness with the Absolute. For me, there is no separation. Just
knowing this makes my life easy, whole and complete. The
absolute wholeness of Spirit is the greater part of who I am at my
center. Therefore, I am complete unto myself. Everyone in my
experience is an individualization of Spirit, whether they know it
or not.
Because I am in the flow of Greater Self-Knowing
acceptance, I am in divine alignment with my highest good. My
consciousness is one of complete unity with Spirit. Therefore, I am
in harmony with every aspect of life. Good flows to me and through
me. I am one with the One Creative process of Spirit within me
and all things. I accept that everyone in my world is a part of the
greater picture, and an integral part in some way. I release
judgment about others as to how they choose to experience life and
I live my own more freely as a result. I bless them and release
them, and turn my attention to people and things that bring me joy
and satisfaction. I give where I can, and Spirit provides everything
I need to be in the flow.
I am One with all good. I am One with God. This is my

truth. I do my best to see it and know it for others as well and let go of ideas of limitation. There are no limits in the Superconscious Mind of the Infinite. I am One with unlimited good on all levels because I know that the good of Spirit exists everywhere. I call it forth and accept it for myself and others right here and now. Thank God, I am free. And So It Is!

CHAPTER FIFTEEN

Eliminate Struggle

One does not have to be a saint to love God. Most all of the great spiritual teachers I have known, are somewhat notorious in their enjoyment of earthly vices. I myself have learned to play with a hedonistic passion and abandon. Years ago, when I discovered that God was all I required to be high on life, I gave up artificial stimulants almost completely. As I learned to trust myself on deeper levels, I gained an assured confidence that Spirit was always taking care of me and watching out for my highest good.

If we knew for certain that God was in us and not separate from us, we could walk with the kind of Divine confidence and love that Jesus displayed. However, most of humanity suffers it's own moments of doubt during the painful times because it was taught out of a fear-based teaching to not trust neither God nor the self.

As a child, I relied on a Christian upbringing to protect me, never deserting my belief in God even when it was popular to do so. And because of it, I believe that I always led a blessed life. Just as you may have, I wondered at times if my heavenly Father was really rooting for me. I had moments of doubt and sometimes felt alone or terrified, but love and trust in my Divine Parent in times of trouble and good always got me through unscathed. Spirit has been the continuity of Golden Thread revealing Itself to me ever since I was a five-year-old fatherless boy in Iowa. I was a loner and small for my age, roaming the streets and alleys of my small town after kindergarten until my mother came home from work. Even when the bullies twice my size were chasing me, I felt the wings of God beneath my feet as I out-ran them and I knew I was never alone.

"Who Is God Anyway?"

Eventually, along my own path of spiritual evolution, a more expansive and less traditional and limited concept of what this *greater power, God*, really is began to evolve in my mind. It has reveled Itself to be a foundation of belief that is based on love, yet does not necessarily exclude tradition.

I grew into my spirituality through study and classes in Divine Science, meditation, prayer, contemplation of God, self, and nature. I began to see a less contained picture than what I had been taught by traditional religion. **I found this Great Being to** be the *essence* of *Love* and *Creation* working in concert as One Divine Parent, Holy Spirit, and Christ-being that lives within my own soul and that of everyone. As a result, I began to love myself more and utilize my Word to consciously manifest what I required. It took steady uphill work on my own consciousness that stretched over a period of many years. In the process, I began to see with greater clarity and, live life with a sense of relaxed trust. I discovered that the Intelligence of Spirit guides us with purpose, and that we are all connected to a Divine plan for our lives.

These basic truths continue to be revealed to me again and again through the course of time. I become aware of it at moments of peaceful knowing, and by noticing the synchronization of events.

This thing called *God* is in everything and everybody. The Supreme appears to us when we accept that *He, She, It ,Us, You, We Me* lives within us as the greater part of ourselves. The more we acknowledge our *Oneness*, the more aware we become that *we are the thing we have been seeking*.

Goals

Our society teaches that to achieve goals is the chief purpose of life. In America we are so focused on reaching our peak that we put much time and effort into scaling our career mountains and into achieving what we believe to be the ultimate goal: financial security. In the quest for more and better we ignore essential, spiritual aspects of life that contribute to our sense of well- being and to a richer awareness and enjoyment of our life experience. On the climb to the top, often we believe that we are pulling ourselves up to a higher level and that when we reach that place we will have it made. However, just as we think we have arrived because we have scaled to the top of the plateau, we turn and see another mountain looming before us. That was how I looked at my life before I discovered that in traveling the path of least resistance I found the greatest gifts of joy, success and the money I had sought as well!

Many of us are goal-oriented. Goals are essential to forward movement and bring satisfaction as they uplift the quality of our lives. They give purpose and serve others in expansion as they serve us. However, a life spent in quest for gain on the material plane is often seeped in traditional, competitive ways of thinking that teach material success as the ultimate quest. To live it keeps one in the track of never having enough satisfaction. One becomes locked into the effort of struggle. In observing my own patterns, I saw that my values were built on the belief that struggle was a natural and necessary part life. Yet my studies of metaphysics revealed to me that ease in manifestation is a very high tenet of living. As I tested the principles through application, I found it to be true.

The Universe Creates In Ease. The same Creative Principle is in you and I. We can use it consciously to form our own experience.

As I began to manifest my desires and prove to myself that this stuff worked, it was easier to consciously release the old limited belief in struggle and to make real changes in the ways I thought and acted. Struggle may seem normal because we are so rooted in it from childhood, but it is certainly not natural. You and I have the inherent power to manifest ease, and have our needs met at the same time. We were taught struggle. I discovered that we are designed in the image and likeness with the potential to be a part of a greater plan for humanity. It is for us to awaken to Oneness and our Divine heritage so that we may walk with one with God and one another, creating a living heaven on earth.

Struggle is as unnatural as water flowing uphill.

The idea that struggle is part of the natural course of life is a misnomer that many of us were taught since early childhood. I found the idea that a life of ease, enjoyment and fulfillment could be actualized was acceptable to me on spiritual level, but did not seem at all realistic or fit into the paradigm I had been taught to think and act.

What about the work ethic? The harder one works the more success one achieves. One who leads a purposeful, career-oriented, dedicated life naturally gets ahead. When we put focus and energy into our goals, we succeed. So why surrender to an airy, fairy theory that there is some pie-in-the-sky better way to live? The dollars are coming in, bills are paid and everybody is happy. Right? We know there is more to life than collecting our check and paying the bills. Why is it that so many are now searching for more? The most powerful social movements in America today are based on the discovery of self and spiritual enlightenment. There is some work involved in letting go. However, it is only a shift in perception that makes the difference between what which may seem to be an immense task, and what may be transformed into the most rewarding journey of self-actualization possible.

I began to free myself from the belief in the need for struggle by affirming that my growth need not be painful. Instead of thinking of the tasks ahead, I asked and affirmed that my life lessons would become joyous. It began to work. I observed my experience becoming more effortless over a period of time as I began to be easier and more loving to myself.

I became particularly clear on the issue of struggle when I was painting custom mural work for a fantastic and wealthy client in La Jolla, California. (pronounced La Hoya).

Sending Struggle Off Into The Sunset

My client Georgiana and her husband own an exceptionally unique contemporary, Mediterranean house on the slopes of La Jolla Shores. They bought this glitzy, villa from a former Las Vegas showgirl. Georgiana's good taste and charm transformed it from a brassy Hollywood set to a unique and classy home. I like to think that my artwork adds a grace that complements the ocean views wrapping nearly every room. I completed a major mural in the dining room and was working to finish a painted, detail around the high arched floor to ceiling windows in the kitchen. The design comprised of Italian grape-vines painted around the arches, with fruit motifs nestled realistically into the foliage.

Georgiana purchased a beautiful array of fruits and spread them on the counter to inspire me for use as a working model. I completed handsome interpretations of the grapes, strawberries, and pears successfully. But when it came to the lemons, I painted them over and over. Time and again, they just would not come out right. Georgiana came into the room just as I was beginning to paint them for the fourth time. I said to her, "Georgiana, I cannot get these lemons to look right. I am really struggling with them." "Come down off that ladder." She replied. "I don't want you struggling with anything in my house. I don't even allow my children use the word. Let's go to lunch and figure out something else to paint instead. I don't want the energy of struggle in my home!" It's no wonder she is the wife of a millionaire. She knows how to live with the right attitude!

That day I learned a big lesson in releasing struggle from Georgiana. I decided right on the spot to let go of my belief in it once and for all. I mentally piled the letters spelling it out onto a big raft and sent it free to sail away from me on the ocean. I breathed a tremendous sigh of relief as I visualized it going off into the sunset. If something does not feel good, then release yourself from it. Do not continue to be draw into it. There is always better ways to resolve life's problems. You have the option to return to it the next day with a fresh perspective. Or, perhaps after lunch, a new concept will fill the bill in a better way. A Divine solution is the right answer and is always revealed in right timing when we detach from worry over what does not work. **Let go of focusing on the problem and tune in on the answer.**

When faced with challenges ask for the Divine solution.
Stop asking questions.
Affirm that you have the Divine answer in the now!

There Are No Questions, Only Answers.

In *No Boundaries*, I talk about letting go of struggle and describe several techniques of release. I encourage you to move on to creating and realizing ease. As we practice non-attachment from uncomfortable conditions, we take a break from our problems and turn it over to Spirit. It knows Infinite ways to accomplish everything, and Is the way. Just because we do not enjoy a certain task does not mean that someone else would not. Use the power of your word to create ease and to manifest requirements and desires. The ways, means, and answers always come through the creative principle of focus, Word and faith. The highest and best good will always come to us when we choose the path of least resistance.

When practicing hypnosis with clients and in my personal meditations, I mentally place troubles at the feet of God or Christ on a tray and turn them over to be dissolved. This practice gives the subconscious a powerful mental picture to work with. You can do the same. Be willing to surrender to Spirit the burdens you cannot handle.

We were trained to accept that we must suffer, or to work long, hard hours at things we do not enjoy, just to survive and to pay the bills. The false belief in struggle will be true for as long as we continue to service it. Is not the time with loved ones and doing things in a relaxed way a healthier way of living? Are we at last beginning to understand that we do not need to charge or purchase the latest products thrust upon us by the advertisers, when last year's model is just as good? Or that to not keep up with the Jones's who, by the way, are probably drowning in debt, is freeing and creates peace of mind? That the Internet, cellular phones, pagers, faxes and every other convenience although helpful to production are not necessary to a full and rich life?

Many families are locked in service to debt. It has become a common way of life. Our economy thrives on debt; it keeps people engaged and occupied full time to keep it expanding to fulfill the needs of Gross National Product and corporate profit, if one purchases all the products, throws away the excess, disposes of the waste, and keeps up with the demand for newer and better.

I learned to enjoy my time off from working to support the system by exploring and discovering alternate means of increasing my enjoyment of life by maintaining my liquid cash. I shopped garage sales, bargain stores and just plain watched my spending, and in particular, my charging on credit cards. I did not buy anything that I was not prepared to pay for in full at the end of each month. I stopped going to the big department stores to buy another pair of jeans, shoes, or whatever and only went when I really needed them. Even so, I bought one of what I required, not a whole bag full, only to take them home to hang in the closet. When I came out of a store, I congratulated myself for getting off easy! It was a good experiment. I learned much and in many ways lived better than before when I had tons of cash to spend and credit to utilize. With more cash in our account it is easier to maintain balance. One pair of dress shoes suffices for each occasion. One pair for casual, one for painting, and one for hiking, etc. It's all just stuff!

Speak Your Word and Release Struggle

There is One Power, One Mind, One Infinite Knowingness. It is the Universal All Present Divine Mind. I accept that the Divine connection is in my own Mind. I am One with Infinite Spirit. I am in harmony with this magnificent intelligence. Since It knows everything about me and every person and situation, I unconditionally accept that it knows how to free me from any limitation of pain or struggle. No matter what my past looks like I accept that it can change here and now.

I accept freedom from struggle. I release the belief in it no matter how deeply ingrained it is within me. I speak these words of intention, decision, and commitment to accept the newer, higher path of least resistance. I am free from struggle. I invite this new sense of joy and lightness into every aspect of my mind and into the out-picturing of my experience. Since Spirit is in every person, place and experience, I accept perfection revealed as I go along. I trust God to take care of the details and to dissolve the old patterns of belief here and now. I release this treatment in gratitude, accepting full Divine realization and the joy of the freedom to be who I am. I release and am free from the belief the necessity of struggle at last. Thank God I am free. And So It Is!

CHAPTER SIXTEEN

You Make It Happen

Choose To See On The Inside
What You Desire On The Outside

There was an enormous natural disaster on earth. St. Peter lined up many helpers to assist him in processing and orienting the throngs of new arrivals at heaven's gate. Still, there were just too many. So in order to ease the load and create efficiency, he decided to send those who were still waiting to the *other place* temporarily. Most of the souls who were sent *down there* found the heat too difficult to bear and began to complain to one another. Being resourceful church-going Christians, comprised of Baptists, Methodists, and Catholics with a few metaphysicians, they got together and decided to find a way to install air-conditioning. In order to pay for it, the Methodists held a bake-sale, the Catholics sponsored bingo games, and the Baptists had a rummage sale. The metaphysicians supported the other groups events by participating fully, however they continued to decline sponsoring any events themselves. When the others asked them why they chose not to engage in the fund raising the spokesperson for the metaphysicians proudly announced; "Its not hot, and we're not here!"

There is a lot to be said for the power of denial. Wearing rose-colored glasses adds strength to positive thinking. It's magic of believing in its effect and its power to dissolve an unwanted situation has served to push me past many a personal challenge. It takes a great deal of inner strength to deny that the boogie man is at your door when you have heard him knocking. However, sometimes ignoring him can be the best way to make him go away. It is not unusual for a metaphysician to use denial in affirming our way beyond apparent barricades of limitation, however, it is important to deal with our feelings in a pragmatic way. In choosing the route of denial in handling a problem, we take a stand for absolutism. It can be a very powerful tool in reprogramming our subconscious beliefs so that it does not happen again.

Use affirmative denial to break through apparent limits. State your desire for a higher truth as already prevailing in Spirit. Speaking your Word in claiming and establishing the state of perfection of God. "There is no lack or fear in God, only love and absolute, clarity in knowing of all things. God is in me, therefore there is no lack or fear in that part, the greater part of me. Only the love and absolute knowing of God prevails in me. Spirit purges anything unlike Itself!" Then get busy acting the part and use wisdom.

If you are on a fearful course rowing in your boat on the river of life: "Pray to God, but row away from the rocks."

You Are The Essence Of Your Dreams!

John is a successful businessman living in Hawaii. He manages an eyeglasses boutique in a fashionable Honolulu neighborhood. A picture of him today shows a trim, happy man with gleam in his eye and a smile of satisfaction on his face. In his wallet, he carries a photo of himself as a four hundred and seventy-eight pound obese man. He has come through a tunnel of change that has revealed to himself and the world the slender, loving guy that he is today. John told me; "I always looked like that in my mind, being at a normal body weight."

At his heaviest, he wore size sixty-six pants! Topping over six feet he now weighs under one-seventy-five and wears a size thirty-four pant. He feels that the biggest change for him is that he now allows time for the physical, mental, and spiritual to meet. He says the physical is really nothing, but what counts is what one thinks on the inside. "My philosophy is that we are already are beautiful to begin with; anything we do beyond that is a bonus."

John was the son of restaurateur parents, so food was readily available twenty-four hours a day. He says that his security came from eating four meals a day with snacks in between. He does not blame his parents for his former love-hate relationship with food. "The brainwashing starts with childhood when kids are told to eat everything on their plates, at a set time whether they are hungry or not." What they learn is to eat out of habit. John learned that candy bars and cartons of ice cream were perfect surrogates for non-existent love, friends and self-esteem.

As a result of the tremendous burden on his body, John could only sleep no more than forty-five minutes at a time. After choking on his windpipe from the weight of a twenty-three inch neck, his doctor drilled holes in his sinuses and prescribed a breathing machine for him on his twenty-eighth birthday. People had often encouraged him to lose weight but offered no solutions. He tried every diet in the book. Yet it was not until he made the decision to seriously get started to reduce and he began to eat wisely and nutritiously, that he saw any progress. He did it all by switching to eating smaller amounts of healthy foods. John recommends that one drink plenty of water, reduce the intake of red meat, fats, salt, sugar, and alcohol, and increase the intake of fruits, vegetables, beans and whole grains. He says that the clincher is to eat until one begins to feel slightly full, and to stop at that point.

Today he eats three vegan meals (no meat products), and pays attention to his body's needs more than to his mind's cravings. "Your body will tell you when it needs fuel. The best day to start is the day after you decide to make changes," he said. "It's no use being hard on yourself.. It's okay to slip some days, as long as you get back on track." John knows the power in being consistent. It is the practice of consistency that always gets us to our goals. When I asked him why he took off the weight he replied, "I wanted to live life for twenty-eight years and I did not. I didn't know life could be so rich. It's not the materialistic part of it at all." **"If I died today, I would feel complete. We fear death because we have not loved life. Death is a part of life that simply opens up another door."** John's story is amazing. He accomplished his goal in two and half years, simply by eating healthy and wisely, proving once again that we have everything we need to live as the whole beings God designed us to be. "Some people are not strong enough to make changes on their own, so they need supportive help of the people around them." John stated that he did not know the first thing about nutrition. Lack of knowledge led him to consult a nutritionist and a doctor before beginning his journey to a new life.

Today when I see John, he always has a smile on his face. When I find myself in a mood to complain I only need think of him and remember how he transformed himself from the inside out. John's story reminds me that life is a rich, plentiful experience. We can choose to see ourselves as beautiful and we have a choice in what we think and do. There are better ways to get to heaven than dying. Each of us can create our heaven on earth by the way we live our lives while we are here.

How Did The Snail Get To The Ark?
Answer....Inch By Inch.

Spirit Speaks!

When I set out to publish "No Boundaries," I spent parts of two winters in Hawaii writing far removed from the usual stresses and business climate I dealt with in Los Angeles. The third year, I stayed closer to home in order to work with my editors. In the summer, I presented a prosperity workshop in Long Lake, Minnesota, at a church outside of Minneapolis, when one participant asked when my book would be published. My answer was "when the Universe gets around to it." She surprised me by jumping to her feet, pointing her finger towards me and firmly stated, "Wrong answer. It is published now!" I laughed and replied, "who's giving this seminar anyway?" Her point was well taken. I needed to put it into the present tense not ambiguously, sometime in the future.

I returned home to California and immediately set out to learn about self-publishing, and to release waiting on the pricey Beverly Hills agent I had so dearly paid to find a publisher. Had I not put my own energy into the process, I might still be waiting. She never did get around to supplying me with any working results.

Anything you want to do in life requires your energy, your hand, and your time, thoughts and commitment to make it a success. You can get people to help you, but the thrust of the work must come from you and you alone. Midas might have had a golden agent but it was his consciousness of that brought wealth and success. If you desire success, you must have self-esteem, love and enthusiasm for what you do, and the desire to serve and benefit others as a product of what you passionately create. Recognize that **God is your Source. The source of the idea within you knows the ways and means to bring it to fruition.** You have the unlimited wealth of the Universe at your disposal. You only need to access it. Take time to be quiet and listen, your questions will be answered. All is known in the space of silence.

I did not let my lack of knowledge of publishing stop me from moving forward. I began with what I knew. I researched the rest and took it one step at a time. You do not have to know everything all up front. Relax. Spirit within you has all the knowledge you will ever require! You are covered. It is up to you to get to work creating, unfolding, and birthing your dream. The rest will fall into place as you continue to move forward in a committed way towards the vision of your goal. As you take each step into your vision the next will be revealed in Divine Order. The passion of your vision will be the juice that your subconscious mind is consciously pouring into the cosmic blender of Spirit that ultimately brings it to tangible in form!

Speak Your Word to Activate Manifest Your Desires

There is One Creative Power. It is my source, I am one

with the Absolute. Within myself and the Greater Knowing of Spirit lies all answers and solutions. Because Knowing exists, I accept the peace of acceptance in ease. Whatever I require, is already known in Spirit. Therefore, that which I desire, I accept in ease.

Any and all action required is automatic within me. I live, move, and breathe in Spirit. I am the out-picturing of it as my individualized self. I accept a new freedom in my knowing and actions. I release having to figure out anything and accept that all comes in ease. I cannot make a mistake, because God is always right and I am speaking my word to stay in right knowing and right activity. Right action flows through the knowingness of Spirit in me. I move on what I am guided to do and go where I instinctively am led. There is no effort, stress or strain in Spirit. Because God is moving and knowing within me at all times, I relax into knowing and being my greater good in action. This is my Truth, my Peace and my Allness, expressed. I know that I am one in the One living true to my purpose and expressing the joy of being One with God. For this I am grateful. And So It Is!

CHAPTER SEVENTEEN

Dare To Be Different

Bill is a typical Southern California businessman. He is comfortably on top of his life by the way the world measures success. He drives a more practical than stylish, newer model car. He goes to work faithfully every day, whether he is feeling well or not. He is so deeply involved with his career that it is not unusual for him to stay at the office long past the dinner hour. Frequently he goes to the office on Saturdays just to keep up with his regular work load. He is getting ahead, or at least managing to keep up. He has never been late with a mortgage payment on his slightly above average, ocean-view hillside home. His wife works to ensure that their children will never be in want of anything.

Like millions of other Americans, Bill and his family have a good life. Hard earned as it is, he has plenty of money most of the time. He works about sixty hours a week just to keep up interest payments on credit cards. His daily commute takes him inland from the beach, about forty-five minutes each way in heavy traffic. At the end of a day, he is too tired to talk to his wife and children. He nods out in front of the TV watching anything that is of mild interest to him before falling into bed exhausted. Tomorrow will be another version of the same day.

Bill and his family eat prepared foods, seasoned for taste, color enhanced, and packaged for easy microwaving. They are unaware that the food they digest contains all kinds of chemicals. Like most grocery store foods, it has been grown in soil long ago stripped of its natural minerals. Bill's dinner rounds out a machine-vended, chips and candy bar lunch, washed down with an artificial diet cola, all while deeply engaged with his constant companion, his computer screen. He drinks bottled water like many Americans because the tap water is so heavily laden with chemicals and bleach to minimize the toxicity of the pollution it contains. The water depleted of its natural, life-giving mineral content has been declared to "contain safe levels of carcinogenic materials" by the U.S. Food and Drug Administration.

Bill is envied and considered well off by his co-workers. With the addition of his wife's income, he is able to be free on Sundays and spend time with his children. He may be able to pay for college for them if he can keep his work pace and income until he retires. Bill is typical of millions of other Americans. The nine-to-five, working couple, scrambling just to keep up with the Jones's syndrome has advanced considerably. Today a classic *Donna Reed,*

Leave It To Beaver household of the fifties would be rare. Most families would be hard-pressed to fit under that halo of perfection espoused as an idealistic, American dream.

Bill is fortunate. He has a devoted wife and mother for his children as well as a partner who shares the financial load. His kids are drug-free and exceptional students. His family has a strong spiritual foundation and lives happily. There is nothing wrong with Bill's life, nor the one most of us lead. The common gripe Americans all share has little to do with the style in which we live. It is more about what we do not do, or are not able to do, that depletes our energy and diminishes the quality of our lives.

"The problem with running the rat race is that even if you win, you are still one of the rats." Lily Tomlin

If we examine Bill's experience purely from a physical point of view, we see that he operates in a state of fatigue much of the time. Fueled by frequent sugar and coffee rushes, his nervous system conforms to the daily jump-start pattern. He swallows a handful of vitamins, all claiming to give him the "daily required minimum" of what he needs to be a winner at work. The fact is that the foods which he and most Americans eat lacks the nutrition of Mother Nature's, rich breadbasket that our parents and grandparents were raised on. During the nineteen-fifties, chemical fertilizers began to be added as a supplement to the land in order to boost production. As it was added to the soil and continued to build up year by year, it seeped into the water tables, flowing back into the rivers, fully toxic with DDT and other chemical additives.

Generations of children were raised on sugar and artificial sweeteners added to chemically, laden foods. Most pre-packaged, name brand, but natural labeled, mass-produced items are full of several forms of toxins. Only foods organically grown contain the life giving nature of the mother soil from which they spring. Even so, their mineral content may be low by comparison to the diets of our hearty ancestors. And the "experts" continue to wonder why the disease and death rates in the economically progressive nations of the world are so high. Hundreds of thousands of our brothers and sisters suffer from cancers and every other type of body and nervous dysfunction possible.

Trace Minerals, Natures Formula For Balance

During the same period of the introduction of chemicals

into the land, a quick cure was discovered by veterinarians for farm and zoo animals. When an infirmity set into the livestock, a shot or dose of an appropriate, natural trace mineral would be added to the diet of the creature as a sure, corrective measure. This simple supplement has kept the farm and zoo animals healthy and robust, free of the affliction of aging that has become considered to be common to human beings. Farm animals do not suffer long from the ailments of the barnyard. Whether they live to maturity or not, past their age for slaughter, they are treated with injections of trace minerals as a sure and quick cure for all ailments. Trace minerals for humans are available at any health food store or homeopathic pharmacy. Of course if trace mineral cures were introduced into mainstream medicine, the whole industry's high profit, chemical drug, surgery, infirmary, ambulatory, real estate leasing, and insurance mega businesses would surely be at risk.

High in the mountains of Tibet, and other high-altitude regions, natural, glacial runoff feeds the water supplies and enriches the soil that foods are grown in. Cancer and other well known modern-day diseases associated with old age are practically non-existent. People live to an average age well over one hundred years without most of the afflictions of what we call the developed or civilized world. Mineral-rich, stone-washed water is full of high amounts of natural, trace minerals.

Our bodies were designed to last far longer than what today we consider to be a normal life-span. Our Creator made them to last and for us to enjoy them in a youthful, agile and healthy state. As long as humankind believes that disease and aging are a normal part of life, we will create ways to perpetuate and support a decline of its existence. Perfect health is natural. When we life in balance spiritually, physically and mentally, the idea of disease and aging becomes obsolete and absurd. The time will come when it happens.

The Shangri-La and fountains of youth we seek to discover and have read about or viewed in the movies are possible. The formula for perfect physical health and lasting vitality is in our own bodies and psyche. Those ways are only now beginning to be explored. New vistas on anti-aging and ways to stay young and fit will be realized and perfected in the twenty-first century.

The body Mother Nature gave us is designed to maintain optimum health, with natural vitality. It is a perpetual temple of self-renewal. All the nutrients required to run our magnificent body machines are found naturally growing upon the earth. You and I are made of the same elements found here. We require the same life-giving oxygen and pure mineral-rich water to maintain balance. God gave us everything we need in nature to thrive. It is our human responsibility to preserve and maintain our majestic but delicate ecosystem for future generations. However, the earth's environment is distressed. The weather is changing. Year by year, we observe conditions becoming more extreme.

The Lights Are On. Is Anyone Home?

We live and travel surrounded by electrical systems that effect our bodies immensely. Wires in the car, home and office surround us day and night. It is no wonder that life seems intense. Perhaps I am more aware of it because I have always worked out-of-doors as much as possible or within the quiet simplicity of home.

Several years ago, I was hired to paint an enormous mural for a large national insurance company, headquartered in California. It was to be a depiction of a computer, operations center. The commission was particularly challenging because it lined the walls of the top three stories in a fire stairwell of a high-rise, building. Used by the firm as a passage from floor to floor, they wanted it to look finished. Los Angeles city code prohibited any applications for decor other than paint, so it was up to me to make it shine. Dangling and stretching on a teetering scaffold was more than a challenge. However, as I tried not to look down the twenty-story, well I kept my eye on the vision of the completed product and the robust fee I was collecting to do the work. A balloon payment was due to be paid on my mortgage at the same time, so I was grateful that God provided the ways and means to meet it in full, on time.

As part of the research for the project, I was given a private tour of their computer operations center, hidden discreetly in a quonset-style, tin warehouse, located in a low-key part of the city. The room was so top secret that my visit required a special security clearance and an official escort to enter. There was a twenty-four-hour security guard posted at the door just inside the main computer room. The room itself was immense and was constructed with removable metal panels for the floor, walls and ceiling, allowing access to wiring on all sides. As I entered, I immediately sensed an uncomfortable, vibrational buzz from the intensity of the electrical power in the room, from over my head, under my feet and in the air. It felt as though my blood was tingly and all the hairs on my body were charged all the way to the ends of my eyelashes! I turned to the guard and asked him if he could feel the energy in the room. He said that he could not. His job was to stand guard in the over air-conditioned, windowless, florescent lit, neutral colored people-free space.

I have always been overtly sensitive to florescent lights. I visually detect the vibration of the gas that creates the illusion of continuous light. In no time at all, I get headaches from their monotonous glare. I recall attending junior and senior high school and experiencing the problem for the first time from the grayish-white vibrational light. I still refuse to eat in a restaurant lit by them or stay in a room where they are in use for any length of time. Windows that open to fresh air and expansive views are high on my list of priorities as well. I require tons of air, natural light and space, and will do anything rather than sit in stopped or slow freeway traffic, When confronted with it I exit at the first ramp, go shop, eat, or drive miles on parallel surface streets until I can see that the roadway is clear. In as much as I enjoy driving, I will not waste precious moments of life sitting behind the wheel feeling like I am going nowhere fast.

We love the freedom our cars give us. Independence and the auto go hand in hand, but not without a price. Our precious love affair with the car has created a society that is dependent upon commuting. The by-product is isolation. We spend hours of our lives every day as single drivers, virtually locked on concrete sea-ways, separated by steel and glass from people we do not know. We are all engaged in a self-perpetuating cycle that consumes the benefits of our hard-earned independence. God bless those that must commute. I have tremendous empathy for my fellow humans who do. Some enjoy it. For myself, there is no amount of money that could entice me to commute on a daily basis. Yet, I include my own view not as a judgment but as encouragement and support for those who are ready to throw in the towel and give up commuting in exchange for a less stressful experience.

There is a plethora of ideas available for new development that we can support to make clean and efficient changes in the way we commute and live. Alternate mass transportation could bring the evolution of efficient, fast trains, monorails, or moving sidewalks within a community. They could have seating or cafeterias that move through green parkways that feed the soul as one enjoys traveling to work. Creative developments in transportation would bring great ease and light to our commuting culture. Progress in these areas would increase production and creativity as it provides upliftment to our world, Instead of sitting isolated in polluting cars, we would have time to meditate, converse, eat, or think creatively about our day and lives. Those who develop successful alternative transportation and energy will prosper well beyond current levels.

Recently the county of Los Angeles implemented a number of light-rail trains. One new line runs on rails above the center of a freeway. Not a new idea, but a beginning. It traverses from downtown Los Angeles but stops one mile short of and to the side of LAX International Airport. The motorized private coach, bus and taxi unions lobbied to block it from coming directly into the terminal where it would have been the greatest use to the most people. Consequently, its use is limited to the residents of South Central L.A. Need I say more? Not to judge the unions, They only reflect the consciousness of a nation whose members are not read to act for the greater efficiency and good of the whole of the people and planet.

Each of us can act as individuals and have an effect by the choices we make. The products we purchase, use and discard are a big part of the problem. We can choose to seek out health food and support the growing of organic. Demand creates supply. Price is affected by supply and demand. Awareness of the market's demands forces the growers, manufacturers, and distributors to make changes that meet the demands of the market-place. Our need for effective, clean, cheap energy and transportation currently is geared to what the public is willing to accept. As long as we put up with polluted air and burn fossil fuels at will, we will pay the price in depleted quality of life. Energy-efficient ideas, when demanded, will profit anyone who meets them.

"There is no defense against the excellence of an idea that fulfills the public need." John H. Johnson, Ebony Magazine.

Great wealth will be created for those who are daring enough to create alternate eco-sensitive ways of servicing our populace and meeting the needs of an expanding world. You and I must be the ones who demand change. When we do it with our purchasing power, by how we use it or do not, we send the most powerful message we can to those who have access to the technology and means to create better for all.

In order to support the new, we must we willing to let go of the old. Getting around in a high-powered, fuel injected batmobile may have served us in the past, but it will leave our descendants a contaminated world unable to grow food if we continue to deplete the ozone layers of the earth. As more and more radiation seeps into the atmosphere, the process of photosynthesis diminishes. A doomsday crash-and-burn scenario that makes great movies is not the destiny man and woman were designed to create. We must make choices and demands today in order to preserve our heritage, the paradise of heaven on earth, before it is too late, and if we are to bring it to fruition. I can see it and feel it, so I know that we are to live it in our time.

"Man was free in nature. Now he is in chains.
I want to know what has happened."
Jean Jacques Rousseau,
Eighteenth century, French Philosopher

Samantha

Samantha made her first trip to Sedona, Arizona as a tourist. Accompanied by a couple of girlfriends she visited me shortly after I moved there. Little did she know that her dream of a lifetime would unfold before her. Over the course of a weekend's visit around the town, she was captured by the scent and sights of pine and the dramatic, towering red rocks, set against the so-very-blue Arizona skies. By the end of the weekend, she announced that she had found her true home, the one she had been seeking all of her life. I was not surprised. It is not unusual for strangers to come to Sedona and to fall in love with it.

Sedona is a place that calls to the soul. Everyone who visits is captivated by the majesty of the terrain. The powerful energy of the earth's electromagnetic vortices that are located there cause one to feel a deep connection with the land. The presence of God is so apparent that a sense of harmony and well being prevails among the populace. So strong is the feeling, that even those who doubt the power of the vortices, agree that there is something very special here. Samantha, being a spiritual healer, quickly melded into a state of euphoric bliss. However, she could not imagine how it could be possible for her to live there and make it financially. I advised her not to worry, that once she made the decision and took action towards it, everything would fall into place for her to be supported.

Many people in the world today are struggling to maintain circumstances that they detest. Samantha was one of them. In Los Angeles, she was caught up in the daily grapple, contending with draining conditions at a job just to survive and pay bills. Although she is gifted healer who is always helping others to experience major breakthroughs with challenging personal issues, she had allergies and was unhappy being in L.A.. Her car was repeatedly being broken into, and she felt completely out of place in the city. So when Sedona came into her life, she was thrilled at the prospect of beginning anew.

During the next eight months she thought about Sedona everyday and the way it made her feel. She became depressed with inner conflict, trying to save enough money to move, and working at an office job she detested. She had become gradually more ill with allergies and she had cut back on her healing work. Nothing had improved by waiting. Indeed, everything having to do with the old condition had worsened. She wondered if she might have lingered too long in L.A..

Knowing a return visit would rekindle Samantha's love affair with Sedona, I encouraged her to return. Within three days of her arrival, the allergies subsided, she committed to cut back on cigarettes, took action in seeking employment, and felt renewed and confirmed that indeed she must move. I encouraged her to do it as soon as possible.

Samantha returned to California and began to pack and make ready for the move by throwing out, giving away, and selling anything that was excess baggage. It was as if a new love had taken her heart. When we talked on the phone, she would tell me that she could hardly wait to come, but was still terrified that she would not be able to make a living in small town Sedona. I advised her to let go of the painful struggle and to trust that everything would just work out.

Eventually, Samantha did move to Sedona. When she did, she found what she considered to be the perfect job right off the bat. Its salary was one of the higher paying, but few corporate positions in Sedona. Quickly, she found out that the office scene no longer fit her dream of what she though perfect life would be. Disappointed and disillusioned she resigned. Next she tried a number of hourly, retail positions. Her allergies came back, along with an increase in smoking, and she became desperate about her lack of money.

We take our consciousness with us wherever we go. There is no escaping our problems, our fears. It is the same with our talents and gifts. Whatever is within us, must find a way to express. Sedona with all of its majesty and powerful energy, amplifies whatever it's visitors bring with them, especially the things they need to clear or to work on.

It was several months before Samantha began to settle into getting oriented and in making the kind of life changes that living in a small town bring. When she did, she found peace, support and security. To reach that place she had to leave behind her fears and doubts and her Los Angeles expectations. It was time to surrender to total trust. In doing so, she began to see how the universe supported her when she finally surrendered to seeking her own bliss. It would not be the corporate version that many of have been taught to seek, depend upon and revere. Eventually she began to travel and returned to serving a devoted and expanding list of people who required and appreciated her extraordinary healing gifts and abilities. In doing so she found balance and sustenance that allowed her to live where she wanted and the cash she required to make it all happen.

Our society teaches that to generate money and that to acquire the things it buys will bring ultimate satisfaction. Money can create options and provide financial security. However, we know that having a lot of money does not necessarily bring satisfaction. We all require it and deserve to have enough to flourish. To have an abundance of it creates pathways for flow and movement in our experience. Still, there are many on higher paths of spirituality who miss the mark when it comes to understanding the principles of basic supply. Those who make money an all important goal, and "just want the money" are making it a false god in the material plane part of our existence. What we seek with desperation, eludes us at every *need* and opportunity.

When we seek instead to create and share our ample supply of all good including money, we maintain sustenance and establish a relationship with infinite supply. That is why I encourage us to engage in consistent tithing. It creates balance and takes the pressure from the earthly version of an everyday struggle to just get by. As it releases anxiety, it creates consistent flow and gives breath to creation and it supports us doing what we love.

To be in love with something, someone or an idea and not to act on it is to ignore the gift that God is sending you.

Often we fail to see the potential of empowerment that is held for us in times of change. But when in the middle of it we may not even notice that change is happening until it's past. We may desire to transform our lives or the way we live, but no one left us a road map of how we might begin it. Since each of us is a unique part of God, how could one plan fit all? How do we surrender the old struggle and give in to living our bliss? How could it be possible to follow a dream or become self-employed if we are living in fear? As long as we are in fear we will not find bliss.

In order to live our bliss, it is essential to shift our vibration to loving something that we can be enthusiastic about. It is said that we are either in fear or in love. Both create an energy that determines what we draw to us. We have the power to choose and must choose love if we are to change our personal destiny and that of the way of the world.

Love is the one force in all of the universe that contains all the elements for reaching its object of desire within its own passion and fulfillment. When we surrender to the love of Spirit within, we automatically come into the energy of love. **Be in love with your desire and it will brings everything you require bring it to fruition.** When love for that desire is expressed in feeling and vision and combined with surrender to Spirit, we become free and supported in seeking our bliss.

Surrender Struggle in Reaching Your Desire. The Power of Release and non-attachment to outcome is the magic key to manifestation.

There is a difference between living with feelings of wanting to let go of maintaining something that causes pain, and a struggle to moving in a mindful direction towards something new. Getting from the point of A = struggle, to the point of B = Bliss is the goal. But for one who is working to make ends meet and going nowhere fast just to keep food on the table, it may seem like an overwhelming or impossible task. Many caught in the work-a-day lifestyle, long to be free. But how does one deal with giving up driving the fifty-thousand-dollar BMW or what one's friends will think when they leave the rat-race and it's perks behind? Or for someone who simply cannot take another day of a high-pressure, big-salary career when all they really desire to do is garden? They feel trapped. They love their family and want to be good providers but the job is what they know. After-all they have spent a life-time doing it. Now they deeply yearn for the freedom they have never felt. The freedom to just be, or to enjoy doing something they dream of.

Our world teaches us that to be responsible and to make a living is the highest of duties we can perform. Capitalism, designed to self-perpetuate, insures that there are always more buyers for its products. It creates a never-ending need for more jobs to feed ever more families. As an outgrowth of religion and feudalism, it guarantees that the production of housing, food, goods and services will always hold the center stage of economic focus. An ever-increasing populace seems to ignore a balance with ecology and its growth.

Unfortunately the greatest root sustenance available to humanity is put into a back seat position - the need for a healthy relationship with God. When we give our spirituality first priority, all else will fall into place. It enables us to pursue our livelihoods in a balance with the nature of our individual soul's needs and talents. Some have found it, still many others are locked in struggle. I have been there myself.

At one time, I dreaded going to another construction jobsite only to breathe toxic paint fumes and come home at night exhausted. I was rushing from one job to the next just to collect the checks only to pay it all out in order to keep up interest payments on credit cards. For a long time it felt as though there was no way out. Eventually I found it. In my quest for freedom it became necessary for me to release many investments and possessions or I might never have written and published *"No Boundaries, Let Go of Limits and Create Success."* I related the stories in it and here knowing we all have challenge. Each of us is given what we can handle in order to progress spiritually, and on karmic levels as well. It may not be necessary to release the things I did for one to achieve freedom. Each of our soul's higher knowing can determine what is best to let go of. It may just be an old way of thinking or old habits that are unhealthy. Go within and ask. Continue until you reach knowing of what is personally right for you.

There is within each of us all that is needed at any time to deal with any situation. It is the personalized Divine Knowing of God, and it is available to us at all times. When you surrender to It and ask for help, answers will come. You may require assistance in your own situation or you may know someone who requires it. Do not be afraid to ask for help or to offer it. Asking is inviting the Infinite to expand your faith as you practice it. By offering to assist others you may be an angel to a friend in need. They may be too proud or ashamed to accept help or to share details as I was for a long time. Use wisdom, empathy, tact, and compassion as you offer to reach through the barriers of pain, humiliation, and isolation that carrying a burden includes.

Let Go and Let God.

There is always a way to have our needs met. Finding it requires focus, faith and trust in Spirit and yourself. You can do what you set your heart and mind's eye to accomplish. It may take time. Try not to be hard on yourself. The stress I carried and suffered for over five years is not worth it. **In surrendering struggle, we find joy.** Whatever effort is required to learn to live and love life in new ways is worth it. In surrendering the old painful, toxic work I began to write, and I discovered many gifts. Sometimes, my editor would send the same work back to me two or three times, and I would rewrite it until I got it right. It was a form of struggle. But this time it was different, I was learning something new....a career of service that I would utilize. I knew it would prosper me in ways I could not begin to imagine. I was ready for the journey, so looking at this budding virgin work through new eyes gave me the perspective, challenge and motivation to see beyond my old archetype of struggle. This road had a goal of serving humanity. It was a higher path for me that took advantage of my talents and abilities and was built upon everything that I had already achieved.

Learning to operate a computer was no picnic. Many times, I became so exasperated that I wanted to throw the blessed high-tech little instrument out of the window! Fortunately because of its cost, I did not. Eventually, I arrived where I had set out to go. Finishing and publishing a book for the first time was one of the toughest challenges for a novice writer that I can think of. I am not blessed with natural technical abilities nor a fondness for computers. Many friends would tell me how I would come to love it as I mastered it. NOT SO. To this day, the idea of learning another program is as enticing as disassembling the engine of my car and putting it back together again. So, I had to remain focused and committed to the finished product no matter how tired or how many times I had to redo it. However, the reward of completion and the process of learning to write was a rich experience that enhanced my life infinitely. By the way, the next time around was ten times easier!

You, too, can bring your desires to life and accomplish your dreams. It is absolutely essential for us to let go of struggle and move into acceptance of ease as the natural order of the universe.

You and I breathe effortlessly. The grass just grows. When we focus our energies into joy, with love for what we seek, put our interest and enthusiasm on what we desire, we will see that the magnificence of God within ourselves out-pictures in success.

Learning to accept ease is the name of the game.

Know this truth: Despite any appearance otherwise, the truth is that you are a Divine Emanation of God, individualized, with a mission and purpose. It is to discover yourself, and to let the Creator reveal itself within your own experience as you do the things you love in life. "He maketh Me to walk in green pastures and lie by still waters."
As we refine our path, we will still meet challenges and there will be effort involved, but the way will be illuminated ahead when you surrender to the higher will of God within by detaching from anything that feels like struggle. Samantha could not come to her dream until she was willing to release struggling to support the old idea. Being in Los Angeles no longer suited her, so there was great effort in trying to maintain it. When she finally came to Sedona, to live, and let go of her need to make it be like Los Angeles, all things fell into place almost effortlessly. Her dream was waiting to unfold....so is yours and mine.

We must breathe into our dreams and trust that there is something greater within them that will help us break through to the other side. As you release yourself from the effort of struggle and realize the freedom to be your God/self you will do what you came here to do.

Speak Your Word To Create Ease

I am one with the magnificent power of the lightness of God. Pure Spirit is Ease. I am one with pure spirit. That power within me has all the knowing to create ease within my life. I accept a Divine Awakening within myself to propel me into the arms of ease.

I freely and willingly agree with my higher self to release all the things that cause me pain or struggle. From this moment forward I surrender to Spirit the idea of struggle. In exchange I accept the atmosphere and attitude of ease. I invite the idea and feeling of ease into my life, as it comes from God, it comes to me. I agree to embody as much ease into every area of my life that comes to me. I accept it in work, in play, home and relationships. I am ease because I am one with Spirit. It knows what brings me ease and peace of mind. I accept my life path corrected and flowing in ease right here and right now.

Thank you God. I am one with ease, peace and prosperity. I enjoy all of the health and abundance of living I was designed to live. God is my source of ease. And so it is!

CHAPTER EIGHTEEN

The Limo Of Life

A preacher dies and finally realizes his life-long dream of going to heaven. When he arrives at the pearly gates, he sees that a New York cab driver has a more elevated place and rank in the hierarchy. He says to Saint Peter, "I don't get it. I devoted my entire life to prayer and to my congregation." Saint Peter says, "We reward results here. Did your congregation always pay attention when you gave a sermon?" The preacher looking perplexed replies, "Once in awhile someone would fall asleep." "Well," Saint Peter answers, "when people rode in this guy's taxi, they not only stayed awake, they prayed fervently!"

Oh, the joys of New York taxis. I will never forget those wild, terrorizing rides across Manhattan that are forever ingrained in my memory. One does not truly begin to experience the whole thrill of New York until one abandons all caution and steps to the curb to hail a cab. Just getting one to stop can be risky business. However, being catapulted over pot holes on the West End Highway and running every red light at sixty miles an hour on surface streets, at midnight is truly unforgettable - especially when at the mercy of a driver who speaks some strange dialect unknown to the Western world. To survive the ride without getting one's sacroiliac thrown out, it becomes completely necessary to ride in a state of complete detached abandon. I finally stopped pressing my foot to the floor at every approaching light and turn, let go and trusted that the driver knew what he was doing. I relaxed and became as non-attached as I could from how he chose to do his job. After all, it was his cab.

Another time in Las Vegas, I shared a cab with a lovely, young stranger. We enjoyed a spirited and witty conversation. Curious if she was a visitor or not, I asked what line of work she was in. She sweetly and discreetly told me she was a prostitute. At the end of the ride, she suggested that I take her with me for the evening. After I declined, she offered me a freebie if I was so inclined! I contemplated the generosity and sincerity of her words for a moment and laughed, "No thanks, not today. Where were you, all of those lonely nights when I really needed you?" She perked up one last time and asked, "Why don't you give me your room number!" I again declined and I headed into my hotel. "What a town," I thought to myself.

The Limo

It was an unusually hot morning in Honolulu. I dropped off my rental jeep in Waikiki with the intention of taking a taxi to the airport. The rental car agent, wishing to accommodate me further, insisted that he call me a limo instead. Since he had a special arrangement with a friend, it would cost me the same as the cab. I was surprised when a worse for the wear, dated, slightly lopsided and rusted, but newly washed Cadillac limousine pulled up to the curb. An elderly, Chinese driver dressed like Elvis, all in white, jumped out and hobbled around to collect my luggage. Complete a with cigarette dangling from his lower lip, he casually invited me into the back. Refusing to allow me to help him lift the luggage into the trunk, he sauntered into the street and opened my door. As he reached for his door, the lips parted and the cigarette plopped almost artfully to the street. I was immediately relieved. I was getting nervous about asking him to put it out, especially in respect for his age and obvious pride in his service.

As we started to roll, I stretched out my legs in the rear and began to take in the interior of the car. It was a maroon, crushed velvet, spacious lounge that matched his act perfectly. I chuckled to myself about the in-coach TV, and miles of plastic walnut wood- grained panels. A simple bud vase mounted on one side, complete with faded, but neatly arranged, plastic flowers, added the touch that showed me that he really was doing his best to provide a quality experience. We began to glide along. I reached for the switch to open the sun roof and quickly found that it was in-operable. Next, I tried electric windows. No matter how many buttons I pushed, nothing worked. I felt perspiration form on my brow and the beginnings of claustrophobia as I realized that the air-conditioning was not adequate to combat the high-noon, Hawaiian sun. I had just spent two weeks in bliss, breathing sweet tropical air and reveling in the joy of the trade winds, gently caressing my body and spirit while driving in my open jeep.

When I asked how I might open the windows or the sun roof, he assured me in Hawaiian Pidgin, (a colloquial slang) that the air-conditioning was mo betta (even though it smelled strongly of regurgitated cigarette smoke married with a strong scent of some obnoxious artificial air freshener). By now, I guessed that the aging limo's windows had ceased to work sometime ago. Rather than panic or complain further, I knew in that moment that here was the foundation for a story. I settled back and decided to accept a non-attached and relaxed attitude and enjoy the ride despite the heat.

In our constructed environments, we exchange the pure effects of the natural world for so-called convenience and comfort. Just like our friend, Bill, so many of us wear the corporate suit and work in closed spaces with all the unnatural confinement that is considered to be natural or a symbol of status in the corporate world. Whether we like it or not, it goes with the territory.

The Pope was flying to New York to give a speech to the United Nations. His entourage had arrived earlier to handle the details of his visit. The press was alerted and a special area was cordoned off. The arrangements were all set. Bad weather forced the Pontiff's plane to land in Greenland and to lay over for several hours. On the way to New York, there was another mechanical delay. The flight was forced to return to Greenland for repairs. By the time the Pope's plane landed on the ground in New York, it was five thirty a.m.. His entourage, tired from their long journey, abandoned the wait and went on to the hotel. The press gave up around three o'clock a.m. when they heard that the arrival time was yet undetermined.

The Pontiff arrived at the airport and found no press, no entourage, no reception or apparent escort to town. By now he had less than an hour to get to the United Nations and deliver his scheduled sunrise speech. He was left with no choice but to hail a cab. He instructed the taxi driver to rush him to Manhattan. The driver did his best, but became stalled in the heavy, morning rush hour going into the city. The Pope, becoming exasperated with the situation, and under the gun to get to the UN, asked if he could drive. The frustrated driver, not knowing what else to do, got into the back seat as he exchanged places with the Pope.

As soon as the Pope got behind the wheel, he spied an opening in the stalled traffic. With a bulleted, little prayer and some nifty maneuvering, he got into an open lane and took off. He speeded along, dodging in and out like an Indy 500 driver on the last two laps of a race. When necessary, he took to the sidewalks to avoid getting stuck again. It was the trick that saved the day. As he pulled into Manhattan and neared the UN, a police patrol car spotted the reckless careening cab.

The cop, anxious to make a big score downtown, pulled them over, radioed headquarters, and hailed the Chief of Police. "Chief, you won't believe who I pulled over this time!", he reports. "You didn't stop another Senator, did you?", the Chief asks. "No Sir! This is someone bigger than that!" "I hope it's not the Mayor", the Chief exclaims. "That would mean really big trouble for us". "No Chief, this is someone far more important." The Chief

continues to ask by saying, "Was it the Governor?" "No bigger yet."
"Oh no, not the President." "No Sir, Chief, it's someone far bigger
than that," the officer replied. "Well, who could be more important
than the President?" the Chief asked. "Well, I don't know," the
officer replied, "but, he's got the Pope for a driver!"

There is a subtle difference between taking charge and
being controlling. Sometimes, it is only a fine line of discretion that
makes a distinction between one and the other, and it most
certainly will vary according to opinion. The Pope took charge and
reached his goal on time. Most of us who have taken cabs
frequently can relate to riding in the back and instructing the
driver to take a certain route, or asking him to speed up, etc..
When the meter is running and you know there is a quicker way,
it's just a matter of economics. One who is in the habit of being a
back seat driver definitely reflects a need to control. I have not
heard yet, "If you don't like the way I drive, Buddy, then you can
get out and take another cab." My trick is to offer them a
handsome tip if they can get me to my destination quickly. It
works every time.

The Uniform

I recently observed a group of businessmen in the Century
City area of L.A. walking towards a restaurant in the hot noonday
sun. Each was wearing a nearly identical, standard conforming
grey suit, with its conservative tie, and a starched white shirt. I
watched from the stoplight as they all donned their jackets before
entering a casual eatery. I thought to myself, "what is wrong with
this picture?" I though that lunch was supposed to be a nourishing
and relaxing break from the stress of the workday. Why not leave
the suit coat at the office, loosen or remove the tie altogether, and
prepare to relax and enjoy the meal. Jackets may be mandated in
the workplace, but not by most restaurants these days, especially
in causal, sunny Southern California.

**We are victims of habit, conditioned to conform and
maintain the status quo of convention and so-called
convenience. Do we dare break free and detach from the
habits and ways of the world, no matter how uncomfortable
the seemingly, safe structures feel?**

Choose A New Suit.

I have worn many suits in the past, but when all but one burned along with most of my earthly treasures, I knew that it would be enough to serve me. The Italian suits, various sport coats, and an array of ties went out in a blaze of flaming glory. When they did, I figured it must be time to quit wearing them. I had already turned in my keys to the Hollywood Church of Religious Science to my mentor, teacher and boss, Dr. Robert Bitzer. I needed them when I presided for him at Sunday service and taught classes for him during the week.

Dr. Bitzer, in his ninety-eighth year, was sharp as a tack. As the last living contact to the legendary Earnest Holmes, founder of the Science of Mind, he was well-known for his mastery as the teacher's teacher. I had the privilege of working beside him. I would sit in his office and read to him. Often he would ask me to treat or pray with him. One Sunday morning as I headed for the green room, Mrs. Bitzer grabbed my arm and pointed to a microphone standing on the side of the platform. She wanted me to walk out to the podium ahead of Doctor so that he would not trip on its cord. His eyes were not as sharp as his wit and knowledge. When I mentioned it to Dr. Bitzer, he quickly replied; "If I let you walk in front of me, I'd have to pick you up when you fell!"

Dr. Bitzer and I shared many laughs and some secrets. He was a great teacher and mentor I fondly miss. Many felt he was too rigid in his methods of management. He was too dignified to hug, but always quick to smile with a sparkle in his eyes and shake any extended hand with enthusiasm. He ruled his organization with an iron hand, but taught thousands how to use the Law of Mind to create in successful manifestation. It was right for me to leave when I did, because I preferred a more casual approach and did not feel comfortable wearing the suit and tie.

Dr. Bitzer left this world in his ninety-eighth year. His rightful air to the podium, Dr. Domenick Polifrone, continues to revamp the church experience making it more and more contemporary. The style has evolved from a rigid service to one that addresses today's more casual audience, but the clarity and foundation of the teaching that Dr.s' Bitzer and Holmes established, remains.

The old style church may be on its way out. People today require a user-friendly contemporary experience. They want to be related to at their own level and require fresh, interesting approaches that cater to today's less-traditional family and world. When I presented a seminar at a church in the Midwest, a participant came to me afterwards and complemented me by saying; "You talk with us. Our pastor talks down to us and at us!"

This tells me that if churches plan to serve and survive in the third millennium they must address the people's needs today. More and more people are turned off to the idea of a God outside of themselves. They have had enough of a demanding patriarch based in judgment. Every soul at it's root knowing is aware that God is love.

Media Alert: a business suit and tie and tight protocol are no longer prerequisites for success! A regular, corporate salary and structured environment is not required to live well. An organization that causes undue stress or that fails to recognize and reward personal ability is counter-productive to the basic spirit of human nature.

I once dreamt of producing a screenplay based on making spoof of the conformity involved in the corporate struggle. I starred the outrageous Bette Midler as an office trainee doing her best to be cool with an entry level position. Hired and slated to be groomed for executive training, her quest would be to overcome the bland and banal by being bold enough to be daring in her actions, and dressing for power and by taking command of her position. In this corporate turn-around, only the gutsy, generous and most vivacious would be rewarded with raises and promotions. Of course, in true Bette Midler style, she would succeed as a corporate genius, out-doing others who were less daring in breaking the dress codes and making decisions of their own accord in order to climb the ladder of success.

Howard Stern does the same thing in his own way. I do not care personally for many of the things he says or the way he says them. He has a propensity to be disgusting, negative and degrading. He absolutely pushes our buttons and becomes repulsive and obnoxious to us. However, he has bright moments of illumination and does get his message across. America is a very uptight society. We need to laugh, let go and let Spirit flow through us in whatever way She manifests her insight. If we were free enough to slap each other on the back and openly congratulate our peers for achievement, and be bold enough to spit (metaphorically) in the boss's eye when he gives us a bum rap without fear of losing our livelihoods, the business climate would be a whole lot more robust for all involved.

We need to bring joy and humor into our daily experience. The Howard Sterns, Madonnas, Bette Midlers and other energy busters of our world are trying to tell us

something. They use shock to hit us right between the eyes
with what we need to hear in order to wake us up. They do
for us what we cannot, or will not do for ourselves. That is
why we pay them as well as we do!

Speak Your Word to Be Free

I am that I am, One with the One. There is no separation
between me and God. I am so comfortable with who I am that I
choose to celebrate myself. I choose to embody that part of myself
that loves to be and express individuality. I am me and love who
I am. Nothing in the world can disturb or disrupt the continuity of
who I am. Thank God. And So It Is.

CHAPTER NINETEEN

Environment Earth

In our galaxy is a very special place called planet earth. Compared to it's nearby and barren neighbors the "Blue Planet" is a veritable paradise. For billions of years, Mother Earth existed as she was designed to be: a garden of pristine perfection. Her purpose fulfilled itself providing a home for many species of life: plant, animal and humanity in a beautiful and bountiful natural environment. For all that time, a perfect harmony of air, water, plant, rock, animal and man co-existed in a system of natural symphony unmatched in all of the Universe. Sky, sea and soil were pure and rich with oxygen. Rich, healthy nourishment provided an atmosphere that supported great, natural abundance for all life. A perfectly balanced ecology supported ample and opulent foliage to replenish rich air and to regenerate the cells of life in sustaining her planet's people. Life was simple. Mother Earth provided, humankind took care of the land and lived in respect upon her soil. Mother Earth received the reverence she required to sustain and support a healthy family.

Over a not-so-long period of time, about one hundred years, the people living on the surface began to discover their own ability to create machinery. They developed every kind of machine to make life easier, to travel great distances quickly, and ways to feed enormous groups of people. They marveled at their own genius of conquering over nature. In their quest for speed and efficiency, they became obsessed with profits.

Great fortunes were made. The wealth continued to grow and evolve until several huge corporations eventually dominated the world economy. In their rush to create greater and greater profits, the geniuses of finance disregarded the wonders and sustainability of their natural home. In pursuit of their ambitious and marvelous quest to develop technology, they took for granted her beauty and abundance of self-replenishing clean air, water, and mineral-rich soil. Assuming it would provide them forever, they disregarded the wisdom and the warnings predicted by ecological visionaries of the depletion of clean air and pollution and abundant resources. They continued to dump undesirable wastes into the oceans and into holes in the ground, and left the by-products of fuels to spill into the water and air. With an insatiable fervor to create a higher standard of living and promote economic profits to the far reaches of the globe, they ignored basic sound, logical warnings of an impending damage to their sensitive environment.

The peoples and the governments of this world denied the validity of the warning signs as the weather began to change, growing increasingly more violent and extreme from year to year. The majority of the populace, who daily ingested carcinogens from their food, came to accept the resulting diseases as part of the natural course of life. Over the course of time, they became increasingly more dependent upon science and medicine as the universal panacea for everything.

The paradise, designed to support and nurture beautifully designed God-beings of intricate tissue, fluid, mind and spirit, was slowly becoming a wasted land. As the decades peeled away, signs and warnings were ignored. Forests were stripped, earth, water, and air became more polluted and gradually more toxic. Until seemingly overnight, basic survival became a daily the number-one-concern priority for all.

These innovative and industrious people had created opulence beyond what any royalty could ever have dreamed possible. The ordinary citizen enjoyed unlimited freedoms and could acquire most every luxury and convenience, including personal transportation, in any style or color they so chose. These accouterment of comfort were made available to all. During the late twentieth century, the object of life in the most prosperous country of the world had become geared to the creation and perpetuation and production of goods and services. Commerce, advertisement, and consumerism prevailed as King. The boulevards were lined with billboards, signs and the majority of commercial stores were geared to selling luxury items. The shopping mall occupied center stage in the culture, enjoying the best and most convenient locations to woo and capture the consumer in clever and stylish come-ons. The media entered private homes with commercial advertisement every few minutes, promoting purchase and use of products as the ultimate fulfillment of life.

The populace was obligated to work every day, forty hours a week or more, in order to meet the demands of the consuming system. Just to keep up with rising costs of housing, transportation and food, they worked longer and harder, oftentimes abandoning an education for themselves and time with their children in order to purchase more luxury items. Members of the tribe who could not keep up or were too old to produce and pay the high cost of goods were forced to live on the streets. Because of their plight, they were denied normal health care and a basic human foundation of integrity that shelter, food and expression provide. The opulent society that cared not had banished them to the streets and alleyways and blamed the impoverished for surrendering to hopelessness. Children began to carry weapons, not understanding the basic reverence for life that even the simplest of social structures hold in esteem. This self-centered world who thought itself to be supreme and evolved was of a most primitive nature and functioned at that level.

The nation that promoted, produced and sold its way of life to the rest of the world for profit was directly or indirectly responsible for much of the pollution of the previously pristine environment. The people and government that could create tremendous opulence for the general populace, had the power and ability to change it's ways. Technology was available to create alternative natural, non-polluting products. They had the ability to make wise decisions when it came to the management of resources, but chose instead to increase short-term profitability. What it could not produce cleanly or cheaply at home, it sent other nations to absorb and market. This nation had tremendous natural resources and the ability to transform them into goods. It was able to produce great quantities of food for the entire planet. Yet it surged blindly forward in its own unending quest to increase gross national product as it's chief national goal.

Giant corporations, demi-gods of the economy, continued to introduce new models and styles of personal transportation with innovative gimmicks re-designed annually - each claiming to be better than the competition; when in reality the original concept had not changed. It was still an attractive arrangement of steel, vinyl and glass that rode on four rubber tires, and was propelled by an internal combustion engine that degenerated the atmosphere. It had only gotten slicker, sharper, more aerodynamic and luxurious. The American auto was built to decline as it aged. The theory of diminishing return kept consumers buying new products designed to require replacement every few years, thus insuring production and dependency on future sales of goods and services. This system kept those purchasing the products in constant debt, perpetuating the cycle of work, purchase, debt, more work, ad finitum....and it forced them to breathe polluted air. This *great society* with so much creative energy and great resource refused to look at its polluting ways and to it's future and so set itself up for its own decay and decline.

Is this the history our culture is creating? Is this the legacy we will inherit in our own lifetime? Does it matter that even if we do not see it, our children's children will? Do we have a choice? Can

we can make conscious decisions in our every-day experiences that
have an effect in making a difference?

Much is about education. We can affect and clean up our
future now by starting at home by being conscious of the products
we buy and seriously looking at whether we need them or not. How
many times do we hear the question: plastic or paper? Why either
one? When we go to the store for a loaf of bread, what does the
checker automatically put it in? A plastic bag. Guess what it is
already in! How many plastic bags do we bury in the land daily?
All require oil production and the resulting pollution to produce.
I decided that in 1992, I would refuse both. In every store canvas
bags are offered. I purchased several and keep them in my car and
under the kitchen sink. They are easy to acquire and to keep in the
car and carry into the store with you. What about plastic
disposable diapers, the number one landfill cast-off in America
today? These must be made biodegradable.

We can choose not to purchase the product that is
polluting or wrapped in the offending containers. Let the
manufactures know you will not be buying it until it conforms.
Educate friends, family and strangers. When it came time to
consider getting a new vehicle I chose to re-upholster my seats, get
the car detailed, the carpets shampooed and the paint buffed and
touched up, in lieu of purchasing a new one for thirty-five
thousand dollars plus four years of interest. It was a whole lot
cheaper. The car sill ran like new anyway. I would buy one later.

Our cities and resorts, like Waikiki in Honolulu, Hawaii,
are where hundreds of high-rise, mini-cities are throwing away
hundreds of thousands of plastic cups, paper napkins and products
daily. Multiply that by millions of visitors annually. Tourist
industries flourish, where every attention to detail is taken care of
- from the luxury of a special chocolate on the pillow at bedtime, to
a maid-turned down bed, all at the average price of two hundred-
fifty dollars a day but they cannot seem to support the cost of a
recycling plant. I am told that the island county of Oahu tried to
implement curb-side recycling but it lost money so they canceled
the program. The cost of shipping is greater than the profit it
would create to carry out the recycle process, since all the recycle
plants for re-production are on the mainland. Therefore, all of the
garbage on Oahu goes into land-fill, polluting one of the last
pristine inhabited islands of significant population on the earth. I
am told that many of the exotic, beautiful fish have left the shores
of Oahu. Some days when the trade winds are down, one can
observe smog over Honolulu. A community which voted down light
mono-rail, clean transportation, builds and widens more roads and

crams more housing onto the already small island in search of ways to pull profit from the land.

When will we learn? It is not too late to re-establish the garden paradise that earth was designed to be. We can begin to change our priorities in the way in which we design and arrange our communities, and how we choose to live our lives. We spend most of our time getting to jobs to buy the things that make us feel more secure, comfortable or luxurious. Yet it is the production and marketing of these goods that pollutes our earth and our children's minds, while it trains them to be consumers. Would we even dare consider having only the number of children we can house and educate? Why not make planned parenthood be based on that criteria and enforced with sterilization if need be. We live in a cycle of quest, designed to keep us purchasing in order to acquire and maintain a higher and higher standard of living.

Making the interest payments on newer and better, feeds and self-perpetuates the capitalistic machinery that employs our growing population. It is how the system works. I believe it is a fundamentally good democracy, however until we make significant changes in the ways we go about it, we will be condemned to sitting in traffic as the years of our lives roll by. Years that we could be investing in more satisfying ways of enjoying our lives are spent feeding the machine. What was designed to self sustain support for the many, has evolved into a vicious cycle that keeps them in allure of buying more, engaged in working to maintain it, and enslaved by debt to it. Sustenance and luxury is good, it feeds the body and soul, however over-excess at the cost of the environment is not.

Why not work fewer hours, spend less, be free of the struggle of debt, and have time to be with the people and experiences we enjoy? It can be done. I did it. Not by conscious choice, but because I had no choice. I suddenly came to the realization that after twenty-two years in Los Angeles of going top speed, it was time to seek greener and simpler pastures. I asked Spirit for knowing and to be led to my rightful new home where I could do my perfect work serving God. I wanted to be able to paint, create, write, breathe clean air, drink clean water, and live surrounded by beautiful clean nature. I followed the urge, not knowing how, or even if I would do it. Whether I will stay there or where it will lead next, I do not know, but only that I will not go back to my former life.

Our Culture pays dearly in loss of peace of mind and well being in our effort to maintain what we know we do

not want. Be brave, God is on your side. Out of a new sense of freedom, you can create something new that may serve you and your world in joy. A self-given gift of freedom brings the birth of great wealth in terms of enjoyment of life and often-financial freedom as well. It is a choice to exchange a time clock for ownership of one's own time. Should you desire it, I support you in making that choice. Know that Spirit within you has infinite ways to open new doors, that may or may not be attached to a corporate check. If you are happy with the security and structure then these words may not be for you. If not, what are you waiting for? Thirty, Forty? Fifty? Sixty? It is never too late to change.

Speak Your Word To Release Struggle

There is One Presence, One Infinite Knowingness. It is the all-present Mind of Spirit. I accept my connection to perfect knowing within. God resides within me and my experience. Right here, and right now, I accept that I am moved in all my ways to release any sense of bondage to struggle.

I know that God knows the ways and means for me to be free. I accept Divine Timing, Divine Purpose revealed and Trust the Infinite to provide and to give me guidance when I require it. I am supported in change for the better. That which holds me down, I let go of. I sail to new heights in consciousness. My awareness expands as I move into the new. I boldly go forward, knowing that God moves before me in every good way, lighting my path. I trust that there is always a way to accomplish my goals. I set my sights knowing that I arrive in the right place fully supported along the way. I step easily, carefully but willingly into the new. I give thanks for Divine energy impelling me forward to seek and meet my good. I am magnetized to it and it to me. Thank you, God, for the new awareness and responses in the world that are appropriate and right for me and my changes. Spirit in all, as all sees me home in the right direction. Thank you Spirit in me, and So It Is!

CHAPTER TWENTY

A New World

Change in our world is rapid now. Technological advance, change in governments, policies, politics, and cultural beliefs reflect the personal and global transformation of our time. Dramatic planetary climatic shift, economic restructuring, and new societal attitudes dominate the world news. These changes are the guideposts of initiation into the third millennium. Many of our ancient and beautiful time-honored traditions that nurture and support humanity in its cultural evolution will remain. They continue to provide nourishment for us throughout the changes. However, any philosophy that is opposed to a freeing, evolutionary change is stagnant will not survive. Archaic limits and lies that do not nurture or support a new idea of freedom and truth, fade in the light as truth is revealed in openness. All else shape-shifts to conform and create new form out of the old.

As the militaristic false ideal is de-structured and weapons are melted and turned into the plowshares of new technology, clean transportation and healthy food bring to life a new paradigm for all. Humanity's deep yearning to live a peaceful, harmonious, and prosperous existence finally becomes the primary goal and function of social interaction and governmental, decision making. We begin to restructure the world's economy with a higher priority of feeding all of its inhabitants, not just some. We seek new methods and ways of educating our children and of creating equality and sustenance for everyone. In doing so, each individual realizes an even greater awareness of wholeness and Oneness. When all members of the global tribe are provided for and their needs are met, enlightenment flourishes in the bright light cast by a planet of people in agreement. They celebrate their differences and uphold one another's right to free expression on a pristine earth.

The enlightened world knows on a deep cellular level that all of us are interconnected to one another. The whole tribe will not be free, prosperous, and fed until every one of its members are.

As a result of this shift, everybody is fed, housed and protected. The creative and talented are able to find outlets to utilize their gifts for the betterment of the whole. They become accepted, valued and honored members of their community. Their creativity is channeled to perfect man's products. Environmental awareness of our mother-planet is honored and taught to everyone. The fragile, intricate network of information that comes from living in harmony with nature is supported and interwoven into the daily lives of humankind. The mother garden, valued for the life sustenance she provides, is cared for and restored. Peace is maintained. Paradise Planet thrives balanced in a One-song, harmonic dance. It is choreography of nature and technology directed by a humanity who recognizes its own Divinity, power and responsibility to the whole in one another.

The basic respect for life, joy, ease, health, education and love are valued as the highest attributes a man or woman can give to their children and share with one another. To celebrate each moment as emanations of the Divine Creator is the first order of each day on heaven made manifest on earth. This is my vision I share with you. We can choose to live it now. In fact, we must choose to live it now, if we believe it can be. If each one of us chose to begin immediately to be committed to it and we acted as if it were so, then it would be. Overnight the news would read catapult and celebrate change; **"Life Is! People of Earth Celebrate God's Existence In All! Everyone Wins and Prospers As Environment is Cleaned Up! No More Starving Children!" The idea of a world where anyone goes to bed hungry or sleeps in the street would be a thing of the past.**

"Now clean your plate, dear. You have to eat because there are children starving in China." Everybody's Mother.

When humankind learns the laws of cause and effect and that our thoughts and words are creative, then mankind will cease to perpetuate war, pollution, and disease, and get down to enjoying the garden again. *The fall from the garden represents humanity accepting the belief that we are separate from God. The belief in the duality good and evil came out of feeling separate from God. The garden is here. We have the Divine Seed of Knowing and The ability to Create all within and bring it to full restoration. Until now, the spiritual wisdom and innate knowing has been masked and kept dormant by perpetuating old, limiting beliefs.*

As we awaken to the truth of our being: the creative power and love of the Divine Mother, Father, God is within us all, we create the return to the garden. It could happen in an instant if enough members of the tribe of humankind were to act it and embody it! As we accept it for ourselves, we automatically put it into action for the next, and the next, and on down the line.

Anyone who was born after nineteen forty-five, or was born of their children or their children's children, came from a time when a great shift in the character of life in America had begun to take place. Great numbers of babies labeled the baby boomer generation, came with a common mission. Although most were not conscious to the magnitude of it at the time, they shared a common knowingness, one that came from a deep cellular awareness, one that had little to do with genetics or locale. From all walks of life, children were born into a world that was to become ripe for change by the time they began to mature. This generation arrived wearing the rose-colored glasses of what life could be, and refused to accept its destiny through the blurred visions of the past.

The Mission

This single generation would have an impact upon the earth that was without precedent, one that would mark the awakening of a planet's people, and with it all the knowing and potential that had been asleep in the bounds of materiality for thousands of years. You and I came with a mission. Our parents are a part of it, as they prepared the way, knowingly or not. As a collective awareness for change, we transformed the way young people dressed, danced, wrote and performed music, forever. This generation took up a stand against injustice that differed all historic precedent. In the process, we let the world know that we would not kill in senseless war, would not dress to conform from nor accept the politics or religion of our ancestors just because it had always been. The author Ken Carey poetically tells of our awakening to this mission in his books; *The Starseed Generation and The Coming of the third Millennium*. I recommend reading these fantastic bibles of transformation.

I say this to we the children of the starseed generation and its descendants: We came to earth as children, starseed babies, with a purpose to make change. Out of an innate knowing, we created and celebrated music, the natural love and joy in our bodies, and the desire to make a better world, one that was based in love and openness. Our music contained the primary tones of change that activated and resonated a new life into our culture. It had a profound effect on the world, and continues to. Every piece of music written since, has been effected by it. That music contained the introductory and primary tones for the beginnings of planetary transformation. A generation that volunteered to come here to instill this universal awareness through our music as a primal vibration is now maturing. As we enter the new millennium, we will continue to see greater transformation, as we have in Berlin, South Africa, Eastern Europe, and all over the globe. The love of freedom, expansion of peace and the celebration of life is perpetuating itself like wild flowers on a mountainside in the springtime.

Since it is only the spring season of the new age, along the way we may forget the importance of our life's mission. Or we might think we that we have failed because it seems to have lost its significance in our lives. Involved in the daily tasks of making a living or raising a family, it is easy to get caught up in the spell of matter. Making decisions on how to make money, how to procure mortgages, or how to increase our wealth is time-consuming. Yet the mission continues because we also hold the larger picture in our cells. Remember, as Jesus said; "I am in the world, but not of it." He knew that he was a part of it, He had to eat, dress himself and carry on daily business. He also knew that for spirituality to be embodied on the earth, it has to be the initial foundation of the daily quest.

That is how heaven is restored to earth and that is how a starseed generation installs and vibrates its cellular knowing into an awakening world. It does so by continuing to live the love, peace and understanding that it was willing to sing and march for as a collective of youth.

"The earth has been turned and the soil planted. Now comes the watering and tending. And the face of God in each member of the tribe smiles upon the soil bringing the garden to full life." P.S.

The peoples of the earth have historically slumbered long in the bounds and limits of materiality. They failed to recognize that what they were looking for was already within them. Locked into the illusion of separation, they struggled with primitive thinking and ideals. Bound in shackles of limitation handed down from religious dogma and myth, they fought and killed one another to claim territory in order to rule over one another. Exchanging one dogma or dictator for another only shifted the balance of power every few hundred years until it would shift in another. Failing to realize that each of them was connected to the other on a deep level, they continued to fight. Now as we awaken to the awareness of our true nature, we will begin to take care of one another. Each connected to the other in Spirit, as Spirit, as a One people.

Our generations now have the choice before us to continue to perpetuate fear, pollution and greed, or to begin to live from love with a spirit of generosity and wisdom. We know what is right and wrong. We know what pollutes. We know who is hungry. We recognize injustice. We each have learned our lessons in the ways of the world and of its limits. Take time to listen to the inner guidance and find the wisdom that lies within to break through the barriers and untruths. **We must complete the mission.** Be One with me and commit to live in integrity and peace, and continue to awaken the sleeping giant.

What man seeks to find all his life is his true home in Spirit. When we came to this world, born into its materialistic illusions and we felt torn from our true home. We will only find it here when we surrender to that from which we came.

"If death is man enough, tell him to come to me. I will hold him in my arms dearly and tightly. I take from him eternal life. In exchange he can have my old discolored and faded robe of life. When I die, I go to eternal life." Molana Mohammed Tossi. Iranian Poet

Speak Your Word

I am one with Divine Empowerment. I am so secure in my oneness with Spirit and It in me that I dare to go with the flow. I let go of holding on to the past and its ways. I choose to be one with the higher mission of right now being in the now. God in me knows how to get me into alignment with the divine cosmic shift taking place in my world. I awaken to higher knowing and higher being. I become a lover of life and my world. The divine love of Spirit is my source for living and I acknowledge It in all I do. I accept the divine impetus and energy sparking me forward into action. I act as if heaven on earth were alive today, and I love it. I am a magnet and spark to all that is good. Thank God I am free of the past, and free to live, love and enjoy perfect health, wealth and joy in all I do. I invite greater good into my experience than I have ever known, and I share of it everywhere I go. My truth is this; I am an emissary of light, living in the light, as light. God is my source and I am free to be who I came here to be; healthy, wealthy, joyous and infinitely free! And So It Is.

CHAPTER TWENTY ONE

The Expanding Universe

The mysteries and puzzles of the Universe have intrigued humankind for all time. Sci-fi writers and movie makers tantalize and stimulate our imaginations with their exciting and innovative possibilities. Orson Welles terrified half of New York City with his 1930's live radio tale *War of the Worlds*. Daily, Scientists pose new questions, postulations, and formulation of theories as they attempt to find answers to the unknown. A well known opening line to the classic *Star Trek* television series announces that *Space is the final frontier*. Or is it?

Most of us are familiar with the doomsday scenarios predicted for mankind by Nostradamus in the sixteenth century. Psychic predictions and readings that are subject to interpretation may be helpful and intriguing, but reveal only possible futures we may choose for ourselves. Perhaps their underlying, true purpose is to help awaken us to make the choice to purge our own darkest fears. In choosing to rise to the light and make use of the deeper knowing of Spirit within, we override potential, negative creations. Carl Jung says that conflict exists simply as an opportunity for us to raise our consciousness. Jonathan Livingston Seagull suggests that we go beyond appearances and "look with our understanding,"

We each play an active role in the making of the future of our world. Spiritually, it is up to us to "choose the high watch," as Emma Curtis Hopkins states. Where you and I focus our attention will be reflected back to us directly in what is happening in our lives. In every moment, we can make the conscious choice to accept our Oneness with our Creator. By making our relationship with Spirit our number one priority in all we think, say and do, our Creative process will be in the flow of Divine alignment with all. The I Am in each one of us knows how to reveal the highest and best of Itself in all of us....and in the co-creation of the destiny of humanity.

The Universe, being a very orderly place, proves itself to be perfectly balanced and synchronized in every way. As our mother ship earth hurls through space, she maintains an intricate, ecosystem supporting a multitude of diverse life. Our bodies contain a microcosmic ecosystem of their own. Each is home to a self-perpetuating miniature, entire harmonic Universe within. Everything is working in accordance with all else.

In the not-so-distant past, any logic-based scientist would

have denied the existence of a God or of any kind of master plan. In the nineteen-fifties they would have told you that "Of course we do not believe in God, we are scientists." Today, most of any of them will tell you there absolutely must be a Divine scheme and a Master Creator. Clearly, a shift in awareness is happening.

Now humanity is awakening to the self-discovery of God within Itself vis-à-vis a union of metaphysics and science. We are seeing the effects of its beginnings of embodiment into the culture. As it comes into the full scope of our personal spirituality, it also springs to full life in our surrounding world.

This process and realization of self-completeness shoots through humankind like a bolt of lightning hitting a desolate desert landscape. The ensuing water of Spirit running through an awakening humanity is a rain of truth. This pure self-awareness coming into humanity is like a thunderstorm hitting a parched desert floor. Filling every crack, nurturing every dormant seed, the long-awaited flood of sweet Divine self-awareness washes away the pain of isolation, limitation, disease and fear. As mind and body unite with spirit awakening to its true nature so long denied, man is catapulted into the fantastic future he has dreamed of as the new millennium unfolds.

This One Truth, unrecognized and sequestered is buried deep in the private subconscious chambers of humankind, is our True Reality. You and I, the people of earth knowing we are as One with God, have the power to create change and to heal all of our world's ills and limits. Everything we need to do so is innate within our own beingness. With the realization of a Divinely expressed partnership with Something Greater, comes all we have ever sought and yearned for. **The human outward quest for *the* ultimate answers to life have been ironically hidden within the spiritual self.**

The Something Greater is the bigger part of who you and I truly are. The statement "God lives within us" would have shocked scientists and many theologians alike just a few years ago but now slowly coming to light as accepted truth. Until now we have lived as a mere shadow beneath that truth and light of our being. By denying our real and true nature, we have lived as sheep would, accepting and following a group's collective decisions; to be dominated by limited thinking. These controlling beliefs, instilled into the race consciousness of human beliefs, were designed by institutions of political and religious power. By dictating dogma, they insured a self-perpetuating control over their followers. This structured and limited belief created a feeling of powerlessness in our culture that is a direct result of feeling cut off from God. When separated from its source or parent, a child is guaranteed to flounder and accept what comes along. It will certainly grasp at straws and accept nearly anything in its search for home, especially if those around him are already in the program. Those who originated and evolved the program are long gone, but the legacy of this tribal or pack awareness has been handed down blindly over the ages by institutions and the mores of its perpetuators. Many who preach doctrine fall from grace because they themselves are unable to live within the strict limits they espouse.

A House Divided Is Unstable In All Of Its Ways.

When man feels separate from God, he lives in doubt, is a victim of fear and may be easily controlled. He is unable to identify with the opulence all around him in his natural world. Instead, he feels no choice but to believe in the false idea of scarcity that there is not enough good to go around. As a result he is jealous of his neighbors and feels he must suffer, steal, or make war in order to feel whole and be complete. He accepts the idea of dis-ease, that his body is subject to random outside virus' rather than accepting that health is natural. He does not know that his belief creates his experience and discounts the evidence that his body has all the natural mechanisms necessary for self-healing.

Who we really are lives at the center of our soul.
It awaits our discovery.

Everything mankind is seeking and lacking, we will never find outside of ourselves because it is not there. The empty space we are trying to fill with all the artificial substances, addictions, money, obsessions, and cravings can never be filled with the things we use, abuse and collect. We can never get enough of them to fill the empty space, because **nothing can or will ever replace the desire to be One with Spirit. It is at the center core of all of humankind. We came from a home base of Spirit so naturally the home we seek to find can only be found within as Spirit.**

Man has caved in to a belief in competition, another misnomer that perpetuates the falsehood that there is not enough to go around. He pollutes his earthly home in order to make his personal life more luxurious and for short-term profit, when he already has the ways and means to naturally and cleanly fulfill his needs and to correct any imbalance. He finds ways to vent his anger, stemming from the idea that he is insufficient or imperfect. He becomes violent and out of balance with his surroundings out of frustration, and demands punishment. His belief that he is separate from God has created a dependency and a worship-like relationship with drugs, therapies, and all the various treatments he has formulated to cope with them. From a belief in good and evil, he creates the necessity for self-imprisonment.

I use the vernacular word *man* because the lack of balance in our culture has been birthed and perpetuated from a foundation based on patriarch beliefs. A system that builds itself upon a basic premise that ignores the natural power of the feminine part in everyone and everything cannot survive without wielding a machismo-like dominant way of thought and function. It is what dominates family, government, economics, the balance of world power and the causation of all that is awry in the world. We act in competition with one another rather than in a symphony of creation that could be for the benefit of all because mankind has been out of balance with the feminine principle. The Goddess in all of us was repressed and ignored as the male libido took the lead and continued to dominate and control with wars and production.

Any quest to fill emptiness becomes worship of a false god, and breaks a daily basic Commandment and tenant of life: "Thou shall have no other Gods before me." When we shift our learned and limited perception of focusing on who we are not, i.e., beings of the dust, to an acceptance of ourselves as Divine off-spring with the characteristics of the Parent designed into us, we will consciously alter who we are. As we act and react with one another with Divine awareness, life on planet earth will shift to the paradigm of heaven on earth.

"A human being is a part of the whole, called by us the Universe, is limited in time and space. He experiences himself, his thoughts and feelings as something separated from the rest; a kind of optical delusion of his consciousness. This delusion is a prison, restricting us to our personal desires and to affection for a few persons close to us.

Our task must be to free ourselves from our prison by widening our circle of compassion to embrace all humanity and the whole of nature in its beauty." Albert Einstein.

Change is occurring now. You would not be reading these words if it were not so. Never before has there been a time when as much shift and letting go of old ideas has taken place. The world will never be the same again. History as we know it, is changing. In the twenty-first century, humankind will base its decisions on sound spiritual knowing. Fairness, and concern for the good of the whole will be high priorities. Protection for the environment will take precedent; partly out of eminent need and from an awakening to the reverence nature demands. Children will be fed, as we embody self-love and begin to nurture our world.

It is the quest for Spiritual satisfaction that will turn the tide and ultimately bring heaven to earth. Whether it be through the beliefs of fundamentalists, visionaries or enlightened gurus, global earth changes or climatic shifts, collapse of governments or economies, or personal crisis of every kind, in one way or another man is brought to his knees and ultimately comes home to surrender to God.

Crisis is not necessary for those who already accept and live spiritual Kingdom in their own hearts and minds. Those who choose to live it from day to day will always be taken care of. Others who resist the tide of change leave claw marks on the walls as they do fall in self-destruction.

The second coming the Christians are waiting for is within each one of us. The emptiness we experience in our world is the craving to return to our natural home God. What some prioritize as acceptance of the sacrificial lamb of Christ is simply acceptance of the consciousness of the Christ love and forgiveness for our world within ourselves. The hungry roar of the Lion that Jesus referred to announces the Second Coming of His consciousness in every Man and Woman on earth.

One World One Community

Whether we like it or not, our world is fast becoming a global village. The technology and a worldwide communication network that supports a one-world-community is in place. We can communicate instantly with our neighbors via satellite, fax, on screen, on line, and get an idea to any side of the globe. The message of peace and freedom, the awareness of love and the providence that prosperity brings can be sent or received in a very short period of time. We can be notified of a shortage and have food, medicine, or housing delivered to where it is needed, when it is needed. You and I play vital a part in the transformation. By choosing to live as peaceful children of God on a personal level, we must think expansively, and not in terms of exclusion but inclusion. How is what you and I do related to the highest good of the whole of mankind, not just myself, family, community, team,

or nation? We are a one world family. *Think globally not locally*
reflects the awareness that when we buy or dispose of a product,
or mistreat ourselves or others it somehow affects the whole.

Use these affirmations as conscious tools to aid the peoples
and governments of the world to unite in bringing heaven on earth
to life: **I am in concert with a Divine, global shift to peace
that is happening now. All of my brothers and sisters on
planet earth are now centered in the love of God and share
the joy, prosperity and the enlightenment of Spiritual truth.**
Plug in and play with God in Divine Synchronization to a higher
plan of Unification. Join me in using them and watch the changes
unfold! The collective agreement for peace is stronger than
anything less than itself. It exists at the core in the hearts and
minds of everyone. We are consciously bringing it to the surface as
new paradigm.

Beam Me Up Scotty

It is widely believed that we are being visited by beings
from outer space. The belief is supported in the media with many
first-hand testimonies of those who have witnessed it first hand.
If interplanetary visitors are here, it would be easy for them to
recognize the shoot-first, fear-oriented dysfunctional mentality of
much of the earth's social tribe. I doubt that beings who are
advanced enough to travel light-years through space are going to
land on the white house lawn and invite Tom Brokaw and Barbara
Walters to interview them while the First Lady serves tea.
Perhaps they are waiting for a time when our world becomes
awake enough to communicate openly and peacefully. If they are
here, I believe that we have drawn them to us by our fascination
with the belief that they exist. It may be man's destiny to be a key
player in space travel, exchanging gifts with other cultures and
exploring new worlds as a member of a larger galactic community,
one that up until now we only fantasized about and glorified as
fictional.

Should E.T.s show up, it will quicken our awakening to the
fact that we are a one world people. It will be one heck of a show
to observe the global reaction. Families gathered around the TV
watching military forces being called to arms and fundamentalists
the world over disclaiming their arrival as a hoax or the work of
the devil! What would you do if the spaceships landed? I think I
would turn on the tube and phone out for pizza! I can see Cokie
Roberts interviewing one of them and asking, "Why were you so
elusive for so long, toying with our armed forces and abducting

innocent people?" The E.T. snaps off a quick answer and smiles, "The devil made me do it!"

All life contains Spirit. God has many children and loves them all, no matter what they look like, what sex they are, how they live their lives, what religion they chose to practice or not, or who they choose to be.

Imagine with me that on your way home one day that something shiny moves swiftly across the sky catching your eye. You glance up and ask your self, What was that? Was it my imagination or did I see something unusual? A couple of minutes pass and this time you believe, or want to believe, or do not want to believe you see it again. This time you know you have seen something unique just as it passes from view. It was not at all like a plane or a helicopter. "Oh well," you think, "it probably was a plane." As you near your home you forget about it. Thinking about your evening ahead you walk into the house. The answering machine is in the middle of a message. You recognize it as the person you talk to the most yakking about something, "Are you there, are you there, pick up, pick up!" You grab the phone just in time. As they hang up, you hear, "turn on the TV, call me later" click.

You reach for the remote and think, "Oh, it's probably the latest scandal they are always going on and on about, I'll turn it on and go use the bathroom." You come back into the room and there is some sci-fi adventure thing with spaceships hovering over downtown. "I wonder what channel they meant," you think to yourself as you push the up arrow on the remote. "Same thing again, what's wrong with the TV?" As you push it up again and see the same identical picture you notice the "live" caption on the screen. An excited commentator continues, "This scene has appeared several places in the world in the last hour! Reports are coming in from Harrisburg, Boston, Glasgow England, Beruit, Hawaii and Mexico City!"

Your breath and heartbeat pick up a bit. Many thoughts cross your mind as you sit down on the edge of the furniture. "Can this be real? I always felt this might be possible, but never quite believed it. Oh my God! Now what? I must call my family! I wonder if they know yet? This can't be true. This one will blow the Republicans and the Democrats right out of their seats." You become aware of the announcer's voice again, "The Air Force has sent up planes. Every time they get near one of these things, they go straight up at lightning speed and disappear. We understand that it is impossible to track them on radar!" You think to yourself,

"Of course not. Everybody knows that, you idiot. Get a close up."
He continues, "We have a message confirmed by the White House
that the President has called a press conference and will be
broadcasting momentarily...."
How would you react? I think most of us would pretty
much do the same. I would be excited, not panicked, but probably
tickled that it finally happened. The historic, religion-bound world
we know would never be the same. The date would go down in
history forever as the day "they" landed. Our world would be in for
much change, and we would have many choices to make. Choices
that could affect the future of our planet in many dynamic ways,
positively and negatively. Earth would no longer be a One-World-
Planet.

Those looking for answers outside of themselves might
find new false gods to worship. I call it the beads and mirrors
scenario: Advanced culture arrives on the shores of a more
primitive one. Local natives find new heroes and worship arrivals.
It's an old story that has been the demise of many primitive
cultures. We would have to be clear on who we are, what we stand
for and be alert in order not to be too romanced by the mysterious
stranger bearing gifts of technology and philosophy. More than one
unsuspecting soul has been wooed into the arms of a mysterious
stranger bearing nylons and chocolates.

Will that day come? I cannot answer that. I do get a sense
that we are being prepared for it. The space-alien theme is more
and more on television, in the tabloids, and the news. It is my
guess that they are already here, waiting for us to accept and meet
with them without our feeling threatened or us being a threat to
them. Think in terms of expansion and possibilities. How would
our world improve by establishing a galactic network or bridge
with other worlds and exchanging culture, science and technology
with them? Could we eradicate disease, poverty and hunger?
Would we be more willing to let go of the limitations in belief
imposed upon us long ago and accept the greater picture of Divine
Humankind?

Divine Expansion

The ever-expanding Universe is always making more of
itself. The micro-universe of our minds also has the capability to
expand greatly. It is a known fact that we use approximately ten
percent of our brain power. Could it be that at least in part it is
due to the limits and restrictions we have accepted over the ages?
For about five years before beginning my first book, I yearned to

write and publish a spiritual book that would help the world to understand its own hidden God/Power of Creation. I never would have guessed ten years prior that I could or would do so. For a long time I did not write because I felt I had invested so much into a successful career that I enjoyed and was good at. Why walk away from an art business that rewarded me abundantly? With a degree in that field I felt confident but a bit trapped to be with that line of work for the rest of my life. However, I became bored with it and began to seek something new through prayer to expand my horizons and to set me free at the same time. It was not until I actually began writing that the book fell into place. The editing, publishing and distribution came in Divine Order as I stepped into the act of doing of them.

When I was first guided into the study of metaphysics I knew that my prayer for change had been answered. It had been "God give me something to do for the rest of my life that stimulates me and keeps my interest." Spirit brought just what I asked for. I took the ball that I was given and ran with it. I did it at my own pace. The first book took three years to write and produce. All the while I continued to make a living painting. It is what I needed to do for me. Spirit moved the thoughts, words and understanding through me at the appropriate pace. When you ask for guidance It will give you just what you ask for as well. What comes will be at your level of understanding, because you to grow and fit perfectly into your life pattern. However, you must ask for it, listen to it and be willing to act accordingly, if you wish to reap the rewards.

As a result of following my intuition for change, I took up classes and the formal study of metaphysics. I was provided with essential, constructive tools to redefine myself from the inside out. Before I could be of real assistance to others, it was first necessary for me to learn how to love myself by healing my own buried, wounded parts. Most of us were not taught clear or positive ways of knowing our Oneness with spirit in our childhoods. To live with a healthy, spiritual, self-awareness that we can integrate into our world, we must understand a Spiritual Awakening as it comes from within as a personalized experience. If we were raised with a tight, structured religious foundation, we may have a limited, clouded, or controlling point of view, that translates to judgment of self and others.

Universal truth is free for the asking and user-friendly. It is available for anyone to use in creating change within their own awareness and experience. For those of us who are willing to expand beyond the limited, historic

**religious beliefs that our world teaches, emancipation from
them is just a change of thinking. Perfect physical and
mental health is natural to self-perpetuating a perfect state
of life on earth.** The keys to knowing it are within the very
fibre of the genes, cells and subconscious mind of every
member of the human race. **As we awaken to accept
Oneness and the awareness that goes with it, we
automatically create Heaven On Earth for ourselves.**

The idea that disease, poverty, war, and injustice are
natural is an untruth. Coming from a belief system originally
instilled into cultures in order to maintain power, it was designed
to keep wealth and knowledge in the hands of a few elite. As the
twentieth century closes and the new millennium begins, it is easy
to see that world conditions require an attitude adjustment. We
see evidence all around as families split, violence increases, and
pollution goes on unchecked. We continue to enable our addictions
and dysfunction's to be the scapegoat of our culture. Progress is
occurring. Peace is happening. Dictatorships are crumbling. The
universality of love is spreading over the globe, and we see
Spirituality coming out of the closet giving evidence that a real
shift in consciousness is taking place.
        **You and I are a part of the whole stage of events of
our world at this time. We are each destined to play out our
particular role, making choices every minute of every day.
How will we respond when confronted with change. Will it
be in love or out of fear?**
        If I had succumbed to my old doubts and limits, I would
never have written *No Boundaries, Let Go Of Limits And Create
Success*, the first book that got me started as a writer. It required
of me and demanded faith - at first a blind faith just to begin. The
faith that something greater was working through me and was
behind me in each step is what pushed me through the tedious
editing and publishing. Yet there was a determination from within
to get to the end result no matter what. It was necessary to rely on
the three P's:.patience, persistence and prayer to get me through.
There were days when I simply had to push through the tunnel,
ignoring all the challenges that told me that it was impossible to
do it. There were many. I had to maintain the consciousness of
having a finished product.

**Consciousness is the vibration that goes before you
and makes the crooked places straight.**

Persistent, Fervent Devotion To Your Cause

The strength you require lies within you to complete your goal or realize your dreams. The Divine Seed for those dreams were placed within you as an opportunity to achieve success. Every day we have infinite choices to make. Each decision we make presents us new potential and opportunity to move forward with trust and faith. We can choose to hang out in the shadows that fear harbors or to move into trusting the expansion that faith and love bring. When we follow our guidance and urges, we find our bliss. **"Many are called but few answer."**
Follow the road map Spirit lays out before you. It is not necessary to know the whole route when you begin. Spirit will not lead you astray. You must have the faith to expand by taking the first step and trust that *the power within is in charge*. It knows the way and will get you home on time. Although it helps greatly, you do need to have a vision or mental picture of what the end looks like, but you can associate the feeling of satisfaction and joy with getting to that unknown destination. Know that where you stand and walk on the path is most certainly holy ground!

Use Your Word To Be One
With The Expansion Power Of Love

There is only One Infinite Knowing. The Divine Intelligence of Spirit within me knows all. It is in the highest part of my being. I am One with all the truth and love of the Infinite. I give thanks that It reveals my highest good to me and through me at all times. I accept the guidance I receive from within. I accept that it leads me forward in right activity now and always.
Spirit perpetuates the right activities to support my goals and dreams. It provides all the people, circumstances, money and support to create completion through right activity. I am guided home from within. I accept that the outer picture can and does support me beautifully as well. I move forward confident and clear on my purpose. God is never wrong, therefore I am led to the right decisions for the demonstration of success all along the way. My dream is complete in the Universal Mind of Spirit. I choose to accept success, knowing the idea came from Spirit through me in the first place.
I release any old thinking or belief that I am not enough. With it I let go of conditions that would hold me from my rightful good. I accept that the picture and completion of wholeness is

within the initial idea. Since I choose to carry it out, I accept its completed form in every way right here and now from this moment forward. I give thanks that Spiritual knowing and success are with me all the way. God is the absolute source and knows no limits. I move forward free, seeing the bigger, expanded picture of my life as One with Spirit in every way. And So It Is!

CONCLUSION

**"This is your life now. Be happy now.
This is not a dress rehearsal." Les Brown.**

My journey of the last five years has turned out to be one
of great surprise to this kid from the cornfields of Iowa. There, I
was intimidated and oppressed by a closed culture. So much, that
I grew to be a silent, rebelling young adult, and because of it, I can
sense the vibration of injustice at its first vile hint. When in its
presence, a red flag waves in my awareness, alerting me to its
bigotry and intimidation. However, it was not easy being quiet. I
traveled well into my adulthood with a closed heart. With survival
mechanisms for protection, I was able to avoid many possibly
negative or threatening experiences. At the same time, I missed
much of the good that life had to offer me.

By learning to walk the path of least resistance, I have
expanded enough to open my heart for myself and to others. I had
no choice but to forgive the past and its painful memories in order
to be able to accept freedom and move into the aliveness of my real
purpose and mission of service. It has been a surprising journey for
me to have come from being a complete introvert to a people-
oriented man. Now, I do my best to walk my talk without being
attached to outcome. Often daily, I must call on courage, accept
patience with myself and trust love in order to stay free. It is
important to remain open to the highest good for all despite what
appears to be at stake. You can do it too. You must, if you desire to
be free. A journey of self-exploration and emancipation will serve
your highest interests in life, if you remain non-attached to
controlling outcome. Be open to the Intellignece of Spirit within
yourself and all things as you maintain vision, grace and purpose.

Love yourself, others and Spirit as One....and the way will
be made clear and illuminated before you. Pour unconditional love
into every experience and flow with impassioned non-attachment
in all you do. When unclear or unresolved, ask for guidance.

Be at peace and enjoy the beauty of life. Answers will be
made obvious and unmistakable in all your ways as you remain
committed to the self-discovery of God within yourself and
blissfully non-attached to running the whole show. I send Love and
Light to you and blessings of non-attachment .

Love Never Faileth.

Love never faileth, but whether there be prophecies, they shall fail. Whether there be tongues, they shall cease. Whether there be knowledge it shall vanish away. For in we know in part, but prophecy be in part.
When that which is perfect is come. When that is in part shall be done away.
When I was a child, I spake as a child, I understood as a child, I thought as a child. For when I became a man, I put away childish things. For now we see through a glass darkly. But then for face to face now I know in part. But then shall I know even also as I am known. And even now abideth in faith, hope and love. But of these three, the greatest is love.

Peace be yours. PS I Love You.